Desert Willow

Patricia Beal

Candlelight
Romance
LOVE INSPIRED BY
HIS WARM GLOW

DESERT WILLOW BY PATRICIA BEAL
Candlelight Fiction is an imprint of LPCBooks
a division of Iron Stream Media
100 Missionary Ridge, Birmingham, AL 35242

ISBN: 978-1-64526-254-1
Copyright © 2020 by Patricia Beal
Cover design by Hannah Linder
Interior design by AtriTeX Technologies P Ltd.

Available in print from your local bookstore, online, or from the publisher at: ShopLPC.com

For more information on this book and the author visit: https://www.patriciabeal.com

This is a work of fiction. Names, characters, and incidents are all products of the author's imagination or are used for fictional purposes. Any mentioned brand names, places, and trademarks remain the property of their respective owners, bear no association with the author or the publisher, and are used for fictional purposes only.

All scripture quotations, unless otherwise indicated, are taken from the Holy Bible, New International Version®, NIV®. Copyright ©1973, 1978, 1984, 2011 by Biblica, Inc.TM. Used by permission of Zondervan. All rights reserved worldwide. www.zondervan.com. "NIV" and "New International Version" are trademarks registered in the United States Patent and Trademark Office by Biblica, Inc.TM.

"Scripture quotations from The Authorized (King James) Version. Rights in the Authorized Version in the United Kingdom are vested in the Crown. Reproduced by permission of the Crown's patentee, Cambridge University Press."

Gen. Douglas MacArthur, " Duty, Honor, Country. (May 12, 1962) (acceptance speech Thayer award, Corps of Cadets at the U.S. Military Academy at West Point, N.Y.)

https://nationalcenter.org/MacArthurFarewell.html

Brought to you by the creative team at LPCBooks:
Eddie Jones, Shonda Savage, Karen Saari, Jessica Nelson

Library of Congress Cataloging-in-Publication Data
Beal, Patricia.
Desert Willow/Patricia Beal 1st ed.

Printed in the United States of America

PRAISE FOR *DESERT WILLOW*

Desert Willow is a beautiful story of redemption and forgiveness that will waltz into your heart and leave you wanting more. For in the midst of regret and past mistakes, there is a lyrical oasis of hope and new beginnings just waiting to be embraced.

~Candee Fick
Author of *Sing a New Song*

Wrapped in heart-tingling romance, readers will waltz through the sweet love story of Clara and Andrew, an unlikely couple brought together by the sins and secrets of past generations, lighting the path to forgiveness, redemption, and eternal love. Tissues required.

~Karen Sargent
Author of *Waiting for Butterflies*
2017 IAN Book of the Year

Sometimes, authentic love blossoms despite less than ideal circumstances. Often, it's during those circumstances that God forgives, redeems, and restores, and supernaturally weaves a fresh outlook and a new beginning. Just as Clara and Andrew learn that true intimacy begins with Christ, so it is, too, with our earthly relationships. *Desert Willow* is a beautiful, poignant portrayal of love lost and found. Reminiscent of realistic life scenarios, it's a novel that will move readers to tears...for all the right reasons.

~Cynthia Herron
Author of *Her Hope Discovered*, Welcome to Ruby series

Desert Willow will have a delightful appeal to military families and anyone desiring to find hope and certainty through difficult and unexpected seasons of life.

~Savannah Odom
Army Wife

I highly recommend *Desert Willow* to readers who like Christian contemporary romances with strong and realistic faith elements in the story.

~Narelle Atkins
Author of *Solo Tu: Only You* (A Tuscan Legacy)

Desert Willow is an inspiring journey of love, forgiveness, and family. Patricia Beal has woven a beautiful story that will draw you into Clara Malone's world, waiting with her to learn the contents of the letter that has pulled her far away from her home, and yet much closer to her past and her future.

~Theresa Alt
Author of The Survival series

Praise for *A Season To Dance*

Ah, how this brought back my seasons in the Nutcracker, dancing Juliet, and years of rigor at the barre. *A Season to Dance* is a story of grace in all forms, ultimate romance and finding spiritual center. Thank you, Patricia Beal!

~Tosca Lee
NYT bestselling author

Readers who believe in second chances and a twist in the Happily Ever After will delight in this tale!

~Rachel Hauck
NYT bestselling author

More than a romance, *A Season to Dance* is a layered love story that pulls at the heartstrings while taking you on a trip through dance around the world. I adored it.

~Teri Wilson
Author of *Unleashing Mr. Darcy*
and *His Ballerina Bride*

Patricia Beal has crafted a compelling debut about grace and redemption when life takes unexpected turns.

~Kara Isaac
~RITA Award-winning author

Beal's debut captures the drama and lyricism of the ballet – faith, life and love dance across the story, reaching a satisfying and sigh-worthy dénouement.

~Katherine Reay
National bestselling and award-winning author of *Dear Mr. Knightley*

For 244 pages I was a world-traveling ballerina. This book was not only a captivating story, but an impacting journey. I am changed. Bravo, Ms. Beal.

~Nadine Brandes
Christy finalist and Carol Award winner

Patricia Beal's first novel is a skillfully written tale of a woman's journey to faith and love. *A Season to Dance* will bless every reader.

~**Lorraine Beatty**
Author of the Home to Dover series

Patricia Beal's *A Season to Dance* is gorgeous! Ana's story from emptiness to God's redemption showcases Beal's heart. As a ballet dancer, I loved relating to the well-done, tangible portrayal of Ana's dance and performance life. And how fun to taste, see, and smell her experiences in Germany! Thank you for this heart-tugging look into a professional ballerina's world, travels, and God's faithful dedication to us.

~**Katie Briggs**
Ballerina and former staff with Ballet Magnificat!

A Season to Dance offers readers a beautiful message of redemption and second chances that will dance across the heart. An elegant and graceful journey across two continents as one woman seeks to fill the God-shaped hole in her heart and finally discovers her own season to dance.

~**Candee Fick**
Author of *Dance Over Me* and *Catch of a Lifetime*

A tender romantic tale composed of grace and redemption. Beal's poignant novel gently touches our deepest emotional cords with a panoply of characters who remind us of our friends, family, and ourselves. As a Christian author with autism who has experienced my own battles decoding relationships and the repeated stings of shattered dreams, I could easily relate to Patricia's voice and Ana's struggles. *A Season to Dance* brims with the light of Christ' healing power to mend wounded relationships and make all things new. Patricia's graceful writing style is a joy to read and I highly recommend it.

~**Ron Sandison**
Founder of Spectrum Inclusion,
Author of *A Parent's Guide to Autism: Practical Advice. Biblical Wisdom*

ACKNOWLEDGMENTS

I would like to thank my family for helping me birth another book. I couldn't have done it without you guys.

A big thanks also to the wonderful people who helped me take what started as a "NaNoWriMo in March" adventure back in 2015 and turn it into a real book: Theresa Alt, Kate Breslin, Heidi Chiavaroli, Marisa Deshaies, Jeff Gerke, Joy Avery Melville, Nickie Monroe, Savannah Odom, and Harriett Shooter. Thank you!

Thanks also to Jessica Nelson, Karen Saari, and the whole Candlelight Romance / Lighthouse Publishing of the Carolinas team. We did it!

And I couldn't finish this note without recognizing my wonderful street team and all the people who put in an insane number of hours to promote the work we do. You are the heart of this operation. Thank you so much!

And thank you, reader, for letting me share another story with you. I hope you enjoy *Desert Willow* as much as you enjoyed *A Season to Dance*. This one is a bit different but also has roots that go deep into the story of my life, like *A Season* did.

I hope you will make this journey yours and, like me and Clara, find softness and beauty in the hard deserts we must travel through sometimes.

Love,

Patricia

DEDICATION

For all who could use a second chance.

Chapter 1

Clara Malone sat alone in the airport, her grandmother's labored request crushing through her mind. *My love ... deliver.* Clara had explained that the post office could get the letter to General Medeiros faster and for way less money, but she wasn't interested. *In person ... last wish.*

Last wish? Clara didn't agree with many of the decisions her grandmother had made, but she loved her. And family was family and a last wish was a last wish—not the kind of thing one says no to.

Timing couldn't have been worse though. Fresh out of college, broke, and without a job. Good grief. She'd just expended what meager funds remained to get her from Cincinnati to Texas to fulfill her promise.

And she only had herself to blame. At least for the unemployed and broke part. Everyone knew a degree in dance was not exactly practical. Why did she have to insist that she would be the exception to the rule and that she would find a job?

She surveyed the large atrium of the El Paso International Airport, fanning herself with her grandmother's jasmine-scented, maple-gold envelope. No sign of the general yet. Instead, across a playful and sunny path created by a series of tall arched windows, she spotted *him*—the young Army captain she'd seen at the airport's Placita while falling in love with an overpriced silver bracelet she couldn't possibly afford.

He'd stood close, so close that the subtle soap scent of his freckled skin had reached her with ease. And now here he was again.

No way though. Dating a soldier always sounded like a good idea, but it was never a good idea. Just ask Grandma. Or Mom.

Clara had already learned that lesson too.

She turned her attention to the letter again, lips pressed together. What was in it?

She lifted her eyes and studied the captain's red hair. He was handsome. She had to give him that. *Ginger.* He looked like someone famous. But who?

Hair regulations sure had changed since her dad's stint in the Army. While the captain's thick hair was short and neat, he didn't have the high-and-tight haircut her father sported when he was in the service.

She scanned the atrium again—not for General Medeiros this time, but other soldiers. Maybe one would look like her dad, the late Luke Malone. But none did. He'd been distinguished in his Army uniform, and she liked to remember him that way. She should have kept more photos of that time in their lives.

The captain checked his phone. Clara squinted to read the last name on his uniform, but she couldn't make out the letters on the thin name tape. If only Captain Ginger stood closer.

And that's when he shot a smile her way.

Oh, no. She looked away so fast she startled the pretty blonde who'd just sat next to her. But not fast enough. She now had his warm expression etched in her brain. Why did she have to look at him? She fanned herself with her grandmother's letter again, its floral perfume mingling with the blonde's.

Wait a minute. Clara checked out the girl next to her from the corner of her eye. Midnight-blue silk spaghetti-strap top. Designer jeans. Perfect figure to go with it. Perfect tan too. *You fool. He's not looking at you. He's looking at the blonde.*

He was way too perfect—way too cool. What made her think he was smiling at her? She snorted and tucked a strand of long auburn hair behind her ear. What would a man like him see in a Plain Jane like her?

Not interested anyway. She had already made her own soldier-boy mistake. Go ahead, Blondie. Your turn.

Clara shifted in her seat and tugged at her brown boho-chic dress to cover her knees. She could have worn something nicer instead of walking around El Paso International looking like a campus hippie. College was over. Time to grow up. Her first paycheck—assuming there would be a job and a paycheck one day—would have to go toward new clothes.

A large wave of new passengers arrived, but no one looked like the old officer she was supposed to meet. He was to arrive with his daughter, son-in-law, and three grandkids, all boys.

She studied every group without making a positive match. The last few people walked past her. Nope. No such family on that flight.

Her shoulders dropped and her lungs deflated as the atrium grew quieter, reminding her of the end of morning classes at the University of Cincinnati. There was comfort in the dwindling sounds and crowds, but there was loneliness too.

Was Ginger still there? She straightened her back and searched the area. Of course not. Whoever he was waiting for must have been in that group. Hmm. The sunny path seemed less bright now, and she felt lonelier still. How ridiculous.

Her fingers caressed her grandmother's shaky handwriting. What could be so special about retired General Mario Medeiros to keep him in her grandmother's heart for seventy-some years?

Clara longed to hold the frail author of the letter. The last time she'd made the trip to Brazil to visit her was the year her father died. Too long, and now probably too late.

"Ma'am?"

Captain Ginger. She looked into his forest-green eyes, two shades darker than her own, and disliked the heat his presence sent into her cheeks. What a coincidence that they both had red hair and green eyes. Hmm. Why was he talking to her? He was young, probably her age, but this was no soldier boy—no, sir. His voice was deep and slightly hoarse, in an attractive way. His strong jawline and sharp-but-not-too-sharp chin were sculpture-perfect.

But it was his nose that Clara liked right away. The feature gave his whole face an approachability that was endearing and almost irresistible—almost. It was Prince Harry's nose. That's who he reminded her of. No wonder she was all flustered.

She read his last name on the faded Army combat uniform. "Captain James?"

"Are you Clara Malone, ma'am?"

"Yes." But how did he know her name? She cocked her head. He was obviously not the general's American son-in-law. The son-in-law was a colonel and had to be older.

"I saw you at the store—you're the one." He motioned toward the letter on her lap.

"I'm the—?" Clara cleared her throat.

"You're the one waiting for the Howard family and General Medeiros?" She'd never been anybody's *the one* before.

"The family arriving from Germany with the Brazilian general?" He looked left and right, then behind him, scanning the whole atrium.

"Oh! Yes. Oh, right. Yes. I'm the one." It was fun to say it, even if it meant something else. "I'm waiting for General Medeiros and the Howards." But how did the captain know about her mission?

"Andrew James." He offered his hand. "I'm waiting for them too. We met in Germany a few years ago. Colonel Howard and I served together there and in Afghanistan."

Clara's gold bracelet jingled when she reached for his hand—lightly, like the baby butterflies chasing each other in her chest. His grip was comfortably strong, and his skin warm.

He sat where the blonde had been. When had she left?

She cleared her throat again. "How did you know my name?"

"Colonel Howard told me about you and your grandma. I know General Medeiros too." Andrew's pronunciation of the general's name was beautiful. He lifted the middle syllable like the Portuguese, instead of weighing it down like Brazilians. "They asked me to greet you if I spotted you and to ..." His voice trailed off, and he tapped the rubber heel of his desert combat boot.

"And to what?"

He took a deep breath. Too deep for casual talk. "Clara, I think I have some bad news for you."

"Oh, no." Her hands cradled her grandmother's letter against her chest. "He can't have died."

"No, not that. I'm sorry." Andrew uncrossed his legs and leaned toward her. "I'm so sorry—he's alive and should recover."

"Recover?" Her grandmother was in bad enough shape and wouldn't last much longer. She would be devastated if the general didn't get the letter. "What happened? Recover from what?"

"He's been battling some type of respiratory infection and has a weak heart." He twisted his lips and paused. "Two nights ago, he was struggling to breathe, and they had to take him to the emergency room. They admitted him."

"Wait. The general is not on the flight?" What did this mean? That couldn't be. She'd traveled all the way from Ohio.

"He's not. The Howards had to come without him."

"Why didn't they tell me? When will he come?"

"Soon?" Andrew shrugged. "He seems fine now, but the hospital wants to keep him for a while longer."

"They should have called me." If they'd called her right away, she could have postponed the whole thing without losing money.

"General Medeiros made his daughter promise that she would talk to you in person about his health and about the letter." He paused and narrowed his eyes. "He was afraid you would leave or not come at all if they'd told you he wasn't going to make the flight."

"I wouldn't just leave." She was broke. She needed to be job-hunting. "But I wish I'd stayed home. I could have traveled later when he's actually here. What am I supposed to do now?"

"They thought there was a chance he would end up making the trip. I'm sorry this is happening, but the Howards are good people." Andrew leaned back and crossed his legs at the ankles. "They'll have a plan and will take care of you. Don't worry."

Don't worry? Clara rubbed her forehead with her fingertips. She didn't know them. She just wanted to go home.

Andrew pointed at the envelope. "Can I see it?"

"Sure." What if she said she had to use the restroom and didn't return? Andrew could deliver the letter, and she would be free. *My love ... deliver ... in person.* If she could leave, she would. But she couldn't do that.

Andrew held it carefully. "The general can't wait to get his hands on this letter." He waved the envelope near his face. "Smells good."

"Jasmine."

"Mmm." He handed the letter back to Clara. "Nice."

She smelled her grandmother's perfumed love letter one more time and then placed it in her purse with care.

"Here they are." He stood and pointed to a stylish couple in their forties and three boys who were young, but taller than their mother.

Andrew's genuine smile spoke volumes. It was quite evident he cared for these people, and the friendship went beyond serving together. He was definitely not at the airport just to do a favor for an acquaintance.

All three boys ran to him as soon as they spotted him. "Hi, Brother Andrew!" The youngest threw his arms around him.

Brother? She hadn't heard that since Vacation Bible School. She hadn't been to a church since then either—apart from weddings and funerals. Clara studied the warmth of the men's handshakes and hugs.

Colonel Max Howard placed his massive hand on Andrew's shoulder. "You look great, man."

"Thank you, sir. Welcome to Fort Bliss."

"Thanks for helping us."

The Howards had wrinkled clothes and tired eyes, but their voices were cheerful. Each boy wore a small backpack, and Colonel and Mrs. Howard pulled matching wheeled carry-on bags. Nothing was out of place or out of order.

Mrs. Howard looked at her. "Are you Clara? Or are you here with Andrew?"

Clara blanched at the thought of being there *with* Andrew. "I ..." Nothing else came out.

Andrew took a step toward Clara. "Colonel and Mrs. Howard, this is Clara Malone."

Mrs. Howard's smile broadened. "Oi! Eu sou a Alice. Tudo bom?"

"I understood what you said, but I don't really speak Portuguese. Hi ... Alice." She imitated the woman's pronunciation of the name, but calling her by her first name hadn't felt right. Mrs. Howard was old enough to be her mom and was a colonel's wife—a general's daughter.

"Oh, Clara, you must have heard what happened." Alice gave Clara a warm hug.

"Yes, ma'am. I heard." Clara put her arms around the general's daughter hesitantly.

"Please call me Alice." Mrs. Howard took a step back and removed her leather jacket. "He should be getting out of the hospital this weekend."

"I'm supposed to fly home this weekend." Clara raised both hands and tightened her lips.

"I should have a new flight date for him by tomorrow." Colonel Howard led the way toward baggage claim.

"Clara, you must stay." Alice's voice was soft. "You must."

"I don't know what to do," Clara mumbled.

Alice covered her ears when a passenger's name was repeated over the loudspeaker. "Let's go where it's not so loud."

Why was everything going wrong all of a sudden? Graduating from college should be a good thing. Instead, she was still jobless in what was shaping up to be the worst summer ever. "Unbelievable."

"Pardon me?" Alice turned toward Clara as they walked past an Army reception desk and continued toward baggage claim.

"Nothing." Clara spoke without looking at General Medeiros's daughter. What was she going to do? She had to call Mom after hearing Mrs. Howard's plan—if, in fact, there was one.

The group came to a stop at their baggage carousel.

"We have twelve suitcases coming out." The colonel placed his hand on Andrew's shoulder. "Please tell me you didn't drive the Crossfire."

Andrew chuckled. "We should be fine. I borrowed a van from church—it's a fifteen-passenger van."

What was a Crossfire? The luggage buzzer interrupted the chatter.

"I need each of you boys to get a cart." Colonel Howard handed his wallet to the oldest boy and pointed to the long row of carts behind him. Andrew grabbed a fourth luggage cart, and the parade of suitcases started.

"Clara, you must stay." Alice tightened her lips then closed her eyes briefly before speaking again. "I don't have much to offer right now—"

She continued. "We are headed to the hotel on post, and we'll be there until our furniture arrives. But you must stay. I can help cover your hotel costs, and we can discover some sights together."

Sightseeing in El Paso, Texas, was not what Clara needed.

Alice's eyes became moist. "My dad won't last much longer, and I want to do this for him. It means a lot to me. Please?"

Clara looked at the woman's pale blue eyes. Her voice was husky and pretty. "It means a lot to my grandma too, but why does it mean so much to you? I get your dad and the letter, but why do I have to stay? What is it to you—to him?" *In person ... last wish.*

"He wants to meet you. And it'll be fun. Once you meet him you'll understand. You can't help but love him."

"That's the rumor." Clara stepped closer to Alice to make room for another family with several suitcases and backpacks.

Alice giggled and cocked her head. "Will you stay?"

"I need to talk to my mom. She's in Brazil. I need to see what she thinks." Clara shook her head in slow motion. Unbelievable. "Do you think we're talking five days, fifteen, thirty? I can't stay long."

"I will call you tomorrow as soon as we get an update from the hospital and from travel."

"Travel?"

"The Army travel office." Alice's voice was more animated than before. "They will reschedule his flight once we know when he can make it."

Maybe she could stay. Clara was just a little curious to meet the first man her grandmother had ever loved.

Andrew's luggage cart was the first to fill up. Three suitcases and two Army duffle bags. Would she see Captain Ginger again if she stayed?

"Can I see the letter?" Alice raised her eyebrows.

"Of course." Clara pulled the bright envelope out of her purse and handed it over.

Alice smelled the envelope. "Jasmine?"

"Grandma's favorite scent."

"Can I show it to Max?"

"Sure." Clara followed Alice to where the guys were. Beside them, two more luggage carts were now fully loaded.

"Here's the famous letter." Alice stood behind her husband.

Colonel Howard turned around and his eyes locked on the envelope. "Surreal, no?"

Alice's head bobbed in slow motion.

One of the boys approached them. "Grandpa's famous letter?"

"Yep." Alice kissed his cheek.

Colonel Howard turned to Clara. "I'm so glad you're here, Clara."

"Thanks." She offered him a smile and put the letter away.

The colonel gave Andrew a mock slug. "Hey, how's Tatiana?"

Alice's eyes went wide and she poked her husband's back. He looked over his shoulder. She frowned at him and he shrugged.

"It's okay." Andrew's jaw tightened.

Who was Tatiana?

When he spoke again, his tone was casual. "The usual Tatiana—can't commit but can't let go either. I've seen her once since I got back from Germany. She might come for a few days this summer."

"Don't count on it," Alice snapped.

Tatiana? Clara looked at Andrew from the corner of her eye. Was he not available? What did she care anyway? No soldiers. No.

The colonel loaded the last suitcase onto their last luggage cart. "If she's the one the Lord has for you, it will all work out."

"I know, sir." Andrew led the luggage train toward the main exit.

The airport double doors slid open, and the El Paso air hit them like a blow dryer set on high.

"This heat is unusual for May—even for El Paso." Andrew stayed ahead of the group, his commanding voice easily heard. "It's supposed to cool down for the weekend."

The boys followed him, looking at the massive mountains to the west.

"Cool down to what? The eighties?" Colonel Howard laughed. "It's like being in Afghanistan all over again. Even the mountains look like Afghan mountains."

Alice giggled again and lowered her sunglasses. "Do you need a ride, Clara?"

Clara shook her head. "That's my hotel." She pointed at the Radisson in the distance, one of a dozen two-story hotels encircling the airport's short-term parking lot. "By the giant horse statue."

"That's convenient."

"Yep." *Not.* Everything about her trip to El Paso was very inconvenient, the hotel included. She held her breath to avoid the exhaust smell of a little old car that drove past them.

An airport hotel was supposed to keep her safe from soldiers and all things military—safely removed from Fort Bliss. But it wasn't working. Fort Bliss, like all Army posts, had a way of spilling out. Army equipment, Army personnel, and Army families were everywhere.

One of the boys was still looking at the mountains. "The Franklin Mountains are taller than I thought they would be. Look at that peak." He pointed at the tallest part of the brown formation.

"Wait until you're trying to climb it." Andrew pushed the fourth cart toward a large white van. "It's really tall."

"Will you take me one day?"

"Of course. We'll go up to Elephant Mountain." Andrew opened the back of the unmarked van and loaded the first large suitcase. "I took the fourth row of seats out, so we should have enough space."

"Let me help you load." The colonel grabbed another large suitcase and moved it to the van with ease and purpose. While the men organized the luggage, Mrs. Howard and the boys put smaller bags in the passenger area.

Army families. Families, families, and more families. Everyone's got one. Everyone but Clara Malone. Not the right kind, anyway.

Andrew probably had a great family too. Parents who were still married—dad a career officer and mom a homemaker? Probably. Soon he would marry Tatiana and have beautiful children who would follow in their dad's footsteps.

But in her family, relationships never lasted long, and *forever* was a pipe dream.

Alice got out of the van. "Do you have a car here?"

"No. I don't need one."

"Oh, now I feel even worse. Do you know anyone here?"

"No, but don't worry. I'll be okay." She did the math in her head. It was getting late in Brazil. She had to call her mom.

Alice approached Andrew. "Andrew, show her some sights, will you? Are you busy tonight?"

Where had that come from? Clara's face was hotter than the El Paso sun. Surely not. How embarrassing. "You don't—"

"I would love to." Andrew didn't hesitate. "I need to go back to the office for a couple of hours, but I'm free for dinner."

She lifted her eyes to his face. He didn't look bothered—he wouldn't be doing it just to please the Howards. Or would he? He looked anxious. She should put him out of his misery and just say no already. Why did Alice have to put him—and her—on the spot like that?

"My mom is in Brazil. I have to call her right now." And run away from here, from Ginger, and from Tatiana. "They're four hours ahead. She gets in enough trouble for sleeping at the hospital all the time. She can't have her phone going off in the middle of the night."

"Aww. Your grandma's in the hospital too?"

Clara nodded and swallowed the lump that had formed fast—too fast—in her throat. "They don't think she will be able to leave the hospital." She didn't want to cry in front of The Brady Bunch. It was time to start walking.

"I'm so sorry." Alice hugged Clara. "And I'm sorry I didn't ask sooner."

She released her and looked into Clara's eyes, but Clara gazed at the hotel in the distance.

"Oh, and you will be in a hotel room all by yourself? No. You can't. I won't let you."

"I can really help." Andrew's voice was firm. "You don't have to be alone."

In my room? Clara giggled and Alice joined her.

"What?" Andrew searched every adult face.

Colonel Howard shook his head with a thunderous chuckle.

Then Andrew turned crimson, the crimson of late-season grapes. "I thought we were talking about dinner and sightseeing."

Alice ignored his statement, which suited Clara just fine. "You can come to post and have dinner with us—we'll send a cab. I hear the entertainment area at Fort Bliss is great. Restaurants, pubs, movies, stores. Hmm?"

"I will be okay. Really."

"Nonsense." Alice looked at Andrew, who was tossing the van's keys from one hand to another as if they were a Slinky. "It's decided. You can go be young and let this fine young captain take you out or come to post and hang out with us. But you are not staying here all alone while your grandma is in the hospital and your mom is on the other side of the world. Not happening."

"That's right." Andrew chuckled. "I can help."

Cute. Ginger had a sense of humor. Spending time with him, having him show her around … could she do that? She didn't know him. But wasn't anything better than going to post?

"Go out, you two." Colonel Howard's statement sounded like an order. "Clara needs to call home and make some decisions. Go out tomorrow."

But how about Tatiana? "I don't want to cause any trouble though. Isn't there a girl?"

Alice looked at her husband and shook her head.

"Tatiana is old news." Andrew spoke firmly.

Did Tatiana know she was "old news"? A blue and orange Southwest plane screamed overhead, taking off to who knows where. Anywhere. If only it could take Clara away from El Paso before she got herself in trouble.

"I would love to take you out. Tonight or tomorrow. If you'll let me. Just dinner. I know a great place."

I'm sure you do, Ginger. "Fine. Tomorrow."

His charming grin sent a jolt of heat through her stomach and into her heart.

"Good!" Alice clapped.

Colonel Howard laughed. "Andrew's personal matchmaker is back in business, and we've been together for less than an hour. You're good."

"Maxwell Howard, hush." It was Alice's turn to blush. "Don't embarrass them."

Oh, we were so past embarrassment. "What time, Ginger?" Wait, had she just said that out loud? "I mean, Andrew."

He chuckled. "Seven?"

Clara nodded. "Should I wait in the lobby?"

"How about if I ring the room when I arrive? Friday night traffic in this area can be pretty bad, and I don't want you to be waiting in the lobby if I'm running behind." He tilted his head slightly.

"Okay. I'm in 117." *I'm in 117? I should have given him my phone number instead. What an idiot.*

"All right. Seven tomorrow then."

Too late now. "Okay." She put her bag on her shoulder. "It was nice meeting you—all of you."

Alice smiled. "Nice meeting you too, Clara." All the others echoed some variation of the same. "And I will call you tomorrow."

When she reached the sidewalk, Clara looked back and caught Alice doing a little victory dance, as Colonel Howard patted Andrew's back. Both men grinned unabashedly.

Overhead, a line of Blackhawk helicopters moved slowly, like the El Paso air, and Clara tried to ignore the excitement that overwhelmed her heart, making it beat like the rotors of the helicopters—around and around and with loud whooshes.

She'd just come to hand over a letter. Now what had she gotten herself into?

Captain Andrew James. United States Army. Nineteen hundred hours. Tomorrow.

The palm trees of the Radisson framed a changeable letter sign she hadn't noticed before: Home Away From Home.

Dating a soldier always *sounded* like a good idea, but it was never a good idea.

Andrew drove back to the airport as soon as he got off work.

After taking the Howards to the hotel and returning the church van, he'd spent two hours in his office doing something that resembled work.

The newsletter he was supposed to review and approve got submitted without the usual scrutiny. The Army told people not to micromanage, right? Well, this was it: Andrew James not micromanaging for a change.

His first sergeant wanted him to review some images for a storyboard, but Andrew didn't even open the picture folder. It could wait.

But thoughts of Clara Malone refused to wait.

Returning to the airport to buy a bracelet for someone he'd just met sounded like a terrible idea, but he couldn't help it. A second trip to the airport to buy the bracelet she'd been admiring when he first saw her was an idea firmly planted in his heart since the moment she said yes to dinner with him.

Maybe he would hold on to it to see if things worked out and then give it to her during a future outing? The bracelet wasn't terribly expensive, but she would probably freak out if he gave it to her on a first date.

Andrew drove past her hotel as a group of well-dressed Joes spilled out of the lobby.

Where should he take her? His first thought had been the Magic Bistro, but the L&J Cafe had such a unique environment too and the best Mexican food. Was she expecting Mexican food? Or how about The Garden?

It's just a dinner, Andrew. Chill. Just a dinner.

Maybe he should take her on post? Girls always liked that.

No. Not this girl. Definitely not. Something about the way she'd narrowed her eyes at Alice Howard's suggestion of meeting on post told him Clara had no desire to see Fort Bliss.

Andrew parked at the airport and closed the top of his classic yellow Chrysler Crossfire. He glanced at the Radisson. Please don't be at the window, Clara. Her room probably faced the other side anyway. Besides she'd never seen his car.

But Colonel Howard had mentioned the Crossfire. Did she know what one was? He hurried to the entrance.

Oh, enough. What was the matter with him? He liked her already. That was the problem. Somehow, he liked her a lot. What a beauty! A beauty with red hair and green eyes like his. That didn't happen every day. And *Clara Malone*—even her name was pretty.

He crossed the tall atrium and glanced at the spot where they'd first talked. He suspected her mousy sort of personality was just a façade. After all, she'd been surrounded by six strangers who knew each other well.

But just in case she was always shy and reserved, the Magic Bistro would be their best bet. Their live music was mellow and the singer good. No awkward silences.

Children's voices echoed all around the airport atrium, and the late setting sun shone through the glass roof, forming a path that led straight to the *Placita*.

Andrew walked into the store where he'd first seen her and spotted the silver bracelet she'd held right away. It was the only silver one. How lucky that it was still there. He touched the cold metal flowers, remembering her delicate hands and peach nail polish.

The memory of her sweet perfume and the image of her long willowy figure and toned arms were vivid in his mind, and they warmed his spirit.

Warmed it too much.

Casting down imaginations, and every high thing that exalteth itself against the knowledge of God, and bringing into captivity every thought to the obedience of Christ.

Staying pure until he'd married Tatiana had been easy. He'd grown up expecting to marry soon after college, and even expecting that the year or two before his wedding night would be a challenge. So he'd been prepared.

Keeping it up after being abandoned practically at the altar at West Point on graduation week was not so easy. Being twenty-six and single was not expected. No. Nothing could have prepared him for that.

Bringing into captivity every thought ...

Andrew ran his fingers over the two rows of skinny flowers that made up the bracelet.

"Sir?" the short saleswoman with dark black hair said from behind the counter.

"Yes, ma'am." He continued to examine the bracelet.

"We close in five minutes."

She will love it. "I'll take this bracelet." He approached the counter.

"This is pretty." The woman lifted her glasses. "Love, fun, rest, hope, faith, dreams, joy, wish ..." She stopped reading the tiny petals and rested her glasses on her nose again. "Nice."

"It is." Andrew's voice sounded surer than he felt. "It's very nice."

"A gift?"

"Yes." He pulled his wallet out of his uniform's back pocket.

"Girlfriend?" She smiled and cut the tag, pushing it in Andrew's direction.

"Date." He picked up the tag and tossed it in a plastic wastebasket by the register.

Her eyebrows rose. "Lucky girl." She reached under the counter and showed him a glossy red box with a silver ribbon. "A ruby box for a fairer than ruby lady who will bring you love, hope, faith, dreams, and joy?"

"God only knows if this is the one, but I sure hope so." He tapped his card on the counter while she placed the bracelet on the simple white pad inside the box. Could Clara be the one—the one who would make everything right again? And why did he need a girl to make things right? God should be enough. God *was* enough. Hmm. He handed the saleslady his debit card.

The saleslady handed him the box in a small bag and returned his card. "Well, good luck."

"Thanks."

The atrium was busier than before, and a female soldier in the rental car area looked enough like Tatiana to make him do a double-take.

Would she really show up this summer? He owed her no loyalty—they were not in a relationship. But he'd asked her to come. He'd asked her to reconsider her graduation decision. After four years apart, they were both still single. Her time in the Army was almost up. She could resign her commission and be with him like they'd originally planned.

He crossed the parking lot, baking on the asphalt but aware of the Radisson on his left. As he climbed into the Crossfire, his cell phone vibrated. He removed the ruby box from the small shopping bag and placed it in the glove compartment before checking the phone.

A text from Tatiana?

I BOUGHT THE TICKETS! POP GOES THE FORT. I WILL BE SPENDING THE FOURTH OF JULY 4-DAY WEEKEND AT FORT BLISS 😊

Chapter 2

Clara looked at the mountain range outside her window and exhaled. The hotel parking lot was abuzz with well-dressed people walking to their cars and trucks on a scorching and sunlit Friday evening.

There was no sign of Andrew, though. How late was he? She checked the time on her phone. Seven fifteen.

Clara patted her brow dry and closed the thin curtain. Andrew James didn't know the first thing about the El Paso weather. Some cool down.

Why did she have to say yes? She should have lied. She should have said that she knew people in town or that she had a rental car and a plan.

Instead, she was standing by a window, like a teenage girl, waiting for Prince Charming to show up. She leaned against the wall, parted the curtain, and peeked out.

Nothing.

He wasn't coming. She was so stupid. He'd stood her up.

Her gaze traveled to the spot where they'd said goodbye the previous day. He'd looked so excited. Why would he change his mind?

She let go of the curtains and flopped onto the queen-size bed. The room was still too bright, despite the curtains. She should have closed the heavy curtains too. Could the sun just set already?

Why did she have to say yes? *Why?*

A gentle tap on the door cut through the room's silence.

She jumped off the bed and ran her fingers through the back of her hair. It couldn't possibly be him. He'd said he was going to call the room, not show up at the door.

Clara closed one eye and approached the peephole. *Wowza!*

She opened the door. "You were supposed to call the room."

He stood absolutely motionless and looked like he'd just stepped out of GQ. The two top buttons of his white shirt were fashionably undone, and a tan blazer emphasized his broad shoulders. Stylish brown rectangle sunglasses rested on top of his blown-back red hair.

"Well?" Was he going to just stand there, or was he going to say something and give her the vase of yellow roses he was holding?

"There was a big line at the front desk." He cleared his throat and took a step forward. "I was running behind, and I didn't want to make you wait any longer. I didn't have your number."

Of course, she would never tell him she'd thought he'd changed his mind about taking her out. "Nice flowers."

"I'm sorry." He cleared his throat again. "They are for you."

She accepted his gift. "They're beautiful." He was beautiful. Clara took the elegant clear vase of yellow roses and placed it next to the flat-screen TV. She buried her nose in one of the large blooms and breathed in its sweet and sunny scent, while delicate baby's breath tickled her warm cheeks.

"Glad you like them." He beamed from the doorway.

"Thank you. I love roses—yellow or otherwise." She cocked her head and bit one side of her lower lip.

"You look amazing." He seemed to focus on her lips.

"Thank you." Clara dropped her gaze to the gold sandals that matched her clutch and her necklace. The elegant off-the-shoulder summer dress she was wearing had been a gift from her dad. He'd said its shade of green matched her eyes. It didn't. The dress was emerald green, and her eyes were soft forest green. But she liked the dress. It made her look slimmer and taller than she already was.

"Shall we?" Andrew asked.

"Sure." She grabbed her clutch and closed the door behind her.

"I heard the good news." He walked down the long hotel hallway slightly ahead of her. "Did you cancel your flight already?"

"I don't know that I would call it *good news*, but yes, I've changed my flight."

He paused at the top of the stairs allowing her to walk down ahead of him. Their eyes met as she passed him. His soft cologne was clean and fresh. Nice.

"What's your new departure day?"

"Just before the Fourth of July." Of course, she wouldn't tell him that she couldn't afford the change or the extended stay and that since the Howards were paying for her to wait for the general, they were calling all the shots now.

"What day?" he asked.

"I think the third?" Might as well have been the next century, but when the Howards heard that she was currently unemployed, they had insisted on giving the General Medeiros situation "the time it deserved." It was a letter. What could possibly require so much extra time?

"What day of the week is that?" he asked from a few steps back.

"I don't know." She watched him catch up at the bottom of the stairs. "Why?"

"Nothing." He shrugged. "I hope I can bring you to the airport. That's all."

"I'm *at* the airport." Clara pointed at the terminal as they stepped out of the Radisson.

"But you shouldn't spend all of June here, you know? Mrs. Howard asked me to look into furnished apartments where I live, and they have a few. You can rent a nice one-bedroom apartment for a month, for what you would spend here in a week."

"She didn't say anything about looking at apartments when we talked, but she said she would pay for my stay, so I suppose I'll go where she wants me to go." Why hadn't Alice mentioned this apartment business to her?

"I can drive you there tomorrow, so you can check it out." Andrew stopped by a yellow convertible. "Or tonight even. It's really nice."

"Not tonight." Clara studied the car. "Yours?"

"Yep."

"Wow!"

Andrew grinned and opened the passenger door for her. "Thanks."

The gray and ivory interior was as beautiful as the baby yellow exterior, and the rich leather scent reminded her of her favorite autumn jacket. "What is this?"

"A Chrysler Crossfire."

He turned on the engine and seemed to glance at Clara's tanned legs. "My dad gave it to me when I graduated from West Point."

West Point, of course. She smiled and covered her knees.

He stopped before exiting the crowded hotel parking lot. "I can close the top."

"Please don't." She opened her clutch and pulled out a tiny hairbrush. "I own one of these, and I'm not afraid to use it."

Andrew laughed a delightful laugh, deep and heartfelt.

Why did he have to be in the Army?

She watched his strong hands on the steering wheel. His eyes were fixed on the thick traffic.

What if she did let him charm her for a month? He couldn't possibly break her heart in one month. Could he? It'd taken her ex-boyfriend, Scott, almost a year to do that.

Well, no. That wasn't actually true.

Army Major Scott Taylor had broken her heart in less than 24 hours—a world record, for sure. What had taken almost a year was for her to realize just how irreversible the situation and the damage were. Could she afford to have her heart broken again? She didn't think so.

The sun was nowhere in sight, but the cloudless blue sky was still bright. "Does the sun ever set around here?"

"Yes." He looked at his gray quad watch. "It'll be dark in an hour—maybe less."

"And you know it'll be dark in an hour like you knew the temperature today would be in the eighties?"

"Colonel Howard said eighties. I never said it would be in the eighties. I just said it was supposed to cool down, and it did. Yesterday's high was ninety-eight and today's was ninety something."

"Ninety-eight?"

"Ninety-something, that's less than ninety-eight."

Clara laughed. She would be burning up for a month, and she knew it.

Andrew merged onto a highway, and she closed her eyes, feeling the warm wind on her face.

"That's Mexico." He pointed at a massive metal structure that looked like a red X.

"X marks the spot." She giggled. "Oh, I see the flag!" A giant Mexican flag waved gently in front of a sprawling city. "Do you ever cross the border?"

"To Mexico?"

"No, to Canada. Yes, to Mexico." Clara leaned forward to look at a bridge that connected the two countries. But she didn't see any water. Where was the Rio Grande? She was fairly sure it was supposed to be there somewhere.

"No. The Army won't let us."

"Why?"

"Juarez is violent." He looked toward the border. "It's better now, but I guess they don't feel that we should go yet."

"The Army is funny that way."

"Do you know much about the Army?"

"Some." More than she cared to. "I was born at Fort Benning."

"No way! An Army brat? Me too. I was born at Fort Bragg. My dad served for almost thirty years. He's retired now."

"All right." She forced a smile. This would be a great time to say something clever, but she couldn't think of anything clever to say. Why couldn't she have a normal family too?

"You don't care much for the Army, do you?"

"It's complicated." She didn't want him to be offended. Her family's problems were certainly not his. "Maybe we can talk about the Army some other time."

"Okay." He shrugged.

Next, he would ask her about school and jobs. Just watch. He had to be wondering how she was able to drop everything to stay in El Paso for a month.

What would she tell him if he asked? *Hi. I just got a useless degree, and now I can't get a job.* No. She wouldn't say that.

She could tell him she was still in college and on summer vacation. Simple explanation.

But that would be a big fat lie. She didn't want to lie to him.

She would tell him the truth but word it nicely. No need for more pity parties.

Clara noticed four lines of text on a faraway Mexican mountain. She squinted trying to read the gigantic white letters, but the letters weren't the problem—they were clear enough. The language was the problem. "What does it say?" She pointed to Mexico. "On the mountain?"

"Ciudad Juarez. La Biblia es la verdad. Leela."

"What does it mean?" Something about reading the Bible.

"The Bible is the truth. Read it."

"Cool." Would *Brother Andrew* now ask her if she read her Bible?

"The letters don't look very big from here, but they are huge."

"They do, actually, look very big from here."

"No, really—some of those letters are as tall as a thirteen-story building."

"Wow. That I couldn't imagine."

"True story. I was reading an article about it just the other day." Andrew was driving slightly above the speed limit, but cars and trucks passed them on both sides.

"Big horse, big X, big letters." Clara spoke with her best Texas accent.

"Welcome to Texas, honey." Andrew's attempt at a local accent was much better than hers. She smiled, and he smiled back. She could watch him forever. Yes, he was handsome and couldn't help but be cool. But that wasn't all. There was something else. An easygoingness, maybe, that was uniquely his.

"Do you believe that, Clara?"

"Believe what?"

He pointed at the message on the Mexican mountain, pushed the turn signal lever up, and switched lanes. "That the Bible is the truth and that we should read it."

"I do." Clara had given up on religion a long time ago, but she believed in the Bible and in God. Andrew didn't seem condescending, and the subject was safer than the Army or her career. "We used to go to church off and on, before my parents got a divorce."

"I'm sorry. That must be hard."

She shrugged. "It's okay—old news." *Like Tatiana.* "I got saved in Vacation Bible School during our last summer in the Army. We were at Fort Bragg."

"When were you there?"

"Late nineties. We left in the summer of 2000." Clara fixed her gaze on a large grass-less cemetery next to the highway. She'd been to Los Angeles once, but she'd never been to a place as dry as El Paso.

"We were at Bragg in the early 90s, so you missed me by a few years."

"I suppose I did." She watched him take the exit after the cemetery. Surely they weren't going there, right?

"So what happened after VBS?"

"We moved to Cincinnati."

The light turned green, and Andrew drove toward the mountain—away from the cemetery.

"We left town on the last day of VBS. They picked me up, and we hit the road." Army life was all she'd ever known. She'd cried all the way to Asheville and many times after that, on and off the road.

"So you guys didn't go to church in Cincinnati?"

"No. A couple of weeks after VBS, the church in North Carolina called my mom and talked to her about baptism. She said she was going to look for a church in our area, but she never did." Clara had prayed hard that year. She'd prayed they would go back to their Army life somehow, prayed for a church, and prayed her dad wouldn't leave them. When he left, she'd prayed for him to come back. But her mom had been right. God worked in mysterious ways—too mysterious for Clara. "They divorced that same year."

"How sad." His expression darkened. "I'm so sorry."

"It was a hard time for us." It wasn't until the following year, when the September 11 attacks happened that she'd seen something good come out of her dad's decision to leave the Army after eight years of service. By September 11, 2001, she'd developed a strong hatred for her dad, but she didn't want him to die. Ten years later, he died anyway. Clara shook her head.

"How old were you?"

"Seven or eight."

"I couldn't imagine going through something like that." He looked like he was going to say something else, but he didn't.

"I take it your parents are still together?"

"They are." He nodded. "It hasn't been easy—they've had some rocky times. But they have a godly marriage. They're a tough couple."

"That's good." Godly marriage? Sounded dull. But there wasn't one dull thing about Captain Andrew James. Not at all. He was all kinds of happening. He couldn't possibly have dull parents. And what dull dad gives his son a yellow convertible for graduation? Dull parents don't do that.

"Did your parents remarry?"

"Mom didn't. I don't think she ever stopped loving dad." Pathetic. "Dad did. He was married for five minutes to a girl half his age." The one who broke her family and their hearts.

"And then he didn't try again?"

"No. He dated, but he never got serious with anyone."

"Dated, but doesn't date anymore?"

"Nope. He's dead."

"Clara, I'm so sorry." The next light turned red.

"Seeing soldiers and helicopters, and knowing that the post is right there. It reminds me of him a lot and of our time in the military. They were our happy years. Everything kind of fell apart after the Army."

"Is that why you didn't want to go on post?"

"Yeah ..." One of the many reasons.

"You've had a rough ride, haven't you?"

"I guess you can say that." She shrugged. "Mom always says there's always someone worse off."

"True, but still."

"It's okay. I'm not pathetic, you know."

"I didn't say you were."

"He died when I was a freshman in college, so that, too, is old news."

"Okay." He looked at her and winked.

A jolt of joy filled her chest, like a Mentos in a Diet Coke geyser. He was *so* fine. She didn't want to dump a bunch of sad stories on him.

Maybe they should talk about college. College had been great. It'd been so great that she was considering a master's. She could always get a job later.

Andrew seemed to be following signs to a scenic drive. The hilly neighborhood was old but quaint. The houses reminded her of Clifton Heights and the University of Cincinnati, and some buildings looked just like hers: three floors, exposed brick, and brick balconies.

From time to time, a Mediterranean-style home would take a large corner. Those were quite secluded and had the abundant vegetation the others lacked.

"Where are we going?" Please let food be involved.

"I want to show you a star. Then we're going to a really nice bistro on the other side of the mountain: outdoor seating, live music, really good food ... great atmosphere. It's called Magic Bistro. I think you'll love it."

"I bet I will." It sounded perfect. A magic bistro, a special star, a handsome ginger, and a yellow convertible. What else could a girl want?

A small nagging voice kept saying she was indeed pathetic. But Andrew had said she wasn't.

He was the caring kind and sincere. She believed him.

Too bad he's in the Army.

Chapter 3

The transition out of the Army, by itself, would have been hard enough. But to deal with the divorce too? Ouch. Andrew's heart broke for Clara. He looked at her pink lips and sun-kissed cheeks.

She'd probably prayed a lot around that time. He'd been about the same age when his parents almost got a divorce. His every prayer had been for his parents—for them to stay together. Her pain could have been his. But he'd been spared.

Their eyes met.

She wasn't a sad person, though. Quite the contrary. He'd never seen eyes so beautiful—sparkly green and full of life. "Almost there."

"Okay."

Even with her father's death, her grandma's illness, and her mother's absence, there was something vibrant about Clara Malone. She was different one on one. Where did that spark come from? Work? School? A boyfriend? Please let there be no boyfriend.

"Looks like it will get dark at last." She sat tall and looked toward Juarez.

"See?" He pointed at his watch. "Told you."

Her smile was warm and youthful. Her shiny lips and sparkly white teeth reminded him of early-night fireworks—the first ones you see after an expectation-filled afternoon.

Suddenly, his heart turned into lead and sank to the bottom of his chest with one thought: The Fourth of July. He'd done the math. Clara's stay in El Paso and Tatiana's would overlap by at least two days.

He couldn't and wouldn't pursue two girls at the same time, so if things went well with Clara, as he sure hoped they would, he would have to ask

Tatiana to cancel her trip. That simple. Considering what she'd put him through at the Academy, she shouldn't be surprised.

Coulda, woulda, shoulda. One thing at a time.

"How do you live in the middle of all this brownness?" she asked.

"You get used to it." The Star on the Mountain wasn't lit yet. "You find a nearby oasis or two for when you just need to see a green landscape."

"I take it this drive is not one of your green oases." She sat back, a smirk on her lips.

"No ... This is the Chihuahua Desert at its best." He slowed down by the short rock wall that separated the road from the cliff below. His favorite spot was free.

She chuckled. "This scenic drive is nice though. Thank you for bringing me here."

"You're welcome."

Andrew parked close to the star and hurried to her side of the car to open the door for her. Had she seen the star on postcards already? Did she arrive at night? Had she seen it from the plane? He hoped she hadn't. Now if he could only get the star to light up right in front of her eyes. Hmm.

He pointed at a particular portion of the stone wall. "Let's go over there."

"Sure. Do you mind if I put my clutch here?" she asked, lifting it toward the glove box.

He'd planned to give her the bracelet toward the end of the date, or maybe even in a couple of days, depending on how they hit it off. He didn't want her to think he was weird. Who gives an expensive gift on a first date, right? But before he could answer, she'd opened the glove box.

Andrew slammed it shut.

"I'm sorry." She held the bag against her chest and stepped out of the Crossfire. "I'll just carry it."

"I'm so sorry—"

"No. It's okay. I shouldn't have." She walked to the stone wall stoically— her delicate sandals and the uneven rocky ground seemed to be no match for her determination to get away from the Crossfire and from him.

Way to go, Andrew. Now she really thinks you're weird. He could save the situation and give her the bracelet right there and then. But had she even seen the box? Had she seen the bow? Definitely weird, but he should still wait for the right time. Right now it would be all wrong. He shook his head and walked toward her.

On the highway, she'd twisted her hair and held it against her chest. Now she used her small brush to loosen up her dark red waves again.

He couldn't remember the last time he'd watched a woman brush her hair, but he was pretty sure it'd been at home.

Clara's hair was full and reached down almost to her elbows. How appealing and feminine to witness the intimacy of her simple action, performed near the mountaintop, with a metropolitan area of one million at her feet. The goddess at home.

Juárez and El Paso looked absolutely stunning. She was stunning. Did she even know how beautiful she was?

She put the brush away when she saw him. "I love watching the world at dusk, don't you?"

He approached her. "I do." If she'd been at all offended by the whole glove box thing, she'd let it go. He got on the short wall with ease and stood next to her. On heels, she was close to his height. If he were to stand immediately in front of her, his lips would be at the height of her brow, where stubborn hairs from her side-part hairstyle often danced.

"So which star are we looking for?" she asked.

A warm breeze blew her hair in his direction, and he breathed in her sweet perfume. "I will let you know when I spot it."

El Paso and Juarez lit up slowly. The highway first, then the downtown buildings, and then the homes. The stars were always last.

"Does this star have a name?" Her gaze was fixed on the sky over Mexico.

Andrew looked over his shoulder. "Be patient." *God, help me with the timing. This will be so cool—if I time it right.*

"Be patient?" she asked, scanning every piece of the Paso del Norte sky now. "That's a funny name for a star."

He couldn't help but chuckle.

"I think your star is AWOL tonight. There's nothing out there."

She was even cuter when she said Army things.

She rested her eyes on him and bit one side of her lower lip like she'd done at the hotel, when he'd picked her up.

Did she know what that smile could do to a guy? Did she know what it could do to a guy who'd never known a woman?

Every thought ... every thought into captivity ... the Star on the Mountain ... let's not miss it ... He touched both her shoulders and turned her toward the north to face the rocky formation.

Clara trembled under his touch.

Her flowery scent was now mixed with sweet perspiration. She turned slightly, moving her gaze to his eyes in slow motion.

But if they cannot contain, let them marry: for it is better to marry than to burn. That's all I'm asking for, Lord. Please, let me marry—my way—Your way ...

The thought of his lips on hers made him exhale hard. He lifted his eyes staring firmly at the south face of the Franklin Mountains. *Give this woman to me, Father.*

Clara looked at the mountain too.

And then it happened. Right in front of their eyes, stretching some 500 feet toward the sky and almost as wide, the Star on the Mountain lit up the south side of the Franklins with 459 light bulbs.

"The Star on the Mountain." Andrew's voice was throaty.

"How beautiful! I love it!"

Perfect.

She faced him, causing his hands to separate from her shoulders. "Thank you!"

"You're welcome." He looked at where his hands had been with longing. *You're welcome, sweet Clara Malone.*

She looked up at the star again, and he watched her glow under it. "Hungry?"

"I thought you would never ask." She directed her radiant eyes toward his. "I'm starved."

"Then let me feed you." Andrew jumped down and offered his hand.

Yes, his heart broke for her. There wasn't much he could do about her past, but he could certainly give her a lovely June in El Paso, Texas.

And a lifetime, if God willed and if she would let him.

Chapter 4

Why hadn't he kissed her?

As they drove past a local university on the way to the bistro, the image of his lips so close to hers still teased her. Every memory from that moment by the star still teased her: his scent, his manly presence, the warmth of his hands on the bare skin of her shoulders, the intense desire in his eyes ... oh, those eyes. He'd wanted to kiss her. No doubt about it.

Maybe she shouldn't have worn an off-the-shoulder dress. It'd never made her feel naked before, but on that mountaintop, under his intense gaze, it had.

She respected his restraint, but after the glove-compartment incident, she couldn't pretend his Christian beliefs were the only reason behind it. She'd seen the shiny red present he'd tried so desperately to hide. He'd closed the glove compartment with such urgency and force that she could have lost her fingers in the process.

She turned her eyes to his perfect profile. What else was he hiding? *Ms. Old News?* Probably. He'd told the Howards Tatiana was planning a summer visit—the gift had to be for her.

Don't fall for this guy, Clara. It would be a mistake. She would be a major mess if he were to break her heart.

"We're here." He turned slowly into a long marketplace with a blue gazebo and quaint little shops on both sides of the narrow parking area. A simple sign by the entrance listed a dozen stores under the name Placita Santa Fe.

"The bistro is at the end, but we'll park right here." He pulled into the first parking space available.

Clara had seen a couple of jewelry stores listed on the sign. Maybe one would have a silver flower bracelet like the one at the airport. She should have bought it. Yes, it was a bit expensive, but it was so pretty. She'd returned to the airport store the next day, but they'd sold it.

Andrew closed the convertible top and walked around the front of the Crossfire.

Clara let him open the car door for her. "Thank you." She stepped out and took in the uniqueness of the place.

"What do you think?"

"This is beautiful—so different." She followed him, but her eyes were on an antique garden bench under an arch of delicate white blooms that looked like Spanish jasmine.

"Just about everything you see here is local. Local paintings, local jewelry, local crafts … not sure about all the antiques, but you get the gist."

Her focus remained on the gorgeous landscape. Dozens of pink and purple flowering trees lined both sides of the marketplace. Large terracotta and wooden planters filled with bright blooms decorated storefronts and sidewalks. Flowing fountains and the gazebo added charm to the Placita Santa Fe. *Wow.* "Oasis?"

His eyes sparkled under golden street lamps. "For sure."

A warm breeze ruffled the leaves of nearby trees and made delicate pink flowers rain down from them. She lifted her hands, catching a few of the velvety tubular blooms and then let them fall through her fingers. "Amazing."

They walked slowly, and she scanned the windows of every shop on their path, especially the jewelry ones. But there was no sign of a delicate silver bracelet with thin-petaled flowers anywhere.

What were the words on the petals? Love and dreams were two of them for sure, but she couldn't remember the rest.

The aroma of seared meat, roasted peppers, garlic, and spices filled the air delicately at first but quickly became intense as they walked deeper into the marketplace.

They reached a long stone wall, about seven feet tall, and Andrew stopped. "This is it."

Clara wasn't ready to leave the lusciousness of the marketplace behind, but the beautiful scent of herbs and the promise of a full tummy drew her in. Rosemary? Yum. "I hope it looks as nice as it smells."

"It does. Trust me." He led the way to the still-distant double iron gates of the Alamo-style entrance. Joyful sounds spilled out of the Magic Bistro and accompanied their final steps. Laughter, Spanish, and soft rock mixed with the frantic song of finches that came from the many tall, narrow trees lining their path.

A little gray finch perched on the wall and cocked his head as if studying her. *Shouldn't you be in bed, little one?*

He flew away and into the closest tall tree as if he'd heard her. "What kind of trees are these?"

"I'm not sure. Tuscany tall trees?"

Right. "Scientific name?"

"I doubt it, but there are tall trees in Tuscany that look just like these." He pinched off a little spike from the end of a branch and waved it under Clara's nose. "They smell like the ones in Italy too."

"All I smell is food, so I'll have to take your word for it."

Andrew stopped by the gate and stretched a hand inward, indicating *ladies first.*

To her surprise, the bistro's outdoor patio was not the end of the market-place's luscious beauty. It was the climax.

Wisteria trees grew by the beige building's green window frames and curved over most of the patio, forming a natural roof of soft green leaves and grape-like clusters of fragrant purple flowers.

Delicate geraniums in dozens of long layered planters lent their gentleness to the stone wall, and their pink blooms dazzled the eye in shades ranging from light blush to magenta. Smaller containers with similar combinations highlighted cascading fountains and decorated large circular planters that surrounded two smaller trees in the twelve-table patio.

Seen from the bistro, Andrew's *Tuscany tall trees* added height to the wall, making the space even more secluded and cozy. Orange candles and overhead strings of tiny lights created the magic of the Magic Bistro.

Andrew approached the simple host station. "Hi. Andrew James. Reservation for two."

The young host looked like Bradley Cooper in *American Sniper*, complete with the copper beard. He checked something off a chart and grabbed two thin menus. "Right this way."

They followed him past three wrought iron tables and reached the last one, a corner table next to a flowering tree and a fountain decorated with rustic iron planters and cascading yellow blooms.

"Thank you." Andrew pulled out the chair that offered the best view of the patio for her.

"Your waiter will be with you soon," said the American Sniper. "Enjoy."

She'd expected Andrew to sit opposite her at the round, green table partially covered by a square red tablecloth, but he didn't. He picked up a large iron chair with ease and put it down next to hers.

He winked. "Wouldn't want to block your view."

She chuckled. "That's your excuse, and you're sticking to it?"

"Yes, ma'am." He lowered his eyes to the menu.

Clara glanced at his red cheeks. How cute was that?

A waiter showed up. "Can I get you something to drink?"

"Water for now." The waiter looked like Bradley Cooper too, but without the beard. Maybe the waiter and the host were brothers. They had to be.

"Same here, please." Andrew's gaze returned to the menu.

"Let me get your waters. I'll be right back."

"I think I'll have a Stella," Andrew said to Clara after the waiter walked away.

"I like Stellas too, but alcohol messes up my balance."

Andrew laughed. "I said one Stella, not three."

It was the same hearty laugh she'd fallen in love with at the Radisson parking lot when she'd pulled out a mini hairbrush from her clutch. "It's not that." She laughed too.

"Then what is it?" he asked.

"I dance ballet. Even if I have one beer or one glass of wine, the next day my balances and my pirouettes are off."

"Really? I mean, how off? Do you feel intoxicated in class?"

"No, I don't feel anything. I'm just a little off. It took me a long time to figure it out, but I'm serious. It's for real."

"I'm not doubting you."

"People thought I was crazy for believing that, but the other day there was a story in *Dance Magazine* about this very thing."

"No kidding?" He took the water the waiter handed him and placed it in front of Clara.

"True story."

"Well, I'm not dancing ballet tomorrow." He looked at the waiter. "I'll have a Stella, please."

She chuckled at the thought of Captain Andrew James dancing ballet. "Well, come to think of it, I'm not dancing ballet tomorrow either." Or anytime soon. "I'll have a Stella too, please."

A skinny young guy with shaggy blond hair walked onto the patio with a guitar in hand. He sat on a stool on the makeshift stage near the bistro's entrance, and Clara sat a little taller. She spotted a couple of percussion instruments and a trumpet on the low stage too.

"So you dance?" Andrew asked.

"Not as well as I would like, but that's what I majored in. I have a Bachelor of Fine Arts in Dance with an emphasis in Ballet."

"That sounds cool." He pulled the straw out of his water and placed it next to the tall glass. "What do you do with a Bachelor of Fine Arts in Dance with an emphasis in Ballet?"

"That's the question of the hour." She shrugged. "I just graduated and spent the last several months trying to get into the corps of a dozen small companies, but nothing has worked out so far. I could teach. I could open a studio. I could get a master's. I don't know. There are lots of options, but I haven't figured out what to do next yet."

"That's why it was so easy for you to stay here—you're in transition." He had a sip of water and placed his cup back on the table, exactly where a wet circle indicated it'd been before.

"That's why my mom thinks it's easy for me to stay. She said that it's good to think about life and big decisions away from familiar places." Clara thought it was good to think about life and big decisions away from Army posts and away from ginger-haired young Army captains.

He filled up his lungs. "Something good will come up."

"I know." She returned her water glass to the table, putting it back where it'd been, like he'd done. "It has to, right?" Maybe she should try a few more companies. Maybe smaller ones. A company—the stage—that's where her heart really was. There was no getting around that. But to face more rejections? Not appealing. Not now.

"It will happen, Clara. Believe."

Believe ... She had—the first thirty times she'd tried, she had believed. But now any more believing seemed borderline foolish.

"So how much do you know about this famous love letter?" Andrew ran his fingertips up his cup, drawing small loops on the water drops clinging to the glass. "Why do you think the Howards and the general want you to stay?"

"My mom knows the whole story. I don't know the whole story." Clara paused as the waiter poured their beers into frozen glasses. "Thank you."

"Thanks." Andrew glanced at the menu. "We need a few more minutes."

"Take your time." The words rolled smoothly out of the waiter's mouth, and he walked away.

"My mom won't tell me much about the letter. She says I'm too judgmental."

"Are you?" Andrew's question was partially muffled by the first notes of an unfamiliar song.

"I don't think so." Clara opened the two-page menu and lifted it to eye-level. If people in her family didn't make poor choices, she wouldn't have to be judgmental. Wrong was wrong, and that was that.

"Do you want to share an appetizer?" Andrew's tone was less inquisitive now.

"Sure." A soft ballad she didn't recognize filled the warm night air. It sounded like something Sting would sing.

"Southwest spinach queso?" Andrew tapped the ballad's beat on the table with his fingertips.

"That sounds really good." Everything sounded really good.

"The fish is amazing—I've had the red snapper and the salmon. But everything here is wonderful. You can't go wrong."

They ordered and listened to the music. Talking to him about school and work had been easier than she'd expected. Andrew James made everything easy, somehow.

Unless someone tried to mess with his glove box, of course.

That thought took a bit of magic out of her Magic Bistro experience. What was so special about Tatiana?

The arrival of the Southwest spinach queso put Andrew's ex on the back burner, where Clara wished she'd stay.

"Let's pray." Andrew reached for Clara's hand before she could process the request.

When was the last time she'd prayed? It'd been years. Probably around the time her father died. Another unanswered prayer in her vast collection.

Her hand met his. *That's right, Ginger. You pray for us. He'll listen to you.* She bowed her head, and amid the sounds of multiple animated conversations, some in English and some in Spanish, she let Andrew's words fill her head, soak into her heart, and quietly become hers.

"Father God, thank you for the good company, for this beautiful place, and for the meal we are about to share. I ask that you bless it. Please bless also the time we get to enjoy together, and bless this—your child—Clara Malone. Direct her steps as she decides what she should do next in her life. We pray for these things in Jesus' name, amen."

"Amen." Andrew James was definitely different. Did God answer all his prayers?

Through the course of a meal that pleased the eye as well as the stomach, the musicians switched from rock ballads to jazzier tunes. Before taking a break, they promised to play a block of Armstrong and Etta James when they returned.

"Thanks for suggesting the fish." Clara winked. "Best salmon ever."

"Good."

He finished his pan-seared red snapper and placed his silverware neatly on the square white plate.

The two couples at the table in front of them stood to leave. The musicians were nowhere in sight. Should she use the lull in action and conversation to ask the question that had been in her head since he'd prayed for dinner?

"I need to use the restroom." He folded his napkin and stood.

She watched him walk toward the building. Did God answer all of Andrew's prayers?

Clara pulled her cherry lip gloss out of her clutch and applied the clear liquid to her lips as an older lady walked past her.

The woman made her way to a small waiter station by the door and returned moments later with a white napkin silverware roll. "When you come here all the time, you know where everything is," she said to Clara as she passed her. The two exchanged polite smiles.

Andrew was a few feet behind her and took his seat next to Clara.

"Can I ask a weird question?" Clara shifted in the iron chair.

"No." He laughed, and she followed suit. "Of course you can. Fire away."

"Does God answer all your prayers?"

"No."

"And that doesn't bother you?"

"It does, but there isn't a whole lot I can do about it. I have to trust that somehow, those unanswered prayers are for the best." He grabbed a piece of leftover bread from his plate and put a small crumb on the far edge of the table. "I read my Bible. I look at the history of guys like Joseph, Moses, David, and others. It's obvious, based on their lives, that God often takes His time to make things right."

She nodded slowly. But why? That seemed counterproductive in so many ways. A red-headed finch came to the table and ate the bread. "That didn't take long."

"No, it didn't." Andrew put another small piece out. "But there are many prayers that He answers."

Not hers. Hers seemed to always go unanswered.

"What do you pray about?" Andrew asked.

"I don't know." Nothing, really. Not anymore. She remembered her VBS teacher saying she was supposed to have a relationship with God through prayer. Some relationship. Only she talked. Only she asked. Nothing seemed to happen on the other end. It was just one more one-sided relationship in her life.

"If you only had one prayer to pray, what would it be?"

"One prayer?" Clara pretended to think while playing with the milky pink flower that had decorated her apricot citrus salmon. Should she tell him?

Andrew ran his fingers over his napkin. "Only one."

"A family that would never break." Admitting all she wanted was a normal family had sounded more pitiful out loud than it had inside her head.

"If you follow God's prescription for relationships, courtship, and marriage, you have a good shot."

"A godly marriage?" Whatever that was.

"That's right. If my parents hadn't put God first in their lives, they wouldn't be together today." He took a deep breath and seemed to look through the second finch that came to eat with them. "People split up when one or both parties get selfish."

That sounded about right, but what did he really know?

Andrew looked surprised when the waiter showed up to collect their plates. Where had his mind wandered to?

"Can I bring you a dessert menu?" the waiter asked.

She shook her head. "I'm okay. Thank you."

"Me too." Andrew rested his back against the chair and his smile returned. "I'm fine for now."

"How about you?" Clara asked Andrew when the waiter left.

"What about me?"

"You put me on the spot with the one-prayer-to-pray question. Your turn. If you only had one prayer to pray, what would it be?"

"No, mine will sound weird." He sat back and looked at her. "Can I pass?"

"I told you mine. You can't pass." She laughed.

"All right, all right." He cleared his throat.

She used her fingers as pretend drumsticks on the edge of the table. "Drum roll, ta-ta-da-da."

"Here it goes. Preachers sometimes say that we, Christians, are the only Bible many people will ever read." He paused. "My prayer is that I can be a good Bible—live well, so others will want to know more about God."

He wanted to be a good Christian example?

"I told you it would sound weird."

"No, that's cool." He wasn't selfish like her dad. That was very cool. Good prayer. "Did you go to church a lot as a kid?"

Andrew finished his water. "I grew up in church."

"What's that like?" Growing up, she'd hated going to church in random spurts.

"Fun. I enjoyed it." The waiter appeared with a pitcher of water and filled both their glasses.

The musicians emerged from the indoor dining area, and the trumpet player got the music started. A slow rendition of "La Vie En Rose." Nice.

"I'm still adjusting to life around a majority that doesn't share my beliefs, though. I've been away from home—from my parents—for eight years now, and I still struggle sometimes."

"Is it tempting to do what everyone else is doing?" Clara asked.

"Not really. I think the hardest part for me is to deal with people's reactions when things in my life aren't going well."

That was the first time Clara saw him look tense. "Was Tatiana something that didn't go well?" Had she said that out loud? Oops.

He nodded. "You can say that."

"What happened?" Why did this girl have to exist?

Andrew lifted his arm and got the waiter's attention. "Are you sure you want to hear this story?"

"Pretty sure." Since the girl did exist, curiosity was getting the better of Clara. *Order a drink and tell me, so I know what I'm up against.* Oh, what was wrong with her? She wasn't up against anything. Captain Andrew James was off limits. No soldiers, Clara. No soldiers.

He scratched his head with a boyish I'm-in-trouble-now half smile.

Interesting expression. Did he still like her? *Of course he does, idiot. He's got a gift for her in his car.*

"What can I get you?" the waiter asked him.

"Can I have some tea?"

"Iced tea?"

"Hot tea. Any black tea."

"Earl Grey?" the waiter suggested.

"Sure. That sounds good."

"I'll have the same." Clara smiled.

"So ..." Andrew sat back. "I met her at the Academy. We arrived there together."

That Clara hadn't expected. The girl was a soldier? Hmm.

"There was something between us from the beginning—we just stuck together. With us, it was never a question of 'will we get married one day?' It was always one of 'when would I propose?'"

She'd felt that way about Scott. Instant attractions were evil.

"It took me two years—I proposed exactly after two years of dating. We were planning a big post-graduation wedding at the Academy, like half the other cadets. But one week before the wedding, during graduation week, she told me she'd changed her mind."

"Wow. Why?"

He shrugged. "She did extremely well there."

"You think it kind of went to her head?"

"I think so. I think that ever so slowly, in her mind, marriage became something beneath her somehow."

"Is that what she said?"

"Not like that. Not exactly. She said she wanted to stand on her own two feet and be her own person for a while, before committing to marrying."

"Ouch."

"Yep. That's my sob story."

"I'm so sorry."

He shrugged. "God has a different plan."

"That's so sad, to change her mind so close to the wedding."

"I should have seen it coming. Because of her high grades, she was able to choose her first assignment. Instead of choosing a large infantry post—she's an MP, military police can go anywhere—she chose Italy. There's airborne infantry there, and I'd been to jump school as a cadet, but it's a small post. It was a long shot."

"Did you try to go there?"

"I tried. But I got Germany instead—a weird assignment that would not have been my first choice at all: a separate battalion slated for deactivation."

"Wow." Clara wasn't sure what a separate battalion was, but *deactivation* had to be a bad thing for a young infantry officer fresh out of West Point.

"Here's the kicker: You can't be married while attending the Academy, so as soon as people graduate, they marry. I attended seven weddings the month following graduation. All but mine. Talk about adding insult to injury."

If she hugged him, he would think she was weird. Bless him. "And you've seen her since that time? And she's coming here this summer?"

"That's the rumor." The waiter arrived with two tall white mugs of hot water and shiny silver packets of Earl Grey tea along with a small white container of sweeteners.

Andrew ripped open a packet of tea and dipped the bag in the water. "When she canceled the wedding, she said she hoped I would wait for her— she said she just needed to grow up."

"So here you are waiting for her?"

"Not really. I didn't close any doors, but I'm not holding them wide open either." His expression softened. "I'm here having dinner with you, and you're lovely, and I hope to get to know you better and see where it goes."

"And if I don't measure up, you have Tatiana as your fall-back plan." Whatever. It's not like she intended to have a relationship with him, anyway.

"That's not fair at all. That's not me. I haven't thought about Tatiana romantically in quite some time, but you said you wanted to know the story. Now you know the story."

Andrew James was an interesting man, for sure. But the potential for Tatiana to waltz right back into his life and for him to kick Clara to the side like a dead bug found upside down on the porch in the morning was absolutely undeniable. She'd been right to ask.

He reached for her hand and brought it to his lips.

Her heart did a somersault in her chest. "No, Andrew." They couldn't. She couldn't.

"What is it?" he asked, holding her hand in both of his.

She shook her head but didn't withdraw her hand. "There is something I need to tell you. You seem really nice—"

"Oh no. The you-seem-really-nice-but talk of doom."

She smiled a tight-lipped smile. "I do like you. So much so, by the way, that I will tell you right now that you should not give this Tatiana girl another chance."

"You like me, but?"

"But I don't think I'm the one." The one … the airport. Her heart was suddenly gooey, like the Hersheys bars her mom used to put in her ballet bag when she was little.

"But why?"

She looked at their hands. His touch, the way his hands enveloped hers … it felt so right. But no. No, no, no. She wasn't the one. "I don't date soldiers."

"Why?"

"Don't be offended. It's not you. I just can't." Still, her hand was paralyzed in his.

"But why?"

"Women in my family have had really bad luck with soldiers—three generations of women ruined by soldiers."

"Oh, that sounds so Oprah. Listen to yourself. I'm sure there are unique reasons why each relationship didn't work out. You can't generalize things like that."

She could, and she would. "I can't. It ends with me." Then why couldn't she stop looking at his lips?

"Let it end with you by making your story work." His dark green eyes narrowed. "I would never ruin or hurt anyone, Clara. I'm not that kind of guy."

"Slow down there, Ginger. Who's being all Oprah now?"

"Ginger?" His eyes softened. "I'm just using the words you tossed out there."

She shook her head. "Something would happen, Andrew. It would end up badly. It always does. I would love you, you would hurt me, and then instead of walking away, I would stay, against all common sense. I would be crushed—completely crushed."

"Wow. You sure have it all figured out."

"That's what my grandma did. And that's what my mom did—twice." And she'd done it once already, but she wasn't going to do it again. She remembered the first time she went on post with Scott. She remembered him asking her to duck at a fast food drive-thru. It'd sounded like a joke at first, but he was dead serious. The humiliation burned fresh inside her. "It's enough, Andrew. I'm sorry."

"I would never hurt you."

She shook her head. "I don't want to be stupid like my mother or my grandmother." She withdrew her hand. "It's enough."

"You *are* being judgmental."

"Am not."

"Are too. I can see why your mom is reluctant to share the letter's story."

"What is it to you? Why do you care?"

"I care about people. I care about you, Clara."

Keeps getting better. She focused on the stage.

"Clara." She felt his eyes on her but refused to look at him.

"If this family history upsets you, unsettles you, or whatever it does, you really need to look into it. Make the distance work for you."

"What are you talking about?" She looked at him now.

"The phone. Take advantage of asking questions by phone." He raised his eyebrows. "You can make faces all you want if your mom tells you something that bothers you. Just don't open your mouth to express an opinion."

"Why should I ask?"

He threw his hands up and chuckled. "Discover the real story. This is not even my family's history, and I'm curious. How can you not get excited about it?"

She played statue for five seconds. "Just like that—not excited."

"Why?"

"A bunch of people got hurt, Andrew. Am I the only one doing the math?"

"What do you mean?"

"Nothing." Why wasn't anyone else connecting the dots? General Medeiros had to have known both Alice's mom and Clara's grandma at the same time. Her mom had told her that Alice was the last of several children and that she was a *tempora*, she was born when her nearest sibling was already a teen, and the oldest was already married with kids of his own. It was obvious the general was already married when he met her grandma. She didn't need the details. If she was right, she and her grandma had more in common than she cared to admit. It was much easier to play the judgmental role she'd created for herself than to deal with the truth. The truth would come with guilt—guilt she didn't know if she could handle.

Clara's tea bag was still in the water. It was probably nasty by now. Hmm. And what was the deal with the sudden silence? What happened to the music? Surely they hadn't gone on break again.

"I'm not any of those guys, Clara." He finished his tea. "This is so absurd."

"I know." He was indeed different—not at all like any man she'd ever known. "But it's too much baggage." *Mine and yours.* "I should steer clear."

"Don't steer clear. Don't be trapped by some silly idea." He reached for her hand again. "Spend time with me."

She offered him a tight-lipped smile. *It's not for the lack of wanting, Ginger.*

As her heart dwelled on what ifs, her eyes focused on the makeshift stage. That was different—the percussionist had the microphone. He looked like a young Louis Armstrong. Would he sound like him too?

The trumpet broke the silence, and Clara recognized the melody from an old Marisa Tomei movie.

Andrew had the same boy-in-trouble smirk on his face—the one she'd noticed when he was preparing to tell her about Tatiana. He was probably thinking about her again. Fair enough—she'd just told him they couldn't be together.

The Louis Armstrong look-a-like didn't sound like Louis Armstrong at all. His voice wasn't gravelly. It was young and clean, almost like a female's voice. It was beautiful.

Andrew stood and took a step away from the table, planting himself under the pink flowers and long green leaves of their corner tree.

What was he up to now?

He stretched his hand to her.

He wanted to dance?

"Here?" she asked, surveying the patio. Surely he didn't expect her to dance. No one else was dancing or had danced the whole time they'd been there.

"Right here." He held both arms out and wiggled his fingers.

Clara surveyed the patio again.

"No one is looking, but if you make me wait any longer, people will start wondering why I'm standing here by myself, my girl just staring at me and making me look foolish."

His girl … Her skin pebbled as if she were in the middle of a Cincinnati blizzard. "No pressure."

"None whatsoever." Andrew stepped closer.

She stood and straightened her emerald green dress. "Only one dance." A tremor that originated in the pit of her stomach traveled to her arms and hands, making her whole chest tingle.

"Only youuuuu," he whispered the lyrics in unison with the musician and stepped into her personal space.

His right arm circled her waist and gathered her body and her thoughts, bringing all of her into the fire of his presence. Clara stiffened.

"Relax, girl." He picked up her right hand and held it to his chest. "Loosen up a little—have some fun."

His heartbeat was strong and steady, like a steam locomotive leaving the station.

Images of the first time she met her ex-boyfriend, Scott, flooded her mind. Not like a tsunami that takes everything down with violence. But more like a slow flood that seeps in calmly under the door and rises slowly and without a sound until the whole house is under water.

But Andrew had said he wasn't like those guys. Not Scott, not the guy her mom had moved to America to be with, not her dad, not Mario Medeiros. He wasn't like any of them, he'd said. Should she believe him?

She tried to relax into his gentle rhythm. He smelled so good. Looked so good. Why did she have to be so broken?

I need a sign ...

The buzzing sound of hummingbird wings startled her. She spotted the tiny bird by the tree. And then another showed up—humming louder and in a higher pitch. They exchanged even chee-dit sounds as they danced around each other, drank from the tubular orchid-like pink flowers of the tree, and departed together. Was this a sign?

Clara froze, and Andrew opened his eyes.

"What is this tree?"

"A desert willow." He stopped too.

"Because it's a willow, and it's in the desert?" She chuckled.

He twisted his mouth. "This one I actually know. There are tons of these in my neighborhood. When my mom visited, she looked it up. It *is* a desert willow."

"It's pretty." But two hummingbirds and a desert willow did not a sign make, did they?

"You're right about one thing." Andrew held her tight.

"What?"

"You don't dance well." He chuckled.

"Andrew!" She chuckled too and slapped his chest.

"I'm kidding." He laughed.

There it was. Delightful. Deep. Heartfelt. "I don't dance well ... you'll see." The trumpet solo started. "Let's dance. I'll lead."

"Sure, you will." Andrew spun her out and then back in to the sound of Clara's giggles.

"Look at you." Why hadn't he danced like that from the start? "Nice." She leaned into him and followed his perfect rhythm. Not bad for a grunt.

"What happened to 'I'll lead'?"

"I only lead if I have to." *Oh, Andrew. I'm so tired of leading.*

Her fingertips rested on the back of his neck—his sweet-smelling sweat inviting a caress. Should she? She experimented with small slow strokes, her fingers sliding easily over his soft skin.

His arms tightened around her. His chest trembled against hers. A long low sound seemed trapped behind his lips.

Oh, Andrew ... Her hand traveled up to where freckled skin met ginger hair.

He spun her out. His hand held hers tighter than before, and the distance imposed by their extended arms did not extinguish the intensity of his gaze.

Clara felt the arm tug of his gentle but clear lead. She spun back to him as the band played the final notes of the song. Must breathe. Her chest rose in response.

His hand supported her back, and he dipped her, like the sailor who kissed the nurse on the day Japan surrendered.

Would he kiss her now and end her inner wars? *Please do.*

The velvety warmth of bergamot on his sweet Earl Grey breath enticed her. He bit his lower lip to the sound of claps and whistles from nearby diners.

A heat wave rose from her chest and settled on her cheeks.

The intensity of his hold changed slightly. No, no, no. It weakened just enough for her to know he was going to lead her to her feet. Why? She swallowed hard and let him help her stand straight.

He held her until she was steady on her feet—his strong hands around her slender arms.

Clara pressed her sweaty palms against the soft emerald fabric that covered her thighs. Why couldn't she think of anything smart to say? *Come on. Say something …*

Their waiter came by with the water pitcher again, and Andrew watched Clara while both their cups were filled to the brim. "Can we have the check, please?"

Chapter 5

A ndrew took the Patriot Freeway toward the Fort Bliss main gate instead of following Interstate 10 back to the airport area. And if Clara noticed, she didn't mention it.

If they were going to spend any meaningful time together, he would have to throw her in at the deep end. Fort Bliss wasn't West Point, and Noel Field wasn't The Plain, but it would have to do for now.

He'd first stood on the east edge of The Plain overlooking the Hudson River when he was eleven years old. They'd traveled to the Academy to bury his granddaddy, who graduated from there in 1962, a Vietnam War hero, and retired soon after serving in Operation Desert Shield and Desert Storm.

He'd known his granddaddy was home with the Lord. But there, on that cold New York winter day in 1999, with his young feet planted firmly on the fresh snow dust of the West Point cemetery, he'd discovered yet another home his granddaddy had. The Corps.

His dad, West Point class of 1986, delivered the graveside eulogy and quoted General MacArthur. He used excerpts from the general's Thayer Award acceptance and farewell address that Andrew now carried folded in his Bible, the pages fittingly dirty and worn from frequent field problems, his time in Afghanistan, and many moves—both as an Army brat and as a soldier.

The long gray line has never failed us. Were you to do so, a million ghosts in olive drab, in brown khaki, in blue and gray, would rise from their white crosses, thundering those magic words: Duty, Honor, Country.

His dad had grown up hearing Granddaddy talk about that speech, about that sunny Saturday afternoon just days before his graduation, and about the legendary general who'd stood in front of the Corps of Cadets in the dining hall and delivered his formidable and now famous farewell address using a 3x5 flashcard with one word on it.

Andrew remembered Granddaddy talking about the MacArthur speech very vaguely, but one thing he remembered quite precisely. He'd said that when the general finished, there were no dry eyes in all of Washington Hall.

The same had been true of Granddaddy's graveside eulogy. Even his dad cried. His voice had stayed steady, but the tears flowed freely and unabashedly from "the twilight is here" to "farewell."

In my dreams I hear again the crash of guns, the rattle of musketry, the strange, mournful mutter of the battlefield. But in the evening of my memory I come back to West Point. Always there echoes and re-echoes: Duty, Honor, Country. Today marks my final roll call with you. But I want you to know that when I cross the river, my last conscious thoughts will be of the Corps, and the Corps, and the Corps. I bid you farewell.

Andrew knew from that day on that he belonged in that long gray line too, with his grandfather, who'd been the first in the family to go to West Point, and with his father, who'd gladly followed suit.

Even when many of his friends were being called into full-time ministry, he knew with absolute certainty that God had put him on this Earth to be a soldier—to lead men. His dad had gone as far as sending him on a church field trip to a Bible college in California during his junior year of high school *just to be sure* he was making the right decision. Andrew was sure. He was sure before the trip. He was sure during the trip. He was sure after the trip. He'd always been sure.

He was now sure that he was everything Clara appeared to despise.

She wiggled her fingers in the direction of the side-view mirror, seeming to enjoy the cool late-night desert air.

If only he didn't like her so much.

She didn't try to keep her hair twisted now. Long strands of dark red hair danced in the breeze, inviting a caress.

If he didn't like her so much, he would drop her off at the hotel and leave it at that. The world had many beautiful girls. There was no reason to spend time with one who didn't date soldiers. He'd met girls like that before in Europe, and he'd simply moved on.

But he liked this one—he liked her too well.

Sure she was a knockout. Her lips had been so close to his that he could still smell the fruity gloss he'd so wanted to taste. Sure the warmth of her skin was by far the loveliest thing he'd ever seen.

But that wasn't all.

He'd felt it again. The same sense of destiny he'd felt at age eleven on the Plain. He'd felt it with her at the Magic Bistro. She was to be his. Or was that his imagination feeding words into his loneliness?

"Those are nice." She pointed at the back of the two and a half story brick Victorian houses, part of Sheridan Street's senior officer housing area.

"Mhmm." *Please don't be mad, Clara.* Andrew took the Cassidy Gate exit, and soon the illuminated M41 Walker Bulldog tank displayed at the entrance came into view. On its base, the words "Home of the 1ˢᵗ Armored Division" and the Dorito-shaped distinctive insignia with the nickname "Old Ironsides" left little to the imagination. They were going on post.

"What are you doing?" Clara's easygoingness vanished—she sat tall, twisted her hair, and placed her free hand on her lap. "Where are you taking me?"

"Noel Field." He turned right and proceeded slowly to the gate.

"What's Noel Field? Why are we here?"

"A parade field." Or should he take her to the flag pole? No—too austere. Noel Field would be perfect. "I'll need your driver's license."

"Maybe I don't have it on me."

He cocked his head and held out his hand, palm up, waiting for her picture ID.

She shook her head while digging it out of her little purse and held it out, making him take it instead of placing it on his hand.

Her eyes riveted on the large brown sign with the Department of the Army emblem.

United States Army
Fort Bliss
Cassidy Main Gate

Andrew dimmed the Crossfire's headlights and stopped next to the soldier at the gate. He took his military ID card out of his wallet and handed both IDs to the sergeant.

The young sergeant took a step back and studied the car. "Nice wheels. What is this, sir?"

"A Chrysler Crossfire."

"She's a beauty." He scanned Andrew's ID card.

"Yes, she is." Andrew glanced at Clara, who was looking away.

"Here you go, sir." The sergeant returned their documents and saluted Andrew. "Welcome to Fort Bliss."

Clara was watching them now.

"Thanks." Andrew returned the salute. "Have a good night."

"You too, sir."

"Here's your ID." Andrew rolled onto post and glanced at the picture of a very young Clara with three-inch-long hippie earrings. "High school picture?"

"Whatever." She grabbed her license without looking at him.

Ooh, she was mad. *Sorry.*

He turned onto Sheridan Street, and she lifted her eyes to the war memorial on the corner of Cassidy and Sheridan.

"The Field of Honor Memorial—dedicated to Fort Bliss soldiers who've died in Iraq and Afghanistan."

She nodded in slow motion, her face glowing in the soft golden light of the monument and of the street lights on Sheridan's median.

Would she want to hear about the post? Or should he keep the narration to a minimum?

"Why are you taking me to a parade field in the middle of the night?"

How could he explain it? *I want to see just how uncomfortable the Army makes you? I want to know if there's hope of reformation?*

"Well?"

"I want to show you something."

"Wow. That explains a lot." She rubbed her bare arms. "Is this it?"

"No. This is not the one. Just work with me. It's not far—it's just up the road." She still held her hair in a twist, but she seemed to relax in her seat again. Good.

"So this is why there are no trees in El Paso." She looked straight ahead and lifted both hands toward both sides of Sheridan Street, an area jam-packed with tall pines, mesquites, desert willows, and Tuscany tall trees, each well-established on perfectly-green grass. "They're all here."

Her voice was playful now. Was he out of the dog house? She was right about the trees—Sheridan was exceptionally green and not at all like a typical El Paso street with landscaping gravel, decorative rocks, and infant trees.

"Let me guess." She looked at Andrew intentionally for the first time since they'd arrived on post. "Senior officer housing?"

"For the most part."

"Commanding general?" She pointed at Pershing House, a large white house completely different from all the others with green windows and wide covered porches.

"It was built for that purpose, I assume—it's called Pershing House, and General Pershing was a post commander here during parts of the Mexican Revolution. But now it's somebody else's house, I think—another general, I'm sure, but not the commander." Was she getting into being on post, or was she being pleasant for the sake of being pleasant?

"A Japanese garden?" Clara asked, sitting tall and stretching in Andrew's direction.

"Maintained by the Japanese."

"Who live here for that purpose?"

"Who maintain liaisons here and have troops who rotate from time to time."

"Oh ..."

"If nothing changes, the Howards will get one of these bungalows." The line of single-story beige bungalows was not exactly impressive, but there was no beating the location.

"Too bad they can't get one of the big red brick ones."

Andrew shrugged. "They could still get it. Just doesn't look like it right now."

"Where did you meet them?"

"We were stationed in Baumholder together." Eventually, he would tell her about being in Afghanistan with Colonel Howard, but tonight he didn't feel like talking about wars.

"Where's Baumholder?" Clara asked.

"Near Frankfurt."

She nodded and looked away, seeming to lose interest in the conversation. Did he say something wrong?

Across the street from senior housing, Center Chapel's mission-like façade shone peacefully in the quiet night. Andrew fixed his eyes on the simple cross.

The 25-mile-per-hour speed limit suited the mood and Andrew's purpose.

God, please give me the words. Help me say them in the right spirit. Soften her heart.

The hot day had become a nice warm night, but as midnight approached, the air was getting cool.

Clara had her hands on her lap—elbows tight against her body. He should offer her a jacket.

"This is it." He pointed to the empty field and approached the small parking lot.

He parked by the entrance of the reviewing stand, and his headlights created a path toward the field.

Andrew considered playing his own music but turned on the radio instead. Let God pick the soundtrack to his attempt to get Clara to lower her guard.

Clara looked left, right, and then straight again. "So, what are you showing me exactly?"

"I want to tell you something." He looked at the radio and cringed. Enough with all the chatter—just play something good.

"Then tell me." She rubbed her arms. "I'm getting cold."

"I have a jacket in the trunk." He did have a jacket in the trunk, right? He got out of the Crossfire.

She twisted in her seat and followed him with her eyes.

Andrew opened the trunk and saw the only option available: the jacket of his Army Service Uniform. He chuckled. This would do—this would do perfectly.

He opened her door and held out the jacket, made heavy by more badges, cords, and ribbons than most guys with his rank and time in service.

She sighed and stared at the ground.

"Come on. Let's go take a look around." *Before the MPs come ask us what we're doing.*

Clara stood and let him help her into his jacket.

He left the headlights and the radio on, grabbed her hand, and led her to the reviewing stand.

In front of them was a sprawling green field—a field of possibilities.

"Clara, I love the Army. I was made for it. My middle name is Lee—after General Lee. I went to the Academy. My dad went to the Academy. And his father before him. This is me." He breathed the green grass. "Duty. Honor. Country. It runs in my veins. The long gray line."

She gazed at the field, her eyes narrow, and her lips pressed together.

"General MacArthur once said that his last thoughts on this earth would be of West Point and of the people, the many generations of people, who've lived the values we learn at the Academy. In a famous speech he gave there, he said, 'I want you to know that when I cross the river, my last conscious thoughts will be the Corps, and the Corps, and the Corps.'"

Clara looked at him, her green eyes glistening, her expression softer.

"That will be me one day. I don't mean a famous general, though that would be great. I mean the sentiment. That will be me. In love with and in awe of the profession of arms and of the people who are called to it."

She nodded. "Like I said before, you seem nice. I meant no offense."

"Clara, I like you. I wish you would give me a legit chance. I wish you could put aside past disasters. I'm ready to put aside my past disaster."

"I don't think I can. It's all too much right now."

"Too much what?"

"Too much … Army."

Andrew lifted his hands toward Noel Field and then dropped them, sticking both deep into his pockets, his gaze low.

Lord, give me the words to speak here.

"I love the Army like you love dancing—I think. But this is not all there is to me, just like dancing is not all there is to you. I'm also a guy who wants to give the world to a girl. And I'm so ready to find the girl." He searched her face. "Be the girl, Clara. Let's get to know each other."

She tightened her lips, and big tears rolled from her eyes. "Why me?"

"You're lovely."

"I'm not that pretty."

"I'm not talking about that kind of lovely—though you *are* stunningly beautiful. You're—" Everything that came to his mind seemed wrong. Vulnerable wouldn't sound right. That she needed him sounded even worse. *Please give me the words.*

"I'm what?"

"You're the woman I've been looking for all along, Clara. I know we've just met, but I can tell that you're different. You let me take care of you. You listen to what I say. You're comfortable saying nothing at all. I love the way you laugh and smile and move. I feel like I've always known you." Andrew touched her unsteady lips. "I feel like I was born to stand on this field with you today—just like I knew I was meant to be a soldier on the day we said goodbye to my grandfather."

"That was beautiful." Clara buried her face on his chest and sniffled.

On the distant Crossfire radio, a soft melody. He recognized it. Casting Crowns. "Broken Together."

His hands reached for her waist under the jacket. Clara trembled but stepped closer, and they swayed cheek-to-cheek to Mark Hall's pleading voice.

Her hesitation to his touch was his signal. He'd taken it far enough. This was not the day for kissing.

But the day would come. She would be his. All his.

Chapter 6

Clara opened her hotel room window.

The early morning sunlight made El Paso look less brown, and a cool breeze ruffled the tall palm trees that stood between her second-floor room and the airport's short-term parking lot.

She dragged a heavy chair to the window and waited for her mom's call.

Crazy weather. Good thing she'd brought a long-sleeved nightgown. She drew her knees up to her chest, pulled the long gray gown with little red hearts over her legs and tucked it under her toes. There. Her freshly-brewed coffee warmed her hands.

The phone came to life, showing a pink zinnia and playing an Argentine tango. *Mom.*

"Make faces—don't express a verbal opinion." She could handle that. Right?

Why was she doing this? Because Andrew said she should? Yeah … She shook her head, swiping the answer icon. "Hi, Mom."

"Hi, *Princesa.*"

She sounded happy. Grandma must have had a good night.

"So, I want to know everything. How did it go with Andrew? Were you miserable the whole time like you thought you would be?"

"Not too terribly miserable." The sweet agony of falling hard for someone she shouldn't love was not the kind of misery Sofia Tomaselli-Malone was asking about. "How's Grandma?"

"She had a good night, but she is showing more and more signs that she is …"

Her mom's silence said everything.

"It'll be okay, Mom."

"Ela está se recolhendo." She sobbed.

"Oh, Mom. I'm so sorry." Whatever *recolhendo* meant, it had to be bad. "It's a positive thing that she had a good night though, right?"

"Yes." Her mom sniffed hard. "She's been peaceful."

Clara nodded. "I wish I could be there to give you both a hug."

"But you're not, and it's okay, because you're doing something very special for your grandmother."

"I know, I know."

"And you can do something special for me too."

"Why am I afraid to ask?"

"Simple. Tell me about your date. Tell me about your ginger."

"Mom!"

"What? You can't say no."

"Yes, I can. 'No.' Just like that."

"I've been practically living in hospitals for almost two months now— with my dying mother, mind you—I need word from the outside world, and I need to know about my only baby."

"Oh, okay." Clara shook her head.

"Oba! Let me grab my coffee and sit by the window."

Clara smiled.

"Ready. So where did he take you?"

Her mom loved hearing every detail of every date she'd ever had. It was exhausting. But today, Clara didn't mind. Her mom was right. She'd earned some cheering up.

"How big was this Star on the Mountain?" her mom asked.

"Huge—like a two-story home."

Clara remembered the way he'd touched her.

"So you asked for a sign, and right away these two hummingbirds showed up?"

"Yep."

"Wow!"

"I know!"

"And he can dance?"

"I'm telling you. It felt good. And he finished with one of those roll out, roll in, and incline-to-kiss moves, you know? The whole restaurant clapped."

"Sounds like your kind of guy. And meant to be—according to the hummingbirds. Did he kiss you when he dropped you off?"

"He wasn't finished. You won't believe what he did next."

"What?"

"It was almost midnight. He took me to Fort Bliss—to the main parade field."

"No!"

"Yes."

"What for?"

"He wanted to tell me about how proud he is of his service, his intentions of being a career officer, the long gray line, etcetera."

"And you?"

"It was nice to hear him talk about the Academy—he's a third generation West Point grad. He loves the military." Clara shrugged. "He quoted General MacArthur."

"Oh …"

She didn't want to give out all the details. The parade field dance was private. Her wearing his uniform jacket was private. His sweet words about her—private.

The song they'd danced to was stuck in Clara's mind. Broken together … What was that all about? She'd meant to ask him about godly marriages and what exactly that meant. Maybe next time. He'd said his parents had a godly marriage. Did he want a godly marriage? Probably. Whatever that was. Sounded boring. But then again, there was nothing boring about Captain Andrew Lee James. Not. One. Thing. The thought of his hands on her waist made her tremble. Why hadn't he kissed her?

"Will you see him today?"

"We are doing dinner and a movie on post."

"Look at you, on post this, on post that."

"I know, right?"

"Are you feeling okay about it?"

"I told you I thought about Dad a lot when I first got here, and our times at Fort Benning and then at Fort Bragg." On the skies over El Paso, a lonely Chinook helicopter made its way toward post. "But I'm okay now."

"And Scott?"

The sound of his name made Clara cringe. "Mom, that's in the past, and it's off limits."

"Okay."

"I'm all right, Mom. I'm proceeding with caution. Lots of caution."

"Did you see the apartment the Howards are putting you in?"

"No. I didn't see the point."

"Can you email me the new itinerary?"

"Sure."

This would be a wonderful time to hang up without getting into any of the Renata Lambert and Mario Medeiros business.

"All right, *Princesa*. Have fun hanging out on post tonight. I will call you again tomorrow."

Clara looked at the letter, resting next to her yellow roses—a wave of mixed emotions filled her heart. "Mom?"

"Yes?"

"Do you know what's in the letter?"

"Yes and no."

"Wow. That was really helpful."

"It's hard to explain without telling the whole story, but every time I've tried, you get upset."

"Andrew is curious about it."

"Why?"

"He's a Christian. I think he just wants me to listen to you and not be judgmental."

"Or Alice Howard put him up to it."

"No. He's not that kind of guy." So she'd been right all along, Mario knew both her grandma and Alice's mom at the same time and might have been in a relationship with both at the same time. *Gross.* She made a face and bit her tongue.

"I don't know, Clara. Why would Andrew care?"

"He cares about everything? I don't know."

"I would love to tell you. If you can listen with your heart. But I don't think you should tell him."

Could something—anything—be simple? "Then don't tell me, I guess."

"I'm not understanding. You said you were going to proceed with caution—'lots of caution,' and now you want to tell him the whole history of your family?"

The whole history? And the drama began. No, actually, it didn't. No opinions. That was what she'd set out to do. Not judge. On purpose.

"Mom, I want to hear her story—while she's still on this Earth."

"Well …"

Clara held her breath during the silence that followed, exhaling only after her mother began to speak again.

"Your grandmother was the most beautiful and the wealthiest little girl in all of the German colonies of the south of Brazil."

Sounded like she was in for the long version. *Just listen—learn something.* What was it about Andrew's words that made them replay in her head again and again?

"She also became the saddest little girl when her daddy died. She was so young. Fifteen, maybe? Her daddy was the wealthiest man in the region—shoe industry—but his little girl, your Grandma Renata, had him wrapped around her little finger."

"I remember parts of this story."

"Did I tell you about her ball gowns?"

"No."

"She would take her *modista*?"

"No idea, Mom. My Portuguese is lousier than ever."

"Like a seamstress?"

"Okay."

"She would take her to the movies and point out the gowns she wanted, and she would make them even more beautiful than in the movies. At the club on weekends, the band stopped when your great-grandfather arrived. They would play a folk song he loved, "Boi Barroso", and everyone knew Wilhelm had arrived. Then they would play a waltz, and he would spin his little girl around and around the dance floor. She was his pride and joy. He was already in his fifties, I think. All her brothers and sisters were already married when she was born. She brought new life to the house. They loved her so much. Her life was a fairytale. They were royalty in the area."

Clara nodded silently. She had a picture of her grandma at about twenty years of age in her apartment. Shoulder-length light hair, doe-eyed, beautiful smile, even if slightly contained. She wore a dark top and a medallion. Clara labored to imagine that same young woman as a teenage girl in a Vivien Leigh-style ball gown, but she tried, and soon, images of her grandmother waltzing with her dad filled her head. "If she was fifteenish when he died, wasn't she too young to go to balls?"

"Not back then, and it was a family affair. Uncles, aunts, cousins, mom, dad, everybody attended."

"And then what happened? How did he die?"

"Heart attack."

Clara heard her mom take a deep breath.

"It was something else. Your great-grandfather was not just the region's wealthiest man. He was also the town's benefactor. When he died, the whole town mourned. He died out of town during a business trip. When the people heard the news, they all went to the train station to wait for the body—the train station he'd helped build."

"Wow."

"Everyone wore black, and your grandma still talks about these enormous torch-like candles that were everywhere. That's why she still can't stand candles anywhere near her. It reminds her of that day, possibly still the worst day of her life. The end of her fairy tale."

Why did she ask to hear? Now she was heartbroken. She hated being heartbroken.

"When they buried him, his youngest boy played the harmonica next to the coffin as it went slowly down—tears flooding the young man's face and his little harmonica. He played 'Boi Barroso'."

Clara sniffed hard and pressed the palm of her free hand over damp eyelids.

"You come from a strong, brave family, Clara. That town still talks about your great-grandpa. The industry evolved, but he was part of an incredible foundation that people still respect today. There are monuments, schools, avenues, all with his name. We should go one day. Your grandma and I have been there many times. Not lately though, and that's a shame."

"I do want to go one day." Why hadn't she heard any of that before?

"They kept the chimney of the old factory, and let me tell you, the stories of that chimney. It woke up the town; it marked the new year, it represented power. An old gentleman, a local architect who's notorious for being happy all the time, told us in tears, all these years later, that one of the few times he was ever sad was the first time the old factory chimney was silent."

What was it about that whole story that made Clara's throat ache as she tried to stop the tears from escaping her eyes? That wasn't like her.

Was it the dad who didn't get to enjoy a long life with his beloved family and special little girl? The brave town that lost its most prominent figure so suddenly? Or was it the vivid mental pictures that she now carried inside her—pictures of a beautiful past that was doomed to be forgotten?

One could preserve a chimney, but how about the stories? How many could be preserved? How many lost stories for every preserved one?

Clara had to visit that town one day. She needed to thank Andrew for encouraging her to listen. She'd gained something. Something precious.

But how did Mario enter the picture? Did he take advantage of her grandma's broken heart? *Don't judge.* "And what happened to Grandma?"

"Your grandma and her mom moved away from the German community and to the capital city of Porto Alegre. Hitler's Germany was on the rise, and slowly, being a German descendent was a hassle, to say the least, even in the south of Brazil. There were also rumors of missing money, but they still had plenty. It was just good for them to get away somewhat."

"What do you mean by 'rumors of missing money'?"

"Rumors ..." Her mom's voice trailed off as if she were searching for the right words or maybe deciding how much to share. "It's a colorful history—even after his death. I'm talking notorious lottery wins, chairs with possible hidden compartments, papers flying when there were no windows open ...

People didn't take their money to the bank back then, you know. Think *Midnight in the Garden of Good and Evil* meets *Ghost*."

"It sounds like it." How odd? There had to be a proper explanation, right? A car alarm in the hotel parking lot startled her, reminding her of where she was.

"But money wasn't a problem for your grandma back then. Like I said, they still had plenty. Eventually, the *modista* would be going to the movies with your grandma to copy more extravagant gowns."

"How hard was the whole transition on grandma?"

"Hard. I've never seen or heard of anything like it. I wouldn't even believe it if I didn't have sweet aunties tell me the stories of how my mom didn't utter a single word for two long years. No one could get her out of her shell."

"What did they do? What happened?"

"Lieutenant Mario Medeiros happened. Brazilian Army. Academia Militar das Agulhas Negras graduate, the Brazilian version of West Point."

"How did they meet? I'm assuming that if she wasn't talking, she wasn't participating in society either."

"He drove past her downtown apartment window in his Ford Barata every day for weeks. He had no idea someone was watching him, but oh, someone was watching him. Expecting. Dreaming."

"One day she decided she absolutely had to meet the handsome blond officer with thin lips and tilted cap."

"Did she wait outside and wave him down or something?"

"No. Back then they had license-plate books, like phone books. You could look up the plate and get the owner's name. So that's what she did. The next day when he drove past she started speaking again—screaming actually." Mom chuckled. "Mario! *Na janela! Oi!*"

"And he heard her?"

"Sure did. He was almost ten years older than her. Mature, handsome, and very much in love with her."

"And in uniform."

"Of course."

"He loved her so much, *Princesa*."

Apparently still did.

"They dated for a whole year. On the beach, in the city, in the mountains. She still missed her dad, but her life was a fairy tale once more. She had someone exciting to lean on, who loved her deeply. She talks about that year-long courtship like it happened yesterday. Dreams about it too. All the old ladies we share hospital rooms with want to know who is this Mario guy because as soon as she closes her eyes it's Mario this and Mario that."

"That's cute." But why did he leave her? "Why didn't they marry?" Did he just get tired of her? Did he meet Alice's mom? She just knew he'd done the heart breaking, but she didn't know the specifics.

She couldn't hear her mom. Was there something wrong with the phone? "Mom?"

"I'm here."

"Thought I'd lost you."

"I'm here. This is just hard to talk about."

"I'm sorry. You don't have to."

"It's not hard because it's sad, though it is. It's hard because she's my mom, and I know she did her best. And I won't have my 22-year-old child judge her choices."

"Ah ... We are getting to the part you think I'm too judgmental to hear. I see it now."

"Don't be cute about it."

"Sorry." She wasn't being judgmental or cute. She was just hiding her fear and guilt.

"After their long courtship, he asked for her hand in marriage."

"Grandma said yes, of course?"

"She did, and her mom, my grandmother, planned a gorgeous engagement party for all of Porto Alegre society—an Easter day party."

"And he didn't show up?"

"Oh, he showed up."

"And?"

"His wife showed up too."

Clara couldn't breathe. No ...

"She'd seen the Ford Barata outside the building, asked the doorman or whatever they had back then if Lieutenant Medeiros was in the building, and the doorman said 'yes, he's getting engaged.'"

"No." Clara's voice was weak—her throat dry. Whatever happened next must have been humiliating, and poor grandma was probably still dealing with the loss of her father. Now this. She should have stayed mute. She would have been better off.

"Mrs. Medeiros walked in, found her husband, slapped him on the face in front of everybody and left."

Oh, those poor women.

"Your grandmother disappeared as soon as she figured out what was going on. Mario wrapped himself at the feet of your great-grandmother and stayed there begging for forgiveness until she kicked him away."

"Good for her." What was he thinking? What was his plan? "I'm assuming he stayed with his wife?"

"He did."

"Of course." Clara was young, but she'd already learned that men lie, and then when the truth comes to light, they run to the wife. Why should she be in El Paso waiting to deliver a letter to this creature, and more importantly, who else knew the whole story? How humiliating. And how incredibly similar to her story. Fresh tears filled her eyes. "What was he thinking?"

She heard her mom take a deep breath. "The story isn't over."

Clara held her breath. What else could possibly have happened?

As her mom explained every detail of all her grandmother had accepted and gone through, Clara's heart sank more and more. When the story had truly ended, she shook her head but didn't say anything.

"Even though she still loved him, she begged him to disappear. He loved her so much. He didn't want to say goodbye. But he knew that he'd ruined her and that he had to let her go. He made only one request."

"The letter."

"He said that since he couldn't have the one thing he wanted the most, her, he would settle for the second thing he wanted the most, her forgiveness. He asked her to—when ready—write him a letter letting him know he was forgiven, so he gave her a point of contact in the Army."

"That must have been more than seventy years ago. Did she forgive?"

"I think so. I didn't read the letter."

"Why not?"

"It's a letter for Mario, and she sees fit that he be the first to know what's in it."

Clara's eyes riveted on the letter. What key to forgiveness could it contain? She'd noticed the envelope seemed heavy—a more-than-one-page kind of heavy. Grandma Renata must have had a lot to say to Mario.

"And now you know the story." Her mom's voice sounded suddenly younger. Or maybe having heard such an old story, everything seemed young to Clara.

Still, no part of that story explained why she had to deliver the letter in person. She had no part in any of it.

Or did she?

"You don't think we're related, do you?"

"Of course not! Do the math."

"Hey, you don't need to be angry, Mom. I'm just asking."

"Back then, it was very difficult to marry when you were no longer a virgin. She stayed alone a long time. They said goodbye in the early forties, and she married Grandpa Julio in 1950. Then I was born in 1951, as you probably know."

"Hmm." Of course she knew her mom's birth year.

"I need to go, *Princesa*. I'm actually having dinner with an old friend tonight." Ooh, that youthful tone again. "This talk was good. It was needed. Just don't be telling everyone. This is her story, okay?"

"There's no one to be telling. There's just Andrew."

"Be careful."

"I will." What exactly did her mom mean by that? And what was she supposed to do next? All that talking and they hadn't gotten to the issue at hand. The issue that had just become slightly more complicated. "Should I move to this furnished apartment for a month? I feel bad about the whole Alice Howard thing. I'm the grandchild of the woman who must have caused her mother a world of grief. She would hate me if she knew."

"It's move there or fly home to stay, *Princesa*. You promised Grandma you would deliver her letter."

"I know. I just wish there was a better alternative."

"Right now I can't offer anything better. My ticket here was a fortune, and I'm still trying to pay off bills from all the traveling you did during the audition season."

"What a waste of money that was. I should have known."

"You did what you needed to do. Don't be so hard on yourself. Things will work out. You'll see. For now, go to this apartment, wait for Mario, and deliver your grandma's letter."

Clara nodded. If only it were that simple.

"I don't mean to be rude, but I've really got to go."

"Okay, Mom." Who was she seeing? "So you're going on a date?"

"It's not a date."

"Have you ever kissed this guy?"

"When I was fifteen."

"Then it's a date."

"I kissed him fifty years ago—it's not a date."

"Enjoy your date, Mom." Clara tapped the word *end* before her mom could respond. *Enjoy your date, Mom.*

Seventy years to forgive?

She'd forgiven Scott already, and it'd been what? Two years? That had been the easy part. Forgiving herself for her personal moral failures, now that was a heck of a whole lot harder. She wasn't there yet.

Clara looked at the terminal in the distance and closed the curtains. Did they get more of those bracelets? The shopkeeper had said she should check from time to time. She changed clothes to walk to the terminal.

Outside her door, a single red rose rested on the ground next to a small card. How did he know just what to do? Butterflies flew wild in her stomach as she reached down to pick it up. The warmth on her cheeks told her they now matched the rose. Clara beamed unabashedly in the privacy of the quiet hallway.

Andrew, Andrew …

She placed the red rose in the middle of the bouquet of yellow roses from the night before and opened the card.

Just two words. His handwriting was both simple and masculine, with tall and slim capital letters and markedly shorter lower-case letters.

Only You.

Chapter 7

Clara opened the door for Andrew. "Hi." The butterflies were back and flying just as wildly. *Control yourself, girl—woman.* Breathe.

"Hi." He kept his hands comfortably in the pockets of his crisp charcoal pants and grinned. "You look fantastic."

"Well, do I?" She lifted her shoulders and let his compliment warm her heart. She'd worked hard to look nice for their outing. Again she hadn't found the bracelet at the terminal, but she'd found a ruby dress that was a steal for $19.99 plus tax—a welcome find for someone who was living out of a small suitcase and on a tight budget.

"Shall we?" He offered his arm, and Clara rested her hand on it without hesitation.

His gray dress shirt was as soft as his fresh fragrance. She glanced at him. Everything about Andrew was light and pleasant. The two top buttons of his shirt were opened in what must be his trademark look. It suited him. The opened buttons gave his sophisticated appearance a relaxed touch without compromising elegance. Perfection.

"I have a surprise for you, Clara." The corners of his eyes crinkled, and a big smile stretched his lips.

"You do?" She wasn't keen on surprises but smiled as they walked toward the lobby. What was Andrew up to? She'd agreed to dinner and a movie on post. Please let it not be more people joining them or something. Clara didn't want to meet more soldiers and didn't want to socialize with their girlfriends or wives.

"Do you mind if we don't go to the movies tonight?"

"Why?" What *did* he want to do? They reached the busy hotel lobby.

"I discovered an event at UTEP that I think you'll like better."

"UTEP. University of Texas El Paso, right?"

He nodded.

"Of course I don't mind." UTEP sounded great. A university event was right up her alley. That she could handle. As a matter of fact, the night just got better. "Why would I mind the change in plans? You know how I feel about the Army and the whole being on post thing."

"I thought we'd put that to rest last night."

"Can we not talk about it tonight? All's well. I like you." She gave him a quick wink. "Let's just be. Can we do that?"

"Yes, ma'am—I thought you'd never ask." The corners of his mouth turned up. They reached the Crossfire, and Andrew opened the door for her. The top was down.

Clara sat and smoothed her dress. "So, what is this surprise of yours? What are we doing at UTEP?"

"I'm taking you to the ballet." He closed her door as soon as the words exited his mouth.

Now he was talking her language, and she labored to keep from jumping on his neck and hugging him when he took his place behind the wheel. "You are?! Yay! What are we watching?" She hadn't been to a ballet in months. A ballet on a college campus. How perfect.

Andrew handed her two tickets and studied her as she read.

Giselle. She pressed her fingers to her lips. "I love *Giselle*—it's one of my favorite ballets." Did he know the story?

"You're not just saying that? It really is a good one?" He turned on the engine.

"Absolutely." She filled her lungs with the evening air and her heart with ballet magic and wonder as she remembered the story of the peasant girl and her handsome suitor. "It's the most traditional ballet ever. You'll love it. Do you know anything about ballet or about the company?"

"Nope." He glanced at her and lifted an eyebrow. "This will be my first time watching a ballet."

"No!" She scrunched up her face. "Impossible."

"What? Don't tell me I haven't lived." He sped out of the Radisson parking lot.

Clara giggled. "Andrew, my friend, you haven't lived."

What a promising evening. Her heart fluttered as she remembered her first time at the ballet. *Oh, please love it.*

Andrew threaded a hand through his hair. The ballet idea was perfect. Great decision. This was the most excited he'd ever seen her. Now he knew what made her tick. Not that he'd seen her that many times, but Clara was one of those people—though they'd just met, he felt like he'd known her forever. Strange how that happened sometimes.

Clara shifted in her seat and crossed her legs. Her knees made a brief appearance, but she soon covered them again with the beautiful red dress she wore.

He drove in silence as she took in the scenery—her eyes going from Mexico to the U.S. and then back to Mexico as if she were watching a tennis match in slow motion.

Why did he like her so much? He'd seen pretty girls before, so it wasn't just looks. Was it because she was a bit on the difficult side with the whole *no soldiers* thing?

Nope. That wasn't it. He'd liked her all along. He remembered his attraction at the airport. He hadn't known her opinions then, so the challenge wasn't the reason for the attraction either.

Andrew switched lanes and passed the full-size truck that had been ahead of him since he'd merged onto the busy highway.

Most women threw themselves at guys like him. A soldier, an officer, an infantryman, a West Pointer. Did he have to find the one woman who didn't care about any of it? The one for whom those were negative attributes? Mercy. Who would have thought that the Academy and his commission would ever be problems—strikes against him in the dating world. Unreal.

But she had said she liked him. That was a lot better than "I don't date soldiers. I'm sorry." And she'd winked.

Had she seen his cheeks turn red when she winked at him in the hotel parking lot? Probably not. The wink was a friendly wink. Nothing to it, right? It had caught him by surprise, hence the heat that traveled from the pit of his stomach, through his chest, and to his cheeks. But she wasn't flirting. Or was she?

She was more relaxed than the day before, for sure.

Mixed signals and confusion or an increase in trust? *Lord, please let it be the latter.*

His breathing quickened as he remembered the previous night—the warmth of her body under his hands when they'd danced on the quiet parade field. Her sweet scent had stayed with him all night.

His eyes rested briefly on her beautiful profile. She was quiet but didn't seem bothered. "So tell me about this character."

"Character?" Clara's eyes riveted on Andrew's face.

"Giselle." Why was she looking at him with such apprehension all of a sudden? "Tell me about the ballet. Giselle is a girl, right?"

"Oh." Her face lit up. "Yes. Giselle is a simple girl who falls for a handsome peasant. They date for a while, and soon he proposes. But she discovers that he's not a peasant. He's a nobleman. And he's not available. He's engaged to the prince's daughter, Bathilde."

"That doesn't sound good." Maybe he should have checked the storyline first. There he was trying to impress her with ballet tickets to a performance about a guy who cheats? Not good.

"That part is really not good." Her eyelids dropped. "Giselle has a weak heart and goes crazy and dies right there in the middle of the whole commotion."

Definitely not good. "What commotion?"

"The two women end up face to face, Giselle and Bathilde. The guy—Albrecht—shows up too, and the village people and the castle people are all there trying to figure out why both women seem to believe they are marrying Albrecht."

"So the ballet ends with her dying of a broken heart?" Bummer.

"No. That's the end of act one. In act two, we meet the Wilis, the spirits of women who died of a broken heart—women who were lied to and abandoned before their wedding. They rise from their graves at night and seek revenge. They make men who show up in the forest in the middle of the night dance until they die."

Keeps getting better. What had he gotten them into? And why did she like this ballet?

"Note to self: Don't show up in the forest in the middle of the night." Andrew pulled up to the Sun Bowl Parking Garage of the University of Texas at El Paso. "So Giselle is one of the—what are they called?"

"Wilis. They are called Wilis. And the answer is yes and no. They try to make Giselle one of them, but Albrecht comes to the forest as she is being introduced to the group. They want him to dance until he dies, but Giselle still loves him, and she protects him until daybreak when the Wilis have to go back to their graves. Because Giselle is not bitter and forgives Albrecht, she doesn't become one of them. She's able to rest in peace."

Not all is lost. Not the ideal themes for a date, but redeemable. "Okay. I guess I can get into that. I like her already." He held Clara's hand and led her to the Magoffin Auditorium. "Giselle, here we come."

"I'm sure she's your kind of girl. Forgiving, pure, and loving—no matter what happens." She looked at him with a playful smirk.

Where had that come from? "You're my kind of girl, Clara."

"What kind of girl is that?"

"Smart and serious, but in a cute way."

Clara's cheeks turned pink, and she avoided eye contact—her eyes surveyed the exposed-brick buildings around them instead. At least she'd blushed. That must be a good sign.

"Anyone can become loving and forgiving with God's help. Now smart, cute, and laid back, that combination, that's a gift—a gift only a few have."

Clara giggled. "Well, thank you."

It was his turn to wink. And yes, he was flirting. Openly.

Clara wasn't sure what to expect of the production, but she was glad to be going to a ballet—any ballet, any quality even. Those were her people. That was her home.

The Magoffin Auditorium looked impressive on the outside with towering exterior walls, like all the buildings they'd passed. The inside was more like a movie theater. She took the free program from a friendly young woman at the top of the center aisle and thumbed through it as Andrew led her to their seats. They sat about twenty rows back from the stage and were some-what centered. Perfect.

He had a program too and turned quickly to the libretto.

"What? You don't trust my version of the story?" She chuckled without lifting her eyes from the cast list in her program.

"I just want to know more." He shifted in his seat. "Like, why did the guy betray the noble he was engaged to and hurt Giselle?"

"Because he's a guy?" Clara fiddled with her earring. "I'm not sure you'll find much beyond that."

Andrew twisted his lips. "Judgmental Clara. That's right." He snorted playfully.

"Hey!" Clara punched his arm gently. "You are wrong, my friend. This afternoon I heard the entire story of one Ranata Lambert before she was a Tomaselli, and the story of her Lieutenant Mario Medeiros."

"Oh! Good for you." His smile was genuine, and he didn't ask any ques-tions. "How's your mom?"

"She was going on a date." Clara lifted both eyebrows.

"She was?"

"She said it wasn't a date, but she admitted she'd kissed the guy when she was fifteen."

"Whatever it is, I'm sure it'll be a good break from the hospital rou-tine."

"You're right. It will." Clara zeroed in on an ad in the program. The El Paso Ballet, the company dancing *Giselle*, had an advanced summer program in June. *Hmm.* The picture was of a very young company—high school girls, for the most part, but there were a couple of older girls too.

The lights dimmed, and conversations slowly ended, as if someone had turned a volume control knob gradually to lower volumes and then to the off position. Clara put the program away. She needed to watch a good perfor-mance. She wanted to watch a good *Giselle*.

"Happy?" Andrew spoke in her ear and lingered there, waiting for her reply.

She turned. "Yes." With the excitement of the performance and the the-ater environment, she'd forgotten about how handsome her date was.

That kind of proximity reminded her.

His minty breath on her skin was a sweet and welcome caress, his masculine voice a song. She looked at him, his lips so close to hers, moist, defined. "Thanks for bringing me to the ballet."

"You're welcome." He caressed her cheek and ran his fingertips gently over her bottom lip.

Clara trembled and her heart faltered. Would he just kiss her already? She exhaled and squeezed his arm, wanting him closer still.

Adolphe Adam's music started, haunting and urgent. Andrew bit his lower lip with a soft moan.

She looked forward reluctantly, and a sigh tickled her throat.

He wrapped her hand in his and brought it to his heart, placing her palm on his chest. Then he looked forward.

Clara felt his heartbeat and his warmth. Could she become part of it one day—of the warmth and the beauty that was Andrew James? Should she?

He kissed her hand and leaned toward her ear again. "I like you."

Clara beamed and let light and heat fill her soul. She held her breath. She held her breath because she didn't want to do anything to spoil the moment. She held her breath because she didn't want her brain to take over and start thinking of the many reasons this was going to end badly. She held her breath because she'd never felt that way before—not even with Scott. She didn't want to be separate from Andrew. She wanted to be one. She wanted him to assimilate her completely. That didn't even make any sense, did it? What was wrong with her?

The music for Giselle's first appearance snapped Clara out of her Andrew trance.

The dancer was young and had lovely long lines. She was good. Her feet were beautifully arched and fast, her upper body delicate, and her arms full of grace. She moved with precision. An innocent and joyful smile completed the image of an ideal Giselle. Clara exhaled.

Ah, what she wouldn't give to be on that stage. Would she ever dance on stage again?

She would call the El Paso Ballet and ask about the summer program. *Please don't be expensive.* But how would she even get to the studio? She glanced at Andrew, who looked serious while watching his first ballet. Would he let her use the Crossfire?

No. Bad idea. She hadn't driven a stick shift since high school, and she'd struggled. Maybe there was a bus. She used the bus in Cincinnati, many students did. Uber or Lyft would cost too much.

By the peasant *pas de deux* in the middle of act one, Clara had stopped thinking about summer programs, Andrew, cars, and everything. And when Giselle and Albrecht danced again, they had her full attention.

The man playing Albrecht reminded her of Mario Medeiros. She'd seen a picture of him during a childhood visit to Brazil.

Why was it so easy to love Albrecht and so hard to love Mario? Technically they'd done the same thing. Was it because she could see Albrecht's grief in act two and pity him? Would she pity Mario? What would he be like?

On stage, the prince's daughter looked bothered more than heartbroken. If she'd had lines, she would probably be saying something like, "Silly Albrecht, carrying on with a peasant girl—come home now, honey. Let's play nice."

Giselle, on the other hand, was losing her mind. The ballerina's bun was now undone, and mascara ran down her face. Her lips trembled. She grabbed Albrecht's sword and started a mad dance that ended with him grabbing the sword out of her hand.

She ran to all the people she'd always counted on for support, searching their faces for an explanation, searching for relief. But nothing made her feel better. Her mother tried. The honest hunter who wanted to marry her and who'd exposed Albrecht tried too. All useless. And just like that, when she'd run out of alternatives, her heart stopped.

Giselle had wept, convulsed, lost her composure, lost her mind, and lost her life. Bathilde walked around, shaking her head and consulting with her family and friends.

Some seventy years ago, a similar scene played out in the south of Brazil. How was it for Alice's mom? What happened after she slapped her husband and walked out of Clara's grandmother's engagement party? Was she heartbroken or just bothered?

It was easier for Clara to imagine her just bothered, cold like Bathilde, saying something like, "Silly lieutenant, carrying on with a teenage girl—come home now, honey. Let's play nice." It was much harder to imagine a wife heartbroken because of her grandmother.

Images of another betrayed woman filled her mind, and memories of her history with Scott made her eyes burn with hot tears.

The curtains closed on act one.

"I do feel like I haven't lived." Andrew dried Clara's tears with his thumbs. "This is pretty emotional though. Do you need a tissue?"

Clara shook her head. "You like it?"

"I do. I love it. Those guys are crazy strong."

"Wait until you see Albrecht in act two. He has some gravity-defying solos."

Andrew nodded. "Can't wait. Do you want to get up?"

"Not really. If you don't mind."

He held her hand in both of his and drew in a deep breath. "I want to see you dance one day."

"You said I can't dance, remember?"

"I was kidding and you know it." His eyes sparkled—green jewels and beacons of hope.

Clara nodded. "Well, who knows. You might be able to see me dance one day. The El Paso Ballet, the company we're watching, has a summer workshop in June." Clara pulled out the program and showed him the ad.

"What's a summer workshop?"

"Most companies and schools have summer workshops or programs— same thing—intensive classes, from morning to evening for a couple of weeks."

"Oh, like a summer camp." Andrew leaned back in his seat. He looked comfortable in her world. "You should do it."

"Kind of like a summer camp, but not for kids. Though they do have camps for kids too."

"Find out the times. You'll need help getting around." The left corner of his mouth lifted.

"Thanks." Her palms were suddenly sweaty. That was very nice of him— to think of what she needed. She tucked a lock of hair behind her ear.

"I'm getting hungry already. What are you hungry for?"

"A pizza from Uno. Please say there's a Pizzeria Uno here. There's one around the corner from my apartment in Cincinnati, and I'm suffering serious symptoms of withdrawal already."

"Sorry, girl. They don't have those in El Paso."

Clara pouted playfully, and her shoulders dropped.

"A different kind of pizza? There's a place by my apartment—soon to be yours too—I mean, not the apartment, but the apartment community."

"I know what you mean. You don't have to blush."

He blushed harder. "Anyway ... it's a great pizza place." He stood to let two women pass their seats.

She was hoping to stay in the UTEP area to enjoy the college climate she'd been missing. Plus her stomach would be growling any minute. "If you don't mind, I would rather eat near here."

"Let me see something." He pulled out his cell phone. "I think they have a UTEP location on Cincinnati Avenue if I'm not mistaken." He looked up from the phone. "How do you like the sound of that? Cincinnati Avenue?"

"I love it." Clara cocked her head.

"Here it is—on Cincinnati." He showed her a picture of a thin pizza with tomato and basil.

"Perfect. It's the opposite of an Uno four-cheese deep dish pizza with no tomato sauce, but it looks like a Brazilian pizza, and I love those too."

"German pizza looks the same." He flashed his eyebrows and put the phone away. "It's really good."

"I keep forgetting you lived there. I bet it was amazing. I don't know what I would do with myself if I had a chance like that."

"It *was* amazing. I would go back in a heartbeat."

She'd been to Brazil four times and to Mexico once, but she'd never been to Europe. Would she ever make it there? She'd dreamed of dancing in France or Italy one day, but her spring auditions fiasco probably meant dancing wasn't going to get her there.

What if Andrew was indeed different? Was she Army wife material? She, an officer's wife after all? Hmm. She looked at Andrew, who'd found the summer intensive ad in his own program and was studying it. What if they ended up in Europe together one day?

If any of that were to happen, she would have to tell him what she'd learned about her grandma—and tell him about Scott. That would be a most unpleasant day. How would he react?

Almost everyone had returned to their seats. Ballet moms, ballet dads, college students, and a few people who didn't seem to fit any of those categories. The theater was not filled to capacity, but it should have been. The El Paso Ballet had put together a great production of *Giselle*.

"I hope you like act two," Clara whispered to Andrew as the lights dimmed.

"I'm sure I will." He squeezed her hand, then covered it gently.

As thick fog and the Wilis filled the stage, hot tears filled Clara's eyes. Oh, how she loved *Giselle*.

"Why are their arms crossed like that?" Andrew whispered.

"Holding children who were never born—from marriages that never happened." The little hairs on her arms stood.

Andrew's jaw dropped.

Hers had dropped too when she'd first learned about the arms in a Royal Ballet documentary on YouTube.

Giselle was the first spirit that Albrecht saw, and as music that cried with what-could-have-beens and with regret filled the theater, Giselle danced stoically. When Albrecht was in trouble, forced to dance beyond exhaustion, she didn't hesitate. Her love never faltered. She forgave him, loved him, and helped him.

What made her so different from the other women? Their stories were all the same, weren't they?

What was it about Giselle?

And what would Giselle have done if Albrecht had offered to put together a house for her like Mario had offered to do for her grandma? Would Giselle have said yes like her grandma had? Would she have agreed to be his lover if she hadn't died? No, Giselle was too innocent and too pure. But so was her grandmother. Why had she let it happen? And how could she have forgiven him, as she apparently had?

Forgiveness. Such a hard thing.

Clara had forgiven Scott, but in part, because she'd assimilated some of the blame. She blamed him for the first twenty-four hours. But she blamed herself for every moment they stayed together after that. It was herself she hadn't forgiven. Not yet. Ah, the guilt. The stupid guilt. Would it ever go away?

Scott had only lied for twenty-four hours. She'd had a perfect opportunity to walk away when he told her that he was still married on paper.

But she didn't walk away.

When he broke her heart, saying he was moving back in with his wife, did she then walk away? Nope. She didn't. The relationship only ended because he'd made it absolutely clear that there was no possibility of a wedding and a home for them—ever.

She remembered the time she'd felt like a common prostitute with him. That was the last time she saw him—the last time she was with a man at all.

Andrew opened the door of the pizzeria for Clara. This location was smaller than the one by his house, but the environment was the same. Soft lights, candles, comfort foods, laughter, and warmth greeted them as they walked to a small corner table of the busy restaurant. They ordered two pizzas and a bottle of St Clair's Gewürztraminer, made in nearby New Mexico.

Clara had been unusually quiet on the way to the restaurant. Quiet was okay—he'd seen her do that. But this was a different kind of quiet. The sad kind.

"Are you okay?" It'd been a sad ballet. Beautiful, but sad. Was that it?

"I'll be okay. I'm still recovering from *Giselle*." She gave a half smile. "Wasn't it beautiful?"

"It was, but I'm sorry it made you sad." How could he lift that cloud off her features?

"Don't be sorry. Everything was perfect. *Giselle* is achingly beautiful *and* perfect. I will be okay in five minutes." She winked. "Promise."

This is the time. "I need to get something from the car." He stood quietly and slipped out. She'd seen the ruby box at the Star on the Mountain. He would have to explain that he was waiting for the right time.

He returned to the table with his hand behind his back.

"What do you have there?" Clara smiled that perfect smile of hers—pink lips and bright green eyes. She wasn't joking. It'd been about five minutes, and she was all better.

He put the box on the table. "It's for you. I got it the night I met you, and I've been looking for the right time to give it to you."

"Oh, you didn't have to." She touched the box. "Are you sure?"

"Yes." He rested his chin on the palm of his hand. "Are you going to open it?"

"I will … But I feel like I need to tell you something first." Clara made a steeple of her fingers.

"What is it?" What was that all about?

"It's been weighing heavily on my heart. It's the story of the letter and the history between my grandma and Alice's dad. It's pretty bad. They made some huge mistakes."

"What does that have to do with me giving you a gift?"

"I don't know. I just feel like I need to tell you." She blushed.

"I will feel better if you open the gift first. One thing has absolutely nothing to do with the other."

"But what if the story makes my grandma look kind of bad?"

"What does that have to do with us? You're not your grandma, Clara. Just like I'm not like other soldiers you and your family have met before."

She nodded. "Okay—if you insist."

"I do."

She picked up the box and shook it by her ear.

"Open it." Please like it. What if she didn't buy it because she decided it wasn't her style after all? No. It was the price tag. She'd mentioned money a couple of times. She just didn't want to spend the money.

Clara opened the shiny red box slowly and peeked inside before removing the lid completely.

Her jaw dropped when she saw the bracelet.

That was good, right?

"Oh, Andrew! You shouldn't have—but I'm so glad you did."

Oh, thank God. She likes it.

She reached for his hand. "I love it. I've been looking for it and looking for it, and you've had it all along."

"I saw you looking at it at the airport before we even met." Had she noticed him?

"Thank you." She put the bracelet on her arm and read the words on every petal. "Hope, wish, dream, inspire, love, fun, peace, happy, faith, joy, rest, create."

"I'm so glad you like it."

"I do. I regretted not buying it. I even tried to see if they had one at Placita Santa Fe when we went to the Magic Bistro. Just today I went back to the terminal looking for it again. And now here it is. Thank you."

"You're welcome." He tasted his wine, the satisfaction of giving a good gift making a great evening better. In the background, music he remembered from an epic bus tour to Italy completed the moment. "Now tell me. What did you find out about the letter?"

"Okay. Get ready for this one." She folded her arms. "There's way more to it than I'd expected."

"Oh?" He leaned forward. "Shoot."

"So you don't know anything at all?"

"Not a thing. I know the general, and he's a wonderful person—brilliant officer, but he's also a very private man."

"I never did ask. How do you know him?"

Hmm. Where to begin? "I led Colonel Howard to Christ during a deployment to Afghanistan, and then when we got back to Baumholder, I met the family. Soon after, Alice and the kids made professions of faith too." Did any of this mean anything to her? Better go easy. "Anyway, I don't think the general cares for church much—he doesn't believe like the rest of the family does, so I think he sees me as the weirdo who got his family hooked on church." Andrew scratched his head. "Something like that."

"I can see how that would be a little weird, I guess." Clara looked at her glass, then back at him.

"But like I said, I admire him a great deal. We've talked many times. Army stories, for the most part."

"I can imagine." She toyed with a lock of hair, then straightened up. "So … it was quite a coincidence that you took me to see *Giselle* tonight because it totally frames their story and makes it easier for me to talk about it."

"Ghosts and people dancing until they die?" He knew that wasn't it, but it seemed like the right thing to say to keep things light.

"No." She tilted her head. "Act one."

"General Medeiros is a prince?"

"Okay. Forget about *Giselle*." Clara shook her head. "My grandma adored her dad and lost him when she was really young—around fifteen. She was so impacted by her father's untimely death that she did not speak for two years."

"She refused?"

"She couldn't. She was in shock, I guess. And she stayed in shock for a long time." She balled her fists. "And then the general, a lieutenant back then, came along—a graduate of the Academia Militar das Agulhas Negras, the Brazilian version of West Point, mind you." Clara rolled her eyes as she said West Point.

Seriously? He chuckled. "And that just makes you hate me, doesn't it?" He grabbed her hand, making sure his West Point graduation ring was as visible as possible.

She shook her head and laughed.

Good. She got his sense of humor. Did she also know that he was more interested in a good excuse to hold her hand than in a West Point provocation?

"Anyway." She withdrew her hand gently and took a small sip of wine. "They dated for a year, and he proposed. Then, in the middle of the engagement party, Alice's mom showed up and slapped her husband, General Mario Medeiros, on the face. See why I thought of *Giselle* as a frame for sharing this story—the two women face to face, the guy in the middle unable to deny the truth?"

"Wow." Why did men do that? Would he ever be so inclined? That was a scary thought. *God help me not be like this—help me never give in to such thoughts and acts. Please.* Memories of his childhood—of the time his dad almost left them because of another woman—tried to claim a space in the present. *Nope. Not going there.* "Why do people do that? It's worse than in *Giselle*. At least in the ballet, he wasn't married to anyone yet." People were crazy.

"My thoughts exactly." A cloud descended on her face.

"Why would he do that to his wife?"

Clara lifted her head. "I would love to ask him that."

Their waitress slowed down next to the table. "Your pizzas should be out soon." Had they been waiting long? Clara's company and her story were so good that he wasn't concerned about how long it would take to eat.

"And what about the letter?" Andrew asked.

"Wait. I'm not to that part yet. It gets worse." Clara brought her glass to her lips once more.

How could it possibly get worse?

"They didn't see each other for two months, but then they exchanged a couple of letters, met, and decided to become lovers."

He tightened his lips. *Judge not.*

"He got her a house, and she lived there, always waiting for him, for almost three years—three years of lies and stolen moments." She hugged herself. "Can you believe that?"

He gritted his teeth. "No, I can't." They couldn't have been happy living like that.

"This story makes me so sad and so angry at the same time. I don't even know what to make of it. One minute I feel sorry for them, and then soon after I want to choke them both—him mostly, but her too."

"For whatever reason, I keep thinking of your great-grandfather—her dad. Could you imagine his heartbreak? If he'd been alive, that would never have happened."

"Oh, no. Of course not. She was fragile and needy. Even I can see that."

"And I guess one day she realized they were making a terrible mistake?"

Clara lowered her eyes. "One day another officer came by the house requesting her services."

He raised his eyebrows.

"Nothing happened with that guy, but that visit and his assumption woke her out of her craziness. That night she packed one small suitcase, walked through the rain and the mud, and got on the midnight train back to the capital."

"So God used that other officer to get your grandma out of the situation she was in."

"I guess you can say that, but I don't really see God in any of this."

There was no telling how long she would have stayed in that house if the other officer hadn't shown up, so for Andrew, it was indeed God's mercy that brought the man to her grandma's doorsteps. Maybe one day she would see it that way. One big question remained. "Where does the letter fit into the story?"

"He checked on her after she'd disappeared. She asked him to never look for her again, and he promised to honor her request. All he asked was for her to write him a letter when she forgave him."

"So now, all these years later, she finally forgave him and wrote the letter."

"I guess. I sure hope she didn't send me all the way here to watch him open a letter that says 'screw you' or something." She rubbed her forehead.

He shook his head and inhaled deeply. "My goodness." And stories like that happened too often. Andrew heard them all the time. In the news, from his soldiers, friends. And it once almost happened in his family. His own father. An amazing man. A strong Christian. *God, help me do better. Be better. Please.*

"See, so my family is weak. We're terrible people." She bit her lower lip. "Do you want your bracelet back?"

"I don't want the bracelet back, Clara, and your family's not weak. People sin." Granted some sin more than others. *Judge not.*

"I don't understand how you can be religious and not be immensely offended by this story. Both of them acted horribly."

Religious? "If people didn't act horribly, there would be no need for Jesus. He didn't come to condemn the world. He came to save the world. It's a forgiveness Gospel, Clara."

"Still …" Their pizzas arrived, filling the air between them with the smells of tomatoes and cheese and herbs. "Yum."

"I'm sorry it took so long." The waitress moved quickly to make room on the table.

Clara giggled. "These are huge. We'll be sitting here eating pizza all night."

"You two look like you could indeed talk all night." The waitress took a step back. "Can I get you anything else?"

"More water please." The corners of Andrew's mouth lifted up. "So we can talk all night."

"Coming right up. Ma'am?" She looked at Clara.

"More water for me too, please."

"I'll be right back with your refills."

Clara picked up her utensils. "We'll never eat all this—even if we do stay all night."

"If we have any left, you can take it to the hotel. You have two more nights there, and now you have enough food to keep you going until the move to the apartment."

Clara exhaled fast. "About that ..."

"What's wrong?" More complications?

"I don't feel comfortable letting Alice rent that apartment for me for the month when her dad caused her mom so much grief because of my grandmother." Clara's lips tightened. "Do you think she knows all the awful details of their story?"

"I have no idea." That was a hard one. "I can ask if you want me to."

"No. I don't want to throw you in the middle of this mess. In a way, I hope Alice's mom is kind of like Bathilde in *Giselle*. Bothered more than heartbroken. But I don't know. I need to talk to Alice, don't you think?"

"Let me pray for the meal, and then we'll talk it out."

Clara put the utensils back down and reached for Andrew's hand, bowing her head.

She was getting the hang of it. Cute. "Father God, thank you for the good company and for the meal we are about to share. I ask that you bless it. Help us remember the words of Jesus always—judge not. We pray for these things in Jesus' name, amen."

She let go of his hand reluctantly.

"I'm taking the Howards to church tomorrow. We can all go together. We're having lunch afterward. You ladies can talk."

"No. I don't think so."

"No talk or no church?"

"Neither."

"Then what are you going to do?"

"I don't know."

She should really go to church and talk to Alice Howard, but how could he convince her? Maybe she would change her mind through the course of the evening.

They ate two whole slices of Margherita pizza quietly before Andrew broke the silence. "So how old was your grandma when your mom was born? How did she get to her happy ending?" Had she gotten to a happy ending? He hoped so.

"After Mario and that house, my grandma was on her own for ten years before marrying my grandpa and having my mom. So I guess she was in her thirties? My mom had me late too. Mom had a great love when she was young and stayed in the United States after what was supposed to be a six-month study abroad program because of him." Clara put another thin slice of pizza on her plate. "But it didn't work out. She stayed anyway. She got into acting and was happy. Then she met my dad in her early thirties and finally settled down a bit. So yeah, they both had their babies late-ish."

"You're an only child?"

"Yep. My mom only had me. My grandma only had my mom."

"I want at least four kids." Could she handle four kids if they were to be together?

Clara grinned. "Why four? Can't convert them all, just outbreed them?"

"Of course." Cute and funny. Perfect combination.

And she didn't cringe at the four kids idea. Good. How could he get her to join them in the morning? "What do I have to say to get you to go to church with us tomorrow? You'll enjoy it, and you can get this thing with Alice out of the way. Then everyone who should know, knows, and life goes on." And he would get more quality time with her.

"I don't know." She brushed her palms together. A line appeared between her brows. "I feel like if I step into a church, the roof will fall on my head or something."

"That bad, huh?" What had she done? His mouth twisted.

"I don't know if it's that bad, but I'm certainly not the second grader who got saved at VBS at Fort Bragg." She shrugged and went back to her pizza.

Can't be that bad. "You know, it's not a judgmental Gospel, Clara, so the church—at least our church—is not a judgmental church. We just love on people—mainly visitors. Your grandma and the general did the best they could, however wrong, mistaken, sinful ... We all do dumb things. We all sin. The only difference between me and a lost man is that I'm not lost anymore." He needed to be done. He didn't want to weird her out. "Church is for everybody."

"Church is for good people."

What? "No." He finished chewing. "It's for everybody."

"But you have to be good." She sang her statement, her voice just above a whisper.

"No. You have to know that you're a sinner and that Jesus already did all that needed to be done to fix that." *Don't be preachy. God, help me. What's needed here?* She probably didn't remember any of this. "All we have to do is believe in what He did for us on the cross and accept His free gift."

"And then be good."

"And then try to be good—not because you have to, but because you want to. But church is not about being good. Look at the Pharisees. They thought they were living and acting God's way. Jesus made it clear again and again that everything the Pharisees stood for was hogwash."

"Then what is church for?" She played with her napkin—her eyes fixed on it.

"For learning. It's a place to learn the Bible and surround yourself with people who share your beliefs." Why did he feel so uncomfortable having this conversation with her?

"Okay."

"So you're coming?"

"Not this time."

"When you're ready." She obviously didn't know much about church life. *Soften her heart, Lord. She would love it. You would love it. I would love it too.*

Clara nodded slowly—a timid smile coloring her face. That was better than rubbing palms, creased forehead, and the fear that the roof would fall in. Good. *Thank you, Lord.* They finished eating in silence.

He caught her studying him. Head cocked to the side.

"You look like you have something on your mind." Andrew finished his wine. The pale-yellow liquid was now warm but still sweet and fruity.

"I have lots of things on my mind."

"Any one thing in particular?"

She folded her napkin and placed it on the table. "What's a godly marriage?"

"A godly marriage?" He squared his shoulders, but in the pit of his stomach—the same anxious feeling.

"Yeah. When I asked you if your parents were still married, you said yes, and you said that they have a godly marriage."

Where was she taking this conversation and why? "It means 'til death do us part."

"Oh … Like no divorce—no matter what?"

"That's part of it—married 'til it kills one of you." He winked.

Clara giggled.

"But that's not all of it."

"What else is there to it?" She leaned back for the first time since they'd been there.

"It's about being happy doing life God's way."

"Is that boring?"

"I don't think so." It was better than changing spouses and facing the same troubles over and over again, breaking kids' hearts and dreams in the process. "My parents don't act bored. They seem to have a pretty good time, as a matter of fact." Except for that one time when Dad had almost left them, but Andrew had chosen to forgive. He drew in a long breath. "But then again, what do I know? I'm not married."

"Maybe they were meant to be insanely happy with or without God's help. Soul mates."

Not the soul mate talk. How could he debunk that myth without sounding like the Grinch?

The waitress came around and poured more sweet wine in both their glasses. "Are you finished with your pizzas? Can I get you some boxes?"

"Not yet." Andrew cocked his head. "I'm about to explain to my friend Clara here that soul mates don't exist. It might take a while, so I will hold on to the pizzas."

Clara chuckled.

"Good luck." The waitress then turned to Clara. "He's right. It is a myth." She lifted one eyebrow and walked away with a smirk on her thin lips.

"Last to know." Clara ran her hand through her beautiful red hair.

What had he got himself into? "Okay, so …" He cleared his throat playfully. "From the vast experience of one who was practically left at the altar, let me suggest that soul mates don't exist. Is that a good start?"

Clara tightened her lips. "Let me see. You had your heart broken, and now you don't believe in soul mates. Yes, that's a very good start." Clara laughed nervously at first, then openly when Andrew joined her.

"Okay, that was a horrible start." He tapped his feet under the table, looking for better words. "It's preposterous and naïve to think that God created a perfect person for every individual on the globe. That's a selfish notion, and it's nowhere in the Bible." *That came out harsh.* "I mean no offense. That came out all wrong, didn't it?"

"A little. Maybe your original approach was better."

His eyes met hers. There was unexpected kindness there. He folded his napkin and played with it. How could he make it sound right when he still struggled with the idea?

"Is that the end of your explanation?"

Andrew shook his head slowly. "Not really. I thought I had a strong thesis about this, but maybe I don't. It's not coming out right. I can tell you what I've observed, and what I've been taught growing up in church. But the truth is that in my first attempt to apply all that head knowledge to real life, I crashed and burned. I did everything the way I was supposed to, but it didn't work out."

"Sorry." She pressed her hands to her cheeks. "Does that make you question your faith? I mean, why did something like that have to happen to you? You said it yourself, you did everything right."

"No, not at all. That's the good thing about growing up in a church." *One of many.* "You know the Bible stories—stories of people God used, and you know they suffered tremendous injustices and waited forever to receive the blessings God had promised them. Suffering and surprises and waiting, that's just how life works, and God's in it with you."

"So you have low expectations?"

"No. I'm open to surprises."

"What does that mean? How does it work?"

"Well … you're full of questions, aren't you?"

"I'm sorry." She lowered her eyes. "I'm just curious. I've never known anyone like you. But you don't have to answer my silly questions."

"They're not silly—I'm sorry." He'd just never had anyone that interested in his points of view about matters of the heart and faith. She didn't look like she was clowning around or trying to mock his beliefs. She seemed sincerely curious, and that was endearing.

Andrew reached out for her hands. "Let me see if I can make more sense this time."

She lifted her chin, her eyes moist. "Take Giselle and Hilarion, the simple guy who brought her and her mama the rabbits in the beginning. He adores Giselle. Should she have married him instead of being with Albrecht? To me, that would be having low expectations because she was clearly not into the guy."

"If she'd known Albrecht was engaged to somebody else, then she should have invested in a relationship with the rabbit guy. If she didn't love him and couldn't ever love him, she could have waited for someone else. Someone who would honor and cherish her—someone she was 'into,' as you put it. That's living expectant and ready for God's amazing surprises." He winked. "It's not about having low expectations. It's the absolute opposite. It's daring to dream dreams so big that only God can get you there."

"Then you believe in passion?"

"Of course I do." If she only knew the feelings he had toward her that very minute. "That's how people first come together, and it's an awesome season of a relationship. But I don't think the passion lasts forever, and I believe people need a plan for when it wears off. That's what my parents have—a plan. Their plan is God's plan, and it works." Without God, his parents wouldn't be together. But he wasn't ready to tell her that story yet.

"I wish I had your faith."

"Come to church with us tomorrow. Your faith won't grow in a hotel room."

"I don't know."

"Please?"

"Maybe." She touched her new bracelet, her mouth curving into a smile.

"Dessert?" Both their heads snapped in the waitress' direction.

Clara was quick to answer. "No, thank you."

"Just the check, please." *The opposite of perfect timing.*

"Sunday morning is the best time to catch Alice and get that conversation out of the way. Then all your troubles will be resolved."

"All my troubles?"

"Okay, maybe not all your troubles. But the most time-sensitive ones."

"Fine." She held up her hands. "I do need to talk to Alice before taking her up on the apartment offer. After I tell her what I know, she might want me gone altogether."

"She's not going to want you gone." *Make it count preacher—Clara's going to church.*

"So what time is this church of yours?"

"I have to be there at nine."

"Haha. Very funny. What's the real time?"

"I really do have to be there at nine."

"But it's almost midnight again."

"Then we'd better go."

They were the last customers to leave the pizzeria. Outside, the night was cool and still. Andrew put his arm around Clara's shoulders at the corner of Cincinnati Avenue and Mesa Street. "Cold?"

"A little." Her eyes were on the corner sign that read Cincinnati and Entertainment. "There is no Entertainment Street, is there?"

"There's no Entertainment Street or road or avenue, but this is the center of the UTEP nightlife, or so I'm told."

"I like it." A sudden breeze played with her long hair, and loose strands rested on her bare shoulder.

"I really do like you." He wrapped her in his arms and inhaled her floral scent. "How do you make it last?"

"Relationships? I don't know ..."

He tightened his grip. "That too. But I was talking about your sweet perfume." Her face reddened under the street lights—his arms a perfect frame for her young beauty. How could he keep her forever? *You're where you belong, Clara Malone. You don't know it yet. But you're home, in my arms.*

Her eyes were locked on his lips. Her chest rose and fell with rapid breaths.

Andrew kissed the corner of her mouth first. Then her lower lip. Her body melted into his arms and a moan escaped her sweet lips. *Clara ...* He cradled her head, kisses deepening. She was so tiny and perfect, and yes, he could spend a lifetime answering her questions and loving her. His own, beautiful Giselle. Oh, how he wanted to be with her—all of her. Her palms on the small of his back warmed him and brought him closer to her still.

"I need to get home," she whispered breathlessly amid sweet kisses.

"Sure." Taking her home was the last thing he wanted to do, but it was the absolute best thing to do.

She didn't have to say that she liked him for him to know that she was into him. He smiled at the possibilities, her tender kisses alive in his thoughts as they crossed the manicured gardens of the UTEP campus hand-in-hand on the way back to the Crossfire.

Andrew plugged his cell phone by the nightstand and texted Tatiana.

THANKS FOR NOT CLOSING THE DOOR ON ME WHEN I CONTINUED TO COURT YOU AND PURSUE YOU AFTER YOU TOLD ME YOU DIDN'T WANT TO MARRY ME. BUT I'VE FINALLY MOVED ON, SO IT'S BEST IF YOU DON'T COME FOR THE FOURTH OF JULY. YOU'RE FREE FROM ME AT LAST. I KNOW YOU'LL UNDERSTAND.

He turned off the light and began to pray. A buzz interrupted his prayers. He finished then checked the phone.

NO. I DON'T UNDERSTAND. AND I DON'T LIKE CLOSED DOORS ANY MORE THAN YOU DO. I WILL SEE YOU IN JULY, AND WE CAN HAVE THIS CONVERSATION IN PERSON.

Chapter 8

The patio of the Texas Roadhouse on post was crowded with soldiers and families. Crowded and hot. That kind of heat in Ohio came with buckets of humidity. Here it didn't. Clara wasn't sweating at all.

She finished her steak and nibbled on her baked potato. Twice she had opened her mouth to approach the Renata and Mario subject, but twice she had been interrupted.

"How did you like church, Clara?" Alice Howard's eyes sparkled.

"It's very nice—and very big." She had never been to a church that large. There must have been five hundred people—at least—in the service.

"Isn't it?" Alice rested her hand on her husband's arm. "Our little church in Germany was smaller than the kids' chapel here."

"You'll get used to it." Andrew leaned back in his chair. "It helps to meet people in your Sunday school class first and then expand from there." He'd left his suit jacket in the car, but still wore a perfectly-pressed white shirt and light-green tie that made his green eyes look beautifully dark.

Colonel Howard put his arm around his wife and looked at Clara. "What class did you go to Clara?"

"Passionate for Christ? Heart for Christ? Something like that." She'd had more fun with those ladies than she cared to admit.

"We should all check out Andrew's class one day. Don't you think, Clara?" Alice watched Andrew turn crimson and grinned.

"I don't know." Did she really want an answer, or was she picking on him? "Maybe?"

"Sorry, ladies. Men only." Andrew cleared his throat and straightened up.

"That's too bad." Alice shrugged. "What *is* the name of the class you teach?"

"Men of War." Andrew laughed and turned his attention to the colonel. "Sir, do you want to check out the Under Armour store?"

Colonel Howard looked at his wife.

"Go." She took her hand off his arm. "We'll get the check and move over to Starbucks."

"Can we go to the splash pad?" their older boy asked.

Colonel Howard cocked his head. "Aren't you boys getting a little too old for a splash pad?"

"It's hot, Dad, and you guys will be here forever."

"You're probably right." He smiled. "Don't run over little kids, and you boys are walking to lodging. I don't want wet bottoms in the rental."

"Okay." The three walked away together exchanging mischievous looks.

"Next Sunday can we have them in suits?" Colonel Howard finished his iced tea and watched the boys exit the restaurant. "They looked like bums in church today."

"All that stuff is in unaccompanied baggage—we should have it next week." Alice shrugged. "I thought they looked all right. Their khakis could have used some ironing, but I ironed the polos."

"If it doesn't get here on time, we'll pick up something at the PX."

She nodded.

Colonel Howard turned to Clara. "They're getting baptized here next week. You're coming, right, Clara?"

Did she have to? The sermon was good, and the class wonderful, but the early wakeup call had not been good at all. "I'll try." After she told Alice about her grandma, they wouldn't want her anywhere near them. She finished her iced tea.

"Nonsense. You must."

"I'll do my best." *If I'm still here ...* Her palms were suddenly sweaty, and her heart raced. How bad would it be if she bolted out the restaurant door and never returned?

"Talk her into joining us." He smiled at his wife and walked away with Andrew.

"I'll do my best." Alice winked at Clara. "Now it's just us girls."

She took in a sharp breath. How awkward was the conversation going to be?

"You should really come to church with us again next Sunday, Clara. The boys wanted to get baptized in Germany, but they do it at a small river, and when we left, it wasn't warm enough yet. They wait for a good day and take a big group."

"How old are they?"

"Thirteen, twelve, and eleven."

"Wow. I knew they had to be close, but I didn't realize they were that close."

"They're a handful—that's for sure. I do think, however, that I'm in the middle of the calm before the storm. It's the easiest it's ever been. But soon there will be girls, events, social media ..." She stared at her fingernails then adjusted her wedding ring. "I don't know, Clara. I'm a bit scared."

"I don't blame you. I would be apprehensive too." Clara remembered putting her mom through some rough nights—especially when it came to going out after late rehearsals.

"We're praying about those years already. That's why we're excited about a big church. Personally, Max and I would prefer a smaller one. But we want the kids to be social mostly with church kids, and it helps when you have a lot of people their age and a strong program."

"That's nice." It was a good plan—the part of it she had actually heard. Clara massaged her palms. How could she get the conversation to Mario and Renata when Alice seemed so worried about the future?

The check arrived. "Can I help?"

"No way. We told Andrew this was our thank you for the airport pick up and everything."

"Thank you, but I really didn't do much." Clara offered a half smile.

"You're here. And that means a lot to me." Alice put a small stack of crisp twenty-dollar bills in the waitress's cash holder and stood to leave. "How's your grandma?"

"Not very well." That was a smooth transition. Good. Maybe she too needed to change the conversation. "Seems like one week her heart is better and the lungs worse and then it swaps."

"It's hard when they get to that age. I'm wondering if this scare with my dad will be the beginning of multiple hospital stays."

"I hope that's not the case." Did Clara have to bring up the letter and the history behind it? Would it be unkind to say what she was about to say to the man's daughter? Would she even believe her?

They settled at a table under the shade of a desert willow with tall Frappuccinos and a copy of the *Fort Bliss Bugle*.

Clara looked at the willow and searched for hummingbirds. None today. The image of a desert willow at night floated through her thoughts and settled her heart. The memory of hummingbird sounds lifted her spirits. She could do it. She had to talk, had to get the truth out there. It was just the two of them. Andrew's assurance gave her courage. It's a forgiveness Gospel, he'd said. "Alice?"

"Yes?" She waved at the boys who, in the distance, looked like small children playing on a large, round pad with dozens of jets of water.

"What do you know about your dad and my grandma?"

"I know a lot—I think." She took a long sip of her Frappuccino, her eyes on the drink. "How much do you know?"

"I know a lot too." Where could she go next? Where to begin?

"Do you ever wonder why I'm the one taking care of Dad? Why he's not in Brazil with the other kids and grandkids?"

"I probably should have wondered, but no, the thought hadn't crossed my mind until now. I would have guessed he chose you because of your connection with the military—he still likes being around soldiers, living on an Army post?"

"No, though that makes our lives together nice. My dad and my husband have different nationalities, and Dad is almost twice Max's age, but they are incredibly alike. They are soldiers. But that's not why we take care of him."

"Why do you then?"

"Do you know about the engagement party and how Mom saw Dad's car?"

Clara nodded, lips tight, heart hurt.

"After that party, my mom made his life miserable."

"Understandably, I suppose." Clara's voice was just above a whisper.

"Yes. He still feels terrible about everything, if that's any help. He was the only person in that whole equation who had a choice, and he knows it, and that kills him daily. He knew all the relationships involved and all the people involved and made a bad decision that impacted all of them forever—multiple bad decisions. He lived a lie daily for many years."

Andrew's words rang in her ears. *It's a forgiveness Gospel.* That was probably true. Andrew knew his Bible. But how about people? Clara struggled to forgive and suspected others did too. "Did your mom ever forgive?"

"She never did. She died hating him."

"And your siblings knew about it all too?"

"Mom made no secret. She kept that sword over Dad's head for the rest of their lives together."

There were no excuses, of course, but did the unforgiving behavior of Alice's mom lead him to pursue Grandma Renata again? Maybe that's why he'd set up the house and lived a double life for as long as Grandma let him. How sad. Understandable. But how so very sad. "You're right—he had the decision power, knew all the people involved, knew the truth. But living with his mistake, his whole life must have been hard."

"It was, and it is. All day, every day. He was hated for every remaining day of that marriage. Then when Mom died—she was in her sixties—my brothers carried on the hate legacy. They maintained a relationship for a couple of years after her death, but Dad couldn't take it anymore. After he retired, he came to visit us and never left."

"Is that hard on you?"

"Him living with us?"

"Yes."

"It was an adjustment, but he came to us at a time when the boys were young, and we wanted to see Europe. We did two back-to-back tours there. So he was able to help us. We traveled as a family most of the time, but at night, my husband and I could go out and enjoy operas, dining, ballet. It was such a blessing. It's been great during deployments too. I've taken Rhine tours with my girlfriends, Polish pottery shopping trips with the Officers' Wives' Club, day trips to Paris, all while Dad watched the kids."

"That sounds like such a dream life."

"In many ways it is."

"So we're good?"

"Hmm?"

"I was afraid that you didn't know that my grandma had hurt your family—"

"Oh, I know, I know. It's not like she did it on purpose, and I forgave my dad a long time ago."

"So you know everything? The house they had—"

Alice lifted her palm like a traffic cop. "Everything."

"I'm glad we got that out of the way."

"Me too." Alice finished her drink.

That was easier than she had expected. Good. "Is your dad all set for the twenty-third now?"

"Should be." Alice straightened her back. "Here they come."

Clara saw the men in the distance.

"You didn't tell me about Andrew?"

"He's nice." *Last night was amazing.* Maybe she would tell Alice more one day, but not this day. Looking at Andrew, she remembered the corner of Cincinnati and Entertainment, his strong arms and gentle kisses. She swallowed hard.

Alice tapped her fingertips on the table and raised her eyebrows.

"We're getting to know each other."

The two women giggled as the men approached the table.

"I thought you were lost—gone forever." Alice looked at her husband's two shopping bags.

"I'm never lost." The colonel lifted his shades and kissed his wife. "I found the shirt I needed and went by the PX to pick up your conditioner."

"Oh, I'd forgotten all about it. Glad you were thinking of it."

"I had to take the long way back, so we had more time to talk. Our friend here has girl troubles." Colonel Howard put a strong hand on Andrew's shoulder.

Andrew and Alice both snapped their heads in the colonel's direction.

Andrew shook his head and handed Clara the June edition of *Dance Magazine.*

"Oh, thank you." She inspected the cover. "That's really nice."

"Gives you something to do tonight after you're all done packing."

"Sure. Thank you." How nice of him to think of getting her a magazine. And how spoiled would she be if she spent more time with him? He would surely ruin her for anyone else. "I will take it to the swimming pool when I'm done packing. Thanks." It would be a crime to leave the Radisson without going to the pool.

"Clara?" She heard a familiar voice behind her. "Clara Malone?"

She didn't have to look to know who it was. Could she disappear? Could he disappear? Surely personal teleportation devices had been invented, right? Where was hers? What was he doing there?

"It *is* you." Scott stood in front of her now—the same dark complexion making his blue eyes pop. "What in the world are you doing here?" He searched the faces of all the people with Clara.

"Long story." *Please leave.*

"I'm Andrew." Andrew offered his hand.

"Scott."

"These are the Howards." Andrew's voice was different. Reserved. "They just arrived from Germany."

Scott was supposed to be with his wife in Germany for another year. Why was he in Texas, and why was he not wearing a wedding ring?

"I came here from Germany too." Scott crossed his arms in front of his strong torso. "Grafenwoehr."

"I was in Baumholder, but I've been to Graf many times, of course." Colonel Howard seemed to study Scott, who studied him right back. "Quite the contrast—Germany, El Paso—isn't it?"

"That it is, sir." Scott twisted his mouth. "You're Lieutenant Colonel Howard, soon-to-be battalion commander over at First Brigade. Aren't you?"

"That would be me."

"Major Scott Taylor—your soon-to-be XO."

"Oh, wow. Small Army."

Tell me about it. Am I blue from not breathing yet? Scott talked to Colonel Howard with enthusiasm and interest, but he glanced at Clara every three sentences or so. A major already? Hmm.

"Do you still have the same number?" Scott's voice was playful now.

"Me?" Clara shifted in her seat, all eyes on her.

"Yes, you." His mischievous smile set her face on fire.

She nodded in slow motion. She shouldn't have come on post. She shouldn't be in El Paso.

"We have to catch up. I'll shoot you a text."

She wanted to tell him not to, but nothing came out. What could she say in front of everybody?

"I'll see you on Tuesday, sir." Scott offered his right hand to Colonel Howard.

"Sure thing." Colonel Howard's massive hand wrapped the young major's.

"Ma'am." Scott nodded in Alice's direction, and she nodded back.

"I'll see you around—Andrew, right?"

"That's right." Andrew squared his shoulders.

"I'll see you soon, Clara." The corners of Scott's eyes crinkled. "What a lovely surprise."

She didn't care how much heat Scott still managed to generate within her. No, he wasn't going to see her. Not soon and not ever.

He could go back to his car and put his wedding ring back on and leave her well enough alone.

Now if only she could stay mad at him. If only all of that were true. She didn't want to see him and didn't plan to do it, but she couldn't accuse him of walking around without a ring, picking up girls for sport. He'd loved her.

But just like Mario and Renata and just like Andrew and Tatiana, she and Scott had crashed and burned too.

Their love story cut short.

Hopes and dreams dashed.

The relationship equivalent of a firework dud that leaves the mortar full of promise but fails to function properly in the air and returns to the ground unexploded and damaged, having brought joy to no one. No. One.

Fort Bliss. Whose bliss? Not hers.

Chapter 9

"Oh, how beautiful!" Clara put her purse on the kitchen counter, and Andrew placed her small carry-on and airport shopping bags inside the temporary apartment Alice had rented for her. The smell of fresh linen and new leather invited her in. Had anyone ever used the place?

"Look at this kitchen." She ran her fingertips over the cool marble countertops. Not a speck of dust on the smooth surfaces.

The early morning sunlight bathed the rustic tiled floor, and copper pots and pans hung from a simple wooden rack, inviting her to give real cooking a try. She wasn't sure where to get groceries or how, but that didn't matter for the moment—having a kitchen was enough. She was in a home, not a room.

"Check out the rest of the apartment." Andrew leaned against the doorpost and lifted his shades to the top of his head. His eyes gleamed. "Alice asked me to make sure you're happy with the place—the whole place."

"I am very happy." Clara raised both arms in the direction of the stainless-steel stove. "I have a kitchen. I don't need to see anything else to tell you that I'm happy with the apartment."

"Are you a foodie?" He crossed his arms over his chest and looked at her sideways.

"Not at all. I'm just someone who's been eating out too much lately."

"Ah! That makes sense." Andrew massaged the palm of one hand with the thumb of the other. "I wanted to invite you to my place for dinner tonight, but now I'm afraid to ask. I mean, you're so in love with your kitchen … I'm not sure I want to come between the two of you."

"You would have to ask at your own risk. No telling what could happen." He wasn't serious, was he? She would be okay on her own if he didn't invite her, right?

Andrew looked serious as he continued to massage his right hand, his gaze down. Little red hairs on his arms invited a caress, but she resisted. Oh, who was she kidding? She wanted to be with him. She drew her lower lip between her teeth. *Please invite me to dinner at your place.*

His eyes met hers and changed quickly from serious to mischievous. Then loud chuckles—his first, then hers—filled the space between them.

"Hahaha. Very funny." Clara narrowed her eyes. "You can cook for me if you like. No risk. I just don't want to eat out for a while, if that's all right. The kitchen will still be here tomorrow."

His beautiful boyish grin pierced her heart. He would be safe cooking for her. But how about her? Was her heart safe around him, or was she at risk? Would he still be interested in her tomorrow and the day after tomorrow and the day after that?

He inched forward.

Silliness. Of course he would. He was different. He'd said so, and she chose to believe him.

"When was the last time you had a home cooked meal?"

How long had it been? She scrunched up her face. "Two months ago, before my mom went to Brazil?"

"I'm not sure I can compete with your mom, but let me cook for you tonight, Clara."

"Okay. I'm sure I'll love it." The sun was shining brighter into the apartment now, but the warmth on her cheeks had nothing to do with the sunlight. "What're you making?"

"It's a surprise."

"That means you don't know."

"That's right. It's a surprise for both of us." They laughed together, and Andrew took another step in her direction. "The Commissary is closed for the holiday. I'm going to WalMart in a few. Do you want to go with me and pick up some things?"

"Not today. I just want to settle in. I saw a Dollar General when we drove in. That will do. I'll be fine."

He tucked a lock of hair behind her ear. "Are you sure? This kitchen won't do you much good if you don't have groceries."

"Positive." She lowered her gaze. "The truth is, I live on cereal and frittatas. I like kitchens and cookbooks, and I want to learn to cook one day. But I haven't quite started—yet. I'll be fine with whatever I can get at the corner store."

He lifted her chin and looked into her green eyes. "Well, tonight you'll live on more than that. If you don't mind."

"I don't mind. I'm looking forward to it already." Her reflection in his eyes and the warmth of his touch spoke of how dangerously close they were. Why wasn't she running? Why was she doing the opposite of running? Because he had said he was different? But didn't they all?

He hadn't kissed her since the night at the ballet and now looked like he would. Should she take a step forward and bridge the small gap left between them? A drop of sweat rolled down her back. She exhaled.

Nope. She shouldn't. Clara took a step back.

The hand that had lifted her chin held nothing for a brief moment. Then Andrew stepped back too. "I'll stop by at six."

"I can walk over at six. Is your building far?" She picked up the apartment documents that were on the counter and fanned her face and chest.

"Not really, but this place is a bit of a maze." He pointed at the rooftops beyond her living room window. "I'm just a couple of buildings over in that direction. I will walk you today, and then you'll know for next time."

"Okay. Can I bring dessert?"

"Not today. I don't want you to go to any trouble. Maybe you can cook for me one of these days—dessert and all. I'll be your guinea pig."

"One of these days." Was she able to cook a complete meal? They'd better have cookbooks at Dollar General.

He handed her the keys. "Here you go. The card is for the gate, laundry room, gym, etcetera."

"Laundry. Yes. That's important."

"You can bring your laundry to my apartment. I have a little stack-up washer and dryer."

"I'm not taking my dirty clothes to your apartment." How embarrassing would that be? Convenient, but no.

"I don't mind. The laundry room here is a bit of a zoo—all these lieutenants trying to wash their filthy field gear."

"I'm really not taking my dirty clothes to your apartment."

"Okay. If you change your mind, bring it. I promise I won't look."

"I'll see you at six—no laundry."

Andrew nodded. "I'm looking forward to dinner."

"Me too." Normally she wouldn't accept an invitation to go to a guy's home. Normally she wouldn't be with a soldier. Yet, here she was. Why? Why did she feel safe with him?

Was it the church? His relationship with the Howards? Both?

It sure wasn't the Army.

Clara closed the door, kicked off her sandals, and took a deep, cleansing breath. *Home.*

The small living room was beautifully decorated, and a peacock-blue sofa with coral pillows was the highlight. Gray and coral curtains framed a large window that faced the east side of the Franklin Mountains.

She'd visited several apartment communities with her mom when she was little and her parents were getting a divorce. She'd always loved the model apartments with their bold décor and new furniture smell. Now she got to live in an apartment just like those. Her temporary life wasn't too bad.

She should have stayed annoyed about El Paso and her situation, but the truth was that something about this temporary life felt incredibly right. She would love to have an apartment like this for real and to have friends like the Howards to keep. Everybody she knew was divorced. It was fun to spend time with a family for a change. And then there was Captain Ginger, of course. Oh, Andrew … What would she do with him?

Clara approached the bedroom door. Orange and teal pillows accented the gray comforter, and on a pale-blue wall, a large oil dominated the room and proposed peace. Her fingertips touched the canvas. An original? The signature was hard to read. A voluminous turquoise estuary meandered against vibrant gold and red brush. On the horizon, mountains. Beautiful.

Her eyes stayed on the painting as she sat on the edge of the tall bed. A text message came in. Clara's hand reached for the smartphone in her pocket. Probably Andrew.

Unknown number?

Sorry I didn't call or text last night. Something came up at work. What are you doing here? Would you like to see me? I would love to catch up.

With fifteen minutes to spare, Andrew inspected his apartment one last time. Most of his Army gear was stowed out of sight. The only evidence of his service was his West Point diploma and graduation picture. Certainly she wouldn't find that offensive. Or would she? She hadn't found Major what's-his-face offensive.

The hungry way the man had looked at Clara made him extremely uncomfortable. She'd looked uncomfortable too. There was definitely a story there.

Had he contacted her like he said he would? She hadn't mentioned anything about the strange encounter, and he wasn't going to ask. But he wanted to know. Maybe Colonel Howard could help since the two would be working closely together. What were the odds that she would run into somebody she knew?

Andrew looked at his phone. Almost six. He was behind with the cooking, but the place couldn't get any tidier, and the table was already set. The only sign of Tatiana's existence was her text saying she was coming to El Paso to discuss saying goodbye forever in person.

He should empty the dryer just in case Clara needed it. Then it would be time.

What could he say to Tatiana to keep her from coming? After all she'd put him through, she should have accepted his request: don't come. Simple. Best for everyone.

But no. She had to insist and impose herself on him. He gritted his teeth and a low growl grunt caught in his throat.

Would Tatiana accept that it was really over when they talked in person? He didn't want to think about the struggle ahead. But there would be a struggle for sure. She wouldn't travel from Washington State to Texas to make his life easy. There was going to be trouble. No doubt about it.

He shook his head and looked at the clock on the kitchen wall. Six o'clock. *God help me—really Lord. Help me get to know Clara better, and help me put an end to the Tatiana ordeal once and for all.*

Don't drink tonight.

Don't drink tonight? Okay.

That made sense. Having a woman over for dinner, being alone in his apartment, playing music … That could end in intimacy, intimacy he should protect her—and him—from. She could drink if she wanted to, but he wouldn't.

The Roberto Carlos CD he'd just purchased was in the CD player. The voice of the famous Brazilian singer would greet Clara when she walked in. *Let's do this.*

Andrew stepped into the light of the scorching Texas sun, and his black polo shirt heated up instantly. He put his shades on and looked up—not a cloud in the sky. Life in the desert.

He reached Clara's building and spotted her on the balcony. *Wow.*

She wore a simple orange and dark-blue outfit with the triangle pattern that was typical of local everything, from clothing to pottery to carpets. The colors were perfect for her complexion. Pretty. Very pretty. Gold dangly earrings reflected the sunlight and made her smile even brighter. Her image was like a painting. Something he would find at a street market in Spain. Warm, inviting, and beautiful. A tropical vacation in the middle of winter. Undeserved and unexpected but absolutely delightful.

"I can see your building from my building." She waved.

"Hi." His voice caught in his throat.

"I saw you step out. It's right there. I could have walked. I would have found it."

"I'm sure you would have." The shorts of the romper ended halfway down her thighs. That was the most he'd ever seen of her legs. And what lovely legs they were. Tanned and toned. And long. Goodness gracious. He filled his lungs to capacity.

"Well, are you coming all the way up, or would you like for me to come down?" She leaned forward, elbows on the rail.

"I'm coming up."

Her lipstick was coral and shiny and matched her clothes. Was it new?

An uncomfortable heat, more powerful than the West Texas sun, burned him from within. Had the major taken her shopping? He was probably off duty too.

At the top, he wasn't sure if he should kiss her cheek or give her a quick hug, so he did neither. Awkward silence. She smiled at him, and he smiled back. Ah, forget the major. Say something. "Did you buy your outfit here? It's very El Paso."

She giggled. "Can you believe I found it at Dollar General? Don't tell anyone." She stepped out and closed the door. "Isn't it pretty?"

"It's very pretty." Her perfume was different too. Andrew's breaths quickened. Something citrus that reminded him of his mom's favorite oil. It was wonderful. Was Clara into oils too?

She walked down the stairs ahead of him and waited at the bottom for him to catch up. "Look at you all relaxed. I didn't think you owned shorts and sandals. I'd seen you wearing your uniform, blazers, and suits. This is the first time you've dressed down some. Do you own T-shirts too?"

"Not many, but as a matter of fact, I do." Andrew placed his hand on the small of her back, and they walked toward his building. "New lipstick?"

"Yes."

"Dollar General?"

"Yes! How did you know? They have everything."

He chuckled. He needed to relax. There was nothing to that major. "Glad you found something that makes you happy."

"Me too." She looked at his eyes, and a corner of her mouth lifted. "Very glad that I found something that makes me happy."

She was probably still thinking about Dollar General and the items she found.

Or was she?

There was something sweet and special in the way she'd looked at him just now. Was *he* the thing she'd found that made her happy? Was she flirting? How cute was that?

They climbed up to his floor and reached his door. He pushed his sunglasses up and fumbled with his keys. This was the first time a woman other than Tatiana would see his apartment. Please let her like Roberto Carlos. It wasn't too much, was it? Well, too late now. *God, please.* "Welcome."

"Thank you." She stepped in holding her hands behind her back. "Roberto Carlos?"

"Yes, do you like it?"

"Yeah. Do you?"

"I don't know much about him. I learned of him from General Medeiros. He has several Roberto Carlos CDs. I found this one at WalMart today."

"You found a Roberto Carlos CD at WalMart?"

"Sure did. The local Mexican community loves Roberto Carlos. It's always on the radio." Andrew put his keys down. "Do you know this song?"

"I've heard it before."

"Did—I'm sorry, what's your grandmother's name again?"

"Renata."

"Do you think she and Mario listened to these songs together?"

Clara squinted. "Not together. Not this particular song. It can't be more than forty years old.

"Then separately, maybe." He could swear those Roberto Carlos songs were meaningful to the general and related to Renata.

"Maybe." Clara scanned the living room and small dining room.

"An apartment with a bigger dining space would have been ideal, but this one had the better view." Did she like it?

"It's very nice." Clara ran her hand through her hair. "Never skimp on the view." She gave a cute half shrug and then was silent.

Breathe, Andrew. Something to drink. Where were his manners? "Can I get you something to drink?"

"Sure." She approached the kitchen counter. "What are my choices?"

"I'm cooking some pork—I'm a bit behind, by the way—I have iced tea, water, a sweet red German wine and a local white."

"They make wine in El Paso?"

"Not in El Paso, but across the state border in New Mexico. It's from the same winery that made the one we had at the pizzeria the other night."

He pulled a bottle of St. Clair Gewürztraminer out of the fridge. "St. Clair is about thirty minutes from here, if that. Most people don't know this, but there is a huge tradition of winemaking in southern New Mexico. It's America's oldest wine producing region." He was talking too much, wasn't he?

"What's Gewürztraminer?" She labored to read the long word on the label.

"I'm not sure what it means, but when I was in Germany, I learned fast that there were three kinds of wine I always liked. Gewürztraminer was one of them." He should have had a better explanation. "Do you want to try it?"

"Is that what you're drinking?"

"Actually, I'm drinking tea." Would she think he was weird?

"I'll have tea too."

He pulled two thick wine glasses from the freezer and poured fresh sweet tea into them.

"Is that a German thing too?"

"The frozen wine glasses?"

"Yep." She ran a fingertip down one side of the cup he'd put in front of her.

"No. They do it at the pizza place around the corner, and I like the way it looks."

"It does look nice."

"A toast?" He raised his glass.

"Sure." She raised her glass too.

"To sweet tea, Roberto Carlos, Dollar General, and all other hidden treasures of El Paso."

They both laughed. He took his glass to hers gently and let them touch with a "clink" as delicate as Clara.

"That's really sweet."

"Good sweet?" He swirled the liquid in his glass.

"Very good sweet." She put her glass on the kitchen counter.

"Do you mind slicing some mushrooms and chopping herbs while I brown the meat?"

"I don't mind." Clara twisted her hair into a knot and washed her hands. "I'm going to earn my keep for a change. I like that."

Clara Malone, you are too cute. He handed her a box of fresh mushrooms. "The board and knives are over there."

They worked in silence and listened to Roberto's ballads. What was that song that the general listened to again and again?

Clara lifted a board full of sliced mushrooms. "What do I do with these?"

"Nothing yet." He turned off the fire.

"I'm used to seeing this kind of stove in Brazil, but I didn't know they still existed in the United States."

"I think most stoves in El Paso use gas." He reached for his glass. "I'm not sure why. Most people have swamp coolers too. Not apartments, I don't think. Definitely not these ones. But older houses, yes." Andrew spent a great deal of time on roofs, wrapping up swamp coolers for his friends from church, older friends, before the arrival of winter.

"What in the world is a swamp cooler?"

"It cools air using evaporation of water. I'm not entirely sure how it works."

"El Paso is so strange."

"It's unique." He chuckled. "Can you put the mushrooms down and hand me that glass baking dish?"

"Sure."

He placed the pork he'd browned in butter with flour, rosemary, basil, and other herbs in the baking dish and dumped the butter that was left in the skillet into a saucepan with flour. He added chicken broth and stirred. "I'm almost done with the hands-on part. Then we can sit out on the balcony. It's small but has a perfect breeze this time of the day."

"No hurry." She shrugged.

He was in somewhat of a hurry. He wanted to look at her more and look at food less. "Can you add the mushrooms?"

"To your saucepan?"

"Yep."

She had to get very close to reach the pan. He could have moved, but his feet seemed to be planted on the black and white kitchen floor. Her arm touched his as her auburn hair came loose from the knot, brushing his face and filling the air with her sweet smell of flowers—and citrus. He breathed her in.

"Sorry." She shrugged and moved toward the sink with the empty board. "Tight kitchen."

"Uh-hum." For once having a small kitchen was a good thing. A very good thing. He finished mixing the sauce, poured it over the pork that was in the baking dish, and covered it with aluminum foil. "There."

"I am so hungry. This is going to be good—it smells good." She picked up her glass, then filled up her lungs with the vapors from the stove area. "Rosemary, basil, oregano, and?"

"And thyme." She would be a great cook one day. She had a good nose and seemed to enjoy the process. Those were the basics. The rest could be learned.

"You sure know your way around a kitchen." Clara dried her hands and placed the kitchen towel neatly back on the counter. "You must love cooking."

"I'm not sure I love it. But I like it a lot, and I usually don't have anyone to cook for, so when I do, I take advantage of it." Usually? Who was he kidding? More like never.

"Cook away. I will be happy to be your plus-one at the dinner table anytime."

"Good." He would take her up on that. "Let's go outside."

He opened the sliding door of the balcony for her.

"You should sit there." He pointed to the closest patio chair. "You'll have the best view."

"Thanks."

Andrew stopped at the CD player and upped the volume before joining her on the balcony. He left the sliding door open, and the sound was still clear from the outside. Good. A new song started.

"I can't believe I'm in El Paso, waiting for my grandma's love, and listening to Roberto Carlos." She straightened her back. "Wait until I tell my mom about Roberto."

She made the *r* sound like an *h*—just like the general did. Was that a rule that applied to all words beginning with *r*, or was the singer's name an exception? Maybe he would learn Portuguese one day. His eyes rested on her profile. He liked her posture. Most girls didn't sit tall like she did. She'd left her sandals by the door and flexed and pointed her feet for the fun of it, it seemed. Andrew kicked off his sandals too and relaxed against the seat. "How *is* your mom?"

"I told you about her date, right?"

"Briefly."

"I've had a hard time catching her at a good time since. She's either with doctors or going out with this guy."

"So there's been more than one date now?"

"Apparently."

"Good for her."

"I hope it's good for her. I'm afraid she's just lonely and tired. I hope she's not giving him false expectations." A line appeared between her brows. "She'll have to come home eventually."

"I'm sure she can handle her own life. Don't you think?" He winked. "She's your mom."

"I don't know. She's been acting strange lately—since she started going out with him." Clara faced him. "I worry."

"About what? Her giving him false hope? I'm assuming he's about the same age and can handle his life too?"

"Like I said, I don't know. I just have a funny feeling about all this."

"Do you always feel this way when she goes out with someone?"

"That's the thing. She never goes out with anyone." Clara lowered her gaze. "She's usually always busy with me and my life."

"I'm sorry." Andrew reached for Clara's hands. "I assumed that your mom going out on a date was a common occurrence." This was a different story altogether. A bit of jealousy. Fear of a new thing. He couldn't imagine his mom going on a date if his dad weren't in the picture. "Give it a little bit more time. Maybe you'll get used to the idea."

A hint of sadness clouded her features, and he understood the sentiment.

Another song started. "Hey, this is it." Andrew walked to the CD player just inside the door and upped the volume. "The song the general listened to again and again in Germany. This is the one." If only he could understand the words. Some sounds reminded him of high school Spanish, but Portuguese seemed more aired out. More vowels, maybe? He wasn't sure. "Do you know what he's saying?"

"Hmm. Not everything. Did the CD come with lyrics?"

"Let me see." He ran inside and brought the case out. "Here." He hand-ed it to Clara.

She opened the box and pulled out the booklet that was on the cover. "What track is it?"

He stepped in again and looked at the display on the CD player. "Five."

Her eyes were fixed on the back of the booklet. "'De Tanto Amor' is the name of the song." Her fingers flipped through the pages and then stopped. "Roberto Carlos and Erasmo Carlos."

"I once asked him to tell me what it all meant, but he wouldn't. I told you he's pretty reserved, right?"

"You did." Clara didn't lift her eyes from the lyrics. She blinked rapidly, her long eyelashes moist. "I don't speak Portuguese, but I understand a lot of it—this is beautiful. Start the song again. I'll try to translate some of it."

"If it upsets you, you don't have to."

"I don't mind." She put the paper down on the tiny table that separated them and took unsteady fingertips to the outside corners of both eyes. "I just hope I don't butcher it too much. It's like translating a poem. It's hard."

"Tissues?"

She shook her head. "I don't think so."

Andrew played the song from the beginning. The piano introduction felt like a long sucking in of breath and life. Then silence. Then he exhaled in a long "aaaah" and began singing. What did he say?

"Ah, I'm here, love. Just to say goodbye, and the last words of our love you'll have to hear."

Unexpected. Wasn't that what Tatiana was trying to do? Be heard? *You'll have to hear.* He hated thinking about her, sitting across from Clara. But those lyrics.

"I was lost loving you so much. I lost my mind. No one can love like I loved. And I should confess: That was my mistake—my error. I will look at you one more time at the moment when we say goodbye forever." Clara shook her head. "Okay, I'm lost. Sorry."

That second part sounded less like Tatiana. How could someone love so much and then back out? Someone mad in love doesn't back out. "Back to the beginning?"

"Sure. If you don't mind, I will start translating again when I hear the part where I left off." She tapped her fingers on the table at high speed. "Is it even making any sense? My Portuguese is horrible."

"It's making perfect sense." He nodded. "Keep going."

They listened in silence. Then Clara lifted a finger—the new part began.

"I will look at you one more time, at the moment we say our final good-bye. I will cry once more when I look into your eyes." Clara's eyes were closed now. "I know I'll miss you, and please my sweetie, let me at least watch you walk down the street—past me. I promise I won't say anything. Just forgive me if I cry." She pouted and blinked back tears. "Then he repeats the part about crying one more time when looking into her eyes."

"Aww. Do you think the general ever did that? Saw your grandma again without saying a word, just watched her pass him?"

She shrugged. "I don't think so. I don't know."

"Maybe he did. He's really into this song. Thanks for translating." The melody ended, and he reached for her hand.

"You're welcome." She faced the small round table and put her other hand over his. "I just feel like I'm turning beautiful poetry into blah, blah, crazy talk."

"It wasn't blah, blah, crazy talk." He faced the table too and caressed her arm. "It was beautiful. I can see why he's so successful."

"Well. Men don't talk this way, I guess. When one does, it touches many hearts. It's very special."

"Maybe many don't." But he could try. "Don't girls see all the sentimental talk as weakness?"

"I don't know about what girls think." She bit her lower lip as if thinking about what to say next. She lowered her eyes. "I think that whining is weak. But expressing a sentiment that's beautiful is not weak."

"No whining." He pretended to write it down on an imaginary notepad on his hand. "Okay."

"That's right." She smiled.

She'd tasted so good on the corner of Cincinnati and Entertainment. Would she let him kiss her again? He held both her hands on the table. "What's he saying now?"

"He's talking about old times." She looked up as if searching for words or maybe to better focus on the words. "The sweet past that will live forever in their memory. That will feel real again when they listen to their old songs, a time when dreams and reality occupied the same space." She pressed her fingers to her lips.

"I like that thought—I like it a lot." He crossed his fingers behind his head and leaned back in his chair. "Do you remember that, Clara?"

She cocked her head. "Remember what?"

"A time when dreams and reality occupied the same space."

"Every day I was at the University of Cincinnati in the dance program. I loved it and had every hope to make it into a company."

"You have to remember to contact that company we saw dance *Giselle*. Who knows? Maybe you are meant to be here for more reasons than one." For Mario and for her career. And for Andrew. Not for the major though.

"I will. I just don't want to get my hopes up again." She finished her tea. "I'll call them tomorrow."

"I'll help you get around. We'll figure something out."

"Thanks." She nodded. "How about you?"

"What about me?"

"A time when dreams and reality occupied the same place?"

"The Academy and even my Army life now—it's a dream, and it's reality." His time with Tatiana too, to an extent. But he wasn't going to mention that.

"How about a girl? How about Tatiana—before she broke your heart?"

"Before she broke my heart, it was dream and reality, in a way." He needed an out. He didn't want to lie and wouldn't. But to talk about an ex with the girl he was trying to win over was not wise.

"In a way?"

"Well ..." *Lord, please help me walk out of this conversation unharmed.* "We never—If this gets weird for you, let me know, and I will stop." He finished his tea too. "We never ... See, I think people shouldn't be intimate if they're not married. I didn't try to be with her. We were never together in that way, so there was a limit to the intensity of the relationship—"

"You guys didn't have sex. I get it. I know people who've made that same choice."

"Yes." Was that her choice too? "So anyway, it was dream and reality, but without consummating the relationship with marriage and intimacy, it was a very incomplete dream and reality. It was more like a promise that didn't materialize, if you will."

"Did she try to talk you into making love to her? I mean, nowadays, most girls wouldn't be okay with waiting, I don't think."

"Kind of." The kitchen timer went off. *Oh, praise God. Thank you, Jesus.* "Dinner's ready."

He opened the oven and grabbed a dish towel. "You can play something else if you'd like." He used the knife to point at the stereo, and then started working on the meat. Maybe the search for something to listen to would make her forget the conversation they were just having. Andrew added the vegetables to the baking dish and placed it on the table. "Do you want a fresh glass of tea?"

"Sure."

He poured sweet tea for both of them and set the glasses on the table.

"I didn't pick anything." Clara ran her long fingers over the row of CDs on the shelf above the stereo. "I don't know who any of these people are."

"They're mostly Christian singers, but I have some classical music too— things I'm sure you're familiar with."

"You pick something. I'm here to get to know you. If I wanted to do my own thing, I would have stayed in my own apartment—I have one of those now, you know."

"Okay." He placed his iPod on the speaker dock and selected a David Garrett list he thought she would enjoy. Then he replayed her sweet words in his head. *I'm here to get to know you.* He enjoyed the sound of that better than any song under his roof. "Shall we eat?"

"I thought you would never ask." Clara grinned.

He pulled the chair out for her.

"Thank you."

His dining table wasn't too big, but it was long enough that he couldn't reach her hands, so he just bowed his head to pray.

"Amen." Clara whispered when he finished.

"Can I serve you?" he asked.

"Sure." She watched him move, and this time, it didn't make him self-conscious. Outside, night was falling and the room was suddenly too dark. Should he light candles or turn on a sidelight? He walked to her side and placed the plate in front of her. "There you go."

"Thank you." She closed her eyes and breathed the vapors coming from the plate.

Candles.

He found matches in the pantry and placed two tall white candles in silver candleholders he'd hidden all the way in the back of the pantry. He'd hesitated to buy them a few weeks back when he was in the Magic Bistro area for a unit function—What for, right? He didn't have anyone to woo with a candlelit dinner.

But he'd bought them anyway, hoping the right occasion would present itself.

He lit the candles with ease and blew out the match. Andrew looked at Clara's bright green eyes, made even more beautiful by the soft light of the white candles. This occasion couldn't be more right.

He sat and enjoyed his meal.

The rosemary was the most intense of the herbs, as it should be. The juicy pork tenderloin melted in his mouth, perfectly warm. Nice. "Is it good?"

"Very good." Clara ate with purpose—not coyly or pushing her food around between bites. "Thank you."

"You're welcome." She looked happy and satisfied, and that pleased him. They ate in comfortable silence. "More?" he asked when she rested her silverware in the middle of her empty plate.

She shook her head. "Thank you. This was so good. But I don't want to get big in case this summer intensive thing works out." She winked. "Best to be careful with what I eat late in the day."

"Really?" She didn't look like she ever had to watch her figure.

"I don't want to have to diet, so I just slow down late in the day—not here lately with us going out to dinner all the time, but generally, I avoid eating a big dinner."

"I don't want to get you in trouble."

She smiled. "It's not a big deal—just no seconds."

He finished his potatoes and grabbed one more carrot from the baking dish before standing.

Clara stood too and followed him to the kitchen—plate in hand.

"You can go relax. I've got this."

"I am relaxed. We can clean up together."

"If you insist."

"I do." She went back to the table and got their empty cups. "I like your goldfish."

Andrew rolled his eyes. He looked at the rectangular tank with the submerged treasure chest and plastic scuba diver. Two orange fish and one white swam around aimlessly like they always did. Stupid fish. "I hate those goldfish."

"Why do you hate your goldfish?"

"Because they remind me that I don't have a dog, I guess."

"Then why don't you get a dog?"

"I can't. Who's going to take care of it when I'm in the field? Or deployed?" He joined Clara and they continued to clear the table. "Soldiers with families have dogs. Single soldiers have goldfish. That's my sad reality right now."

She pouted.

"Are you teasing me?" He didn't really care if she were. She looked so cute pouting.

"I don't know." Clara finished placing the last items on the counter. "Are you whining?"

"I'm not whining." He wiped the kitchen counter with a handful of wipes. "I'm expressing a beautiful sentiment." He tried to imitate her tone from earlier. That's what she'd said, right?

They laughed together—his new favorite thing to do, laugh with her.

He filled a kettle with enough water for tea for two.

"So what kind of dog will you want the day the family dream and reality occupy the same space?"

"A boxer—preferably a brindle." But any boxer would do. "Are you a dog person, Clara?"

"I think so. I want to be a dog person, but I was never allowed to have a dog."

"Parents never let you?" Pouting was tempting—payback. But something in her eyes said this was no light matter.

"Never." Her gaze was fixed on her hands, but she seemed to be far away. Then she came back. "My mom let me have a hamster once. Now that's a ridiculous pet. You can't do anything with it."

"My sister had one. It was kind of cool—always going around in that circle thing."

"That's right. Always. Day and night. All night."

"So what kind of dog will you have one day?" Maybe he could give her a dog. One day.

She shrugged. "A dog I can cuddle with watching movies and in bed, take for walks." Both corners of her mouth lifted. "Any dog, really."

"Sounds like you want a boxer. A brindle."

"Right. Because that's the only kind that cuddles and walks." She laughed.

He laughed too. "Absolutely."

"I will make a note of that." She pretended to write on an invisible pad of her own.

"Last week I saw a boxer up for adoption at the pet shop. Two-year-old male. Gigolo. He was beautiful."

"Gigolo? That's a funny name."

"I know, right?"

"So you cruise pet shops longing for a puppy, Andrew?"

"No, I go to the pet shop to buy stupid food for the stupid goldfish."

She pouted again, and they both laughed once more. Clara took her fingertips to the outside corners of her eyes and patted them dry.

Andrew got the box of Ahmad English teas out of the pantry and placed it on the kitchen counter in front of Clara. "I don't know if you can find these in other places, but I only see this brand at the Commissary around Christmas time." He opened the large box that held dozens of different teas in small shiny packs. "I prefer black teas, but all their teas are good. The Earl Grey is my favorite."

She picked the Earl Grey. "These tea packs look so beautiful. I'm almost sorry to rip it open."

"Get a couple more for your apartment."

"Have you ever been to London?" She pointed at The Houses of Parliament and Elizabeth Tower, aka Big Ben, on her Earl Gray pack.

"I have." He'd met Tatiana there twice after the big West Point breakup when he was serving in Germany, and she was in Italy. She obviously didn't want to marry him, but she didn't want to let him go either. Considering how often she reached out to him, he was pretty certain she still felt the same way.

Clara looked through the different flavors while he placed two teacups next to the box. The kettle whistled, and Andrew turned off the fire. Steaming water filled their cups.

They placed their Earl Grey tea bags in the water, and Clara put two envelopes of tea by her University of Cincinnati keychain, Romantic Jasmine and English Tea No.1.

Did she even like Earl Grey? Or did she pick it because he'd said it was good? At the Magic Bistro, she'd picked from one of his suggestions too. Looked like he'd found a girl who actually valued his opinion for a change. Nice.

He removed the tea bags from the cups. The candles were still lit on the table. The living room was dark. "Should we take it to the table?"

"Can we drink it outside?"

"Sure." He opened the sliding door and went back for his tea, but she was already carrying both.

"Sugar?" he asked.

"Please."

They stood by the wooden railing and listened to the desert crickets while sipping English tea.

"Stars Over Texas." She held her cup with both hands and looked at the star-peppered skies over the Franklin Mountains.

"Isn't that a country song?"

"Uh-hum." She put her cup down and leaned on the railing. "A waltz."

"Can you waltz?" He almost took lessons once. He loved the rhythm.

"Not well." The reflection of a dozen stars sparkled in her bright eyes.

Hmm. He finished his tea and put the cup on the table. Instead of asking Colonel Howard to find out what the deal was with that major, how about just outdoing the guy? If the man was even in the running for Clara's heart.

All Andrew had to do was be better than him and make sure he had plenty of time with Clara—quality time, unforgettable time.

She hummed the slow country waltz.

Could he win her heart in a month and keep her forever? He took two slow steps in her direction and ran his fingers through her long, silky hair.

She faced him and put her arms around him. That was the first time she'd initiated physical contact, and Andrew could have run one hundred laps around the block with the jolt of energy her small gesture gave him.

His hands touched the thin fabric of her clothes and found their place around her waist. They swayed, humming the waltz together at first, then humming it more and more quietly, and then they swayed silently.

She caressed the skin just below his neck. Her touch was gentle and light.

Touch her back, Andrew. Run your fingers on her bare shoulders, so beautifully tanned. If you hold back like you've done before, you'll lose her, just like you lost Tatiana.

If this is the girl God has for me, I won't lose her. Get thee behind me ...
But I will kiss her.

Andrew lifted her chin and let his lips touch hers, gently at first, but as her embrace grew tighter and more eager, he kissed her deeper, stronger. Her soft moans encouraged him.

Could he take it just one step further, and still be in control? No, he couldn't. He had to stop and take her home.

Andrew's arms held her tenderly as the kisses softened. Her chest rose and fell with rapid breaths against his embrace. His body swayed almost unnoticeably, and he rested his cheek on hers. Her soft skin felt like fresh linen after a week in the field.

She followed his soft rhythm.

I love you, Clara. I want to tell you that so much. I will protect you and love you and honor you. "I'll walk you home." His voice was low, almost a whisper.

She took half a step back and nodded. Glow and tenderness adorned her countenance.

Andrew took her hand and walked her home.

Clara leaned against the closed door. The only light in her new apartment came from a street lamp near her balcony.

He'd blushed. And he smelled of rosemary and basil, and his shoulders were so broad and his red hair so perfect and his little freckles, his baby skin, his lips—oh, my goodness. And did she understand him correctly? Was he really a virgin? A guy couldn't be that perfect. There had to be something wrong with him. Something that would break her heart forever. But what?

She turned to the closed door. "What is it, Andrew?" she whispered. "How are you going to break my heart?"

No. She wasn't having a fear party, a worry party, or a pity party. Enough.

How about happiness for a change. Her feet followed the light, and she stepped out onto her own balcony. Clara dared to look up at the stars. Her evening with Andrew fresh in her mind. His touch fresh on her skin. Her fingertips touched her lips, and hot tears welled up in her eyes as she hummed "Stars Over Texas." Tears, hot with love and desire and hope fell down her cheeks, and she didn't feel the urge to dry them.

Andrew played track five again and imagined she was still there. One day dream and reality would occupy the same space. He knew that with absolute certainty.

But until then and even then, there would always be "Stars Over Texas." Andrew's eyes focused on the stars above El Paso as he hummed their waltz. A new story had started. A new hope. A new love.

Chapter 10

Another text message. Good grief.

Clara put her heavy Dollar General bags on the kitchen counter and checked her phone.

Scott again. *Of course.*

She had to tell him something, so he would stop texting. Ignoring him wasn't doing the trick. She blew out her breath.

Listen, I had no idea that you were here. I'm just in town taking care of some family business. Let's just leave the past in the past. No hard feelings, okay?

There. She flopped into the closest chair and studied her purchases. Both her hands still hurt from walking more than a block with four heavy bags.

Scott wasn't the only one who'd texted her. Andrew had messaged too. His text had come in before eight a.m.—probably right after PT, a soldier's daily physical training that started religiously at six-thirty a.m., after leadership meetings. After exchanging a couple of notes, she'd agreed to cook dinner for him at her place—her borrowed place.

Soon after that, Scott began texting too. But he was too late. Too late by a couple of years. Her phone was quiet now. Good.

What was for lunch? Cereal? Why not? Oats always hit the spot. That would be quick, and then she could start thinking about dinner.

The pocket-sized cookbook she'd grabbed at the store would do. Yes, she was a sucker for impulse buys. She'd looked at every page and found two dishes that were viable without having to go to a real grocery store. She'd chosen bacon and Alfredo on bowtie pasta recipe.

Clara put the groceries away and enjoyed her bowl of cold cereal. There couldn't be a better lunch on a hot Texas day. No way.

Her chin rested on her palm as she studied the recipe one more time. The garlic bread could stay in the freezer until almost dinner time, right? She could do this. What could possibly go wrong? It was pasta.

But what if she messed it all up? It was a gas stove. Would that make a difference? She should have learned to cook years ago. She, a grown woman, was stressing over frozen bread and pasta. Pathetic.

Her nervous fingers played with the new containers of spices and herbs she'd placed on the counter. Her borrowed kitchen looked like a regular kitchen now—full of potential, some food, and the first dirty dishes. *Life.* How many meals would she end up cooking there? She clicked open the basil container and let the dried leaves share their strong, sweet smell with her.

Clara studied the kitchen, her culinary imagination running free. Pizzas, breads, cookies, cupcakes—because happiness wasn't happiness without cupcakes, right?

The roses Andrew had helped her transport from the hotel decorated the counter and were more fragrant than ever. But wait—a couple of them had begun bowing down, their splendor fading. A sad reminder.

The kitchen was borrowed. The apartment temporary. El Paso wasn't her reality. It wasn't her life. Clara put away the basil and her joy. Soon she would be back in Cincinnati, a college grad without a job.

She shook her head and lifted her shoulders, but that hurt. Why did she have to think about reality? Thinking about it didn't change things, did it?

And when had she become such a pity party queen?

Andrew would pout and tease her if he could hear her thoughts.

Ginger. She didn't want his presence in her life to be temporary. But how could she ever keep him? He was so good. Next to him, she felt like damaged goods.

Her phone buzzed again. Scott.

Let me see you. Where are you staying?

What was it to him? It was over. What should she write back?

She raised her chin, and her heart raced as she began stabbing the letters.

I STILL HATE YOU FOR LYING TO ME. I STILL HATE MYSELF FOR NOT WALK-
ING AWAY WHEN I LEARNED THE TRUTH. AND I WISH I COULD TAKE IT ALL
BACK. I WISH I'D NEVER MET YOU.

She gasped for air. Her fingertips massaged the tense area between her
brows.

Delete, delete, delete, delete.

Clara filled her lungs to capacity and exhaled slowly.

I DON'T KNOW WHAT TO SAY. PLEASE DON'T TEXT ME ANYMORE.

It'd been two years since she'd finally ended their relationship, but somehow
he still had the power to ruin her everything. *Unbelievable.* If things worked
out with Andrew, she would have to tell him that she wasn't a virgin anymore. Would he accept that? Probably not … Thanks, Scott. Appreciate that.

Another buzz.

"Argh!"

IF YOU SAY SO. I'M HERE. I'M AVAILABLE. AND I STILL LOVE YOU.

Did he consider that maybe *she* was with someone? If he did, he didn't seem
to care. If only she could have a do-over. She would have handled Scott so
differently.

Her phone vibrated once more.

A call this time. Her mom. Good. Clara exhaled and answered the phone.
"Hi, Mom."

"Hi, honey. How are you? Can you talk for a bit?" Her words came out
in a rush, her voice tense.

"Sure. Is there anything wrong?"

"Not really. I just want to spend some time talking to you." That was
more like her. "I miss you."

"I miss you too, Mom." Clara opened a can of iced tea and lay down on
the cool fabric of the peacock blue couch. "How's Grandma?"

"As expected, I guess. The problem is that what's expected from here on
is not very good. They were talking about trying surgery." There was a silence
on the line. "I don't know if I like that idea."

Grandma was so old and fragile. "Surgery for what?"

"Her heart. The doctor wants to regulate her heartbeats, and nothing else is working."

"Is it fibrillation?"

"AFib. Do you know much about it?"

"Not much." Clara had looked up common heart problems in elderly people when the general didn't show up, and fibrillation had come up.

"Surgery can help, but at her age and considering how fragile she is, I just don't know." There wasn't much conviction or energy behind a thing her mom said. She was pretty fragile too, no?

"I wish I could be there with you, Mom." The air conditioner blew ice-cold air on Clara—too cold. "A hug would be good right now, you know? I think we both need it."

"I know *Princesa*. Soon enough, hmm?" Clara heard her mom sniff hard. "But there's really nothing you can do here. What you're doing right now at Fort Bliss, that's what's important. That's the best thing you can do for her—and for me."

"What are you going to do? How long are you staying there?"

"I will stay for as long as she needs me." Conviction had returned to her mom's voice.

"But what if she lives for another couple of years? It could happen, right?" Her mom couldn't stay gone forever. "Grandma could stay fragile on a hospital bed or in a nursing home for a long time. Then what?"

"That could happen, but it's not likely at all." Her mom cleared her throat but didn't say anything else.

A weird silence settled between them. "What is it, Mom?"

"Clara, don't freak out now."

"What?" What was she trying to say? "What is it?"

"Don't freak out *and* don't worry. My decision is not final—it's up to you at this point."

"Mom, I am freaking out, and I am worrying. What in the world are you talking about? What decision?"

"If you don't want me to, I won't—"

"You won't what?"

"If you don't want me to, I won't move back to Brazil. But I want to."

"What are you talking about? You want to move back to Brazil after thirty plus years in America?"

"I do." Her mom's voice was almost a cry. A long-held breath.

"You can't possibly be serious." Why would her mom want to leave her like that? "It's that guy, isn't it?"

"No. It's not the guy." Her mom paused briefly. "No more guys in my migration decisions."

"You've never mentioned the possibility, so this is a bit of a shock."

"I know. I'm just tired."

She sounded tired. "Of course you're tired, Mom. You've been living in Grandma's hospital room for weeks now. I can help you more, but you have to let me."

"No. Not that kind of tired."

"What kind, then?" Whatever it was, Clara could fix it. She needed her mom.

"I'm tired of being 'the Brazilian who lives in the United States' when I'm in Brazil and of being 'the American who was born in Brazil' when I'm home in the U.S."

Where had that come from? Clara wasn't even sure she'd understood what her mom was trying to say. But the last part made sense. "'Home in the U.S.'—you said it all. America, the United States, is your home, Mom. What's all this?"

"I just want to be me—simple." There was nothing simple about her mom. "I'm tired of having geography as part of my identity. I don't want that anymore."

"This is so out of character. I've never heard you talk like this before. It *is* the guy, isn't it? Please let me talk some sense into you. You're not alone, Mom. Let's forget about this letter, and let me fly out there and be with you." Everything in El Paso was temporary. Her mom had to be permanent in her life. She couldn't leave her.

"No, you don't have to come. I'm doing okay, and the letter is crucial— crucial, Clara."

Apparently.

"I'm fine. I'm enjoying hearing my mama's stories, seeing old places and old friends. It's just making me nostalgic, I guess. I like it here, Clara."

"If you like it there, then why did you leave in the first place?"

"It was a good idea at the time. I was in love. He promised me the world."

"And then he didn't deliver. Why didn't you go back to Brazil then?"

"When I found out he was committed to someone else, I decided to pursue my theater dream—it was a good dream." Her mom snorted. "And there was my pride too. I wasn't about to go home with my tail between my legs to face all the people who'd said moving to the United States was a bad idea."

"Or maybe you stayed hoping he would change his mind." If Clara herself had felt that way, chances are her mom did too.

"You know that I always tell you the truth, so believe me when I say this. Yes, I was heartbroken. But once I knew he was marrying someone else, I disappeared from his life and never looked back."

"Why was it so easy for you to do that and not so easy for Grandma?" *Or for me.*

"Your grandmother had just come out of two years of not speaking. Her grief after her father died was tremendous. She was not capable of making a sound decision."

Maybe Grandma had an excuse. Clara hung her head. But what was *her* excuse? Nothing, right? Life hadn't been pleasant, and her parents' divorce had scarred her for life, but she knew right from wrong.

Her grandma knew right from wrong too, and so did her family. She could have walked away. "Why didn't her relatives stop her from moving into that house and from giving him all of her—her virginity and her future?"

"I don't know. Everyone felt so sad for her. Everyone was in shock. They'd dated—openly—for a year."

"I still can't believe I have to meet this jerk." Clara wanted to hurt him right now. "Can I punch him for her?"

"No. Just give him the letter."

"Okey-dokey. And *you* just come home, like normal people do. Okay, Mom?" And that's when it hit her. Clara shook her head hard, hoping she could shake off the thought that had just flashed through her mind like lightning. "Wait. Are you marrying the guy who's been taking you out? You are, aren't you? That's why you don't want to come home."

"No!" Her mom laughed hysterically.

"What about any of this is funny?" This would be a perfect time to get mad. But all Clara could think of was how much she missed her mom. "Not funny, Mom."

"This conversation is not funny. I'm sorry. What's funny is that you know me so well but at the same time don't know me at all. I am not getting married again, Clara. There's only one marriage—I was married to your dad. The end. So your idea is absurd and laughable."

"I didn't know you felt that way."

"Learned it from my dad. He was never married to that other woman he ended up with after he and Mom separated. I asked him once if he would marry her as I knew that he loved her very much. But he said there was only one marriage and that he was already married. That stayed with me somehow."

"But dad is dead. Big difference. You should marry one day." Clara didn't have a problem with that. "Just don't move."

"I don't want to. One marriage."

Clara nodded in slow motion. "Is that why you took such good care of dad when he was dying?"

"Well, that and also if I didn't, no one else would. Bless him, he was just so broken."

Broken together. Hmm ... One marriage? "I never talked to Grandpa. We saw each other very little, and he didn't speak English."

"I regret not traveling to Brazil more when you were little. You missed so much in terms of family relationships and family history."

"Don't sweat it, Mom. What's done is done."

"I guess. Hey, think about what I told you—about my desire to move. I know how you feel right now. But chew on it, and then we can talk again. Now, enough about me. Tell me about Andrew."

Clara would think about it all right. She wasn't likely to change how she felt about it, though. As for Andrew, where to even start? "I like him a lot. I just wish he weren't a soldier. I get such bad vibes."

"You shouldn't be too concerned about what he does for a living. It so happens we've all had some bad experiences with military people. But it could all be a coincidence. Mama wasn't thinking straight. I ran as soon as I heard George was marrying someone else. Your dad wasn't even in the service when we first met. He joined to make sure you would be born in a proper hospital and have a roof over your head. And your Scott was a dreamer, I guess. I don't know what he was."

"Half Italian, a sweet talker, and a liar. And guess what? Are you sitting?" Her mom wasn't going to believe this one. Clara pushed herself up and sat facing the mountains. "He's here. Scott is here."

"Scott? No!"

"Yep." Clara played with the edge of a nearby pillow. "And divorced. Or so he says."

"Where did you see him?"

"I was outside the Starbucks on post with everybody, and there he was. And check this out. He will be working for Colonel Howard. He's his XO."

"No!"

"Yep. True story."

"Are you going to see him?"

"Absolutely not." If she was going to move on and grow, she had to distance herself from past mistakes.

"So you must like Andrew?"

"I do." She placed her fingertips on her lips and let a breath of fresh air fill her lungs. "He took me to a ballet Saturday night, *Giselle*. Then he helped me move and cooked dinner for me yesterday. Oh, and listen to this. He bought a Roberto Carlos CD for our dinner."

"Wow."

"Wow indeed. I like him."

"And the apartment?"

"It's perfect. Remember the furnished ones we saw when you and dad were splitting up?"

"How could I forget?"

"I'm sorry. Well, it's kind of like those. Beautiful decorations and views. I'm looking at the Franklin Mountains, sitting on my couch right now."

"Well good, *Princesa*. Just be careful, hmm? Has he tried anything?"

Clara smiled. "We kissed twice now—it's sweet. He stops when things start getting too hot."

"Well then, I like him already."

"I'm supposed to cook for him tonight."

"Oops." Her mom cracked up laughing again.

"Mom!" Clara wanted to laugh too but didn't.

"I'm sorry." The laughter died down. "Do you remember that movie with the forest fire people in airplanes—Holly Hunter and Richard Drey-fuss?"

"*Always.* Yes, I remember. What does that have to do with anything?"

"Remember when she orders takeout and then unboxes everything, spreading flour in the kitchen to make the new guy think she cooked the meal?"

"Haha. Very funny. I'm cooking pasta, and I have a recipe." Though the Holly Hunter idea wasn't bad—if she had a car.

"Good luck. Be sure to make a good salad. Did you get quality ingredients?"

"There's a Dollar General half a block from here. It's awesome. They have everything."

"You bought ingredients to cook for a guy you like at Dollar General?"

"I don't have a car, remember? Uber rides are expensive. I've got this, Mom. Plus, what's the point of getting a bunch of fancy groceries at a real store if I don't know what to do with it? I'm going to start small." Maybe she should be more concerned. Why wasn't she? Hmm. "I'm excited about tonight and about cooking. It will be okay."

"Well, good then. I'm happy for you."

Her mom wrapped up their talk and promised to keep Clara posted on the possible surgery, but Clara wasn't done talking. She still had to bring up the summer workshop at the ballet company. Why couldn't money rain from the sky or grow on trees? Bummer.

"There's one more thing, Mom."

"What is it, honey?"

"The company that danced *Giselle* on Saturday has a summer intensive starting next Monday. It runs for two weeks, and then there's a performance on the twentieth."

"Did you audition?"

"It's a school and youth ballet. I don't have to." Here comes. "I just have to sign up and pay by Friday."

"How much?"

"A grand."

Clara heard her mom exhale hard.

"I'm sorry. I know I should be making money now." Her eyes welled up. She'd tried so hard to get into a good ballet company. Maybe it was time to look for a different kind of job—any job—until the right opportunity came along. Now that she wasn't traveling for auditions anymore, she could.

"It's okay. It'll all work out, Clara." Her mom cleared her throat. "Here's what we're going to do. Talk to whoever runs the place. Tell them about your diploma and see if there's anything you can help them with to offset the cost."

"Do I have to? Doesn't that sound a little desperate?"

"You have to, *Princesa*. You have a good degree. You dance well. Try. The worst that will happen is they will say no, and then I will figure something out. I'll come up with the money. I always do, don't I?"

She always did. "I know, Mom. I'll man up and do what you said." She had to grow up and become independent. *Might as well begin now.*

"Call me as soon as you know something."

"Okay." She stood and bounced on her toes.

"Be brave. Be excited about talking to them. Who knows what will come out of it?"

"Okay. Be brave. Be excited." A whole lot of nothing. That's what would come out of it, like always.

"And good luck tonight. Don't fuss over the whole Army thing. Just be young and be happy."

"I'll be happy when I go home and find a job." *So I don't have to beg.*

"Be happy right now. You always have your eyes set on the next thing—the next station. You never seem to enjoy the ride. Open the windows. Enjoy the view. Talk to the other passengers."

Clara nodded in silence. Her mom was right.

"I love you, *Princesa*."

"I love you too, Mom."

Clara ended the call and reached for the sliding door. She stepped outside and let the sunshine warm her body and her spirits.

Twin desert willows packed with light-pink flowers shared the warm breeze and the attention of hungry hummingbirds. Their buzzing sounds had become a familiar song and reached Clara's balcony with ease. They moved from tree to tree and from flower to flower without worrying about who was from where or where they were going.

Why couldn't her mom do the same? Did she really feel like a foreigner in the United States after so many years? No way.

Her mom couldn't move. She was all she had.

A double honk got Clara's attention. She spotted the light-yellow Crossfire leaving the community and Andrew waving. Her heart beat faster, and the sun got ten degrees hotter. She waved back. Dinner. That's right. She had to make dinner happen. *Yikes.*

Chapter 11

Clara smoothed down her emerald dress and opened the door for Andrew, who held a green gift bag and a small box of Godiva chocolates. "Look at you! Come on in."

"You look beautiful." He kissed her cheek and handed her the gifts. "For you."

"Thank you." Andrew's soft soapy smell made her think of things young and fresh and beautiful. His light jeans fit him perfectly, and the green polo shirt he wore matched his eyes and made his red hair look redder. *Captain Ginger* . . .

Her mom had told her to enjoy the ride and talk to the other passengers. Well, she was doing just that. Oh, she was looking out the window all right, and the view was just perfect.

"Check the bag." He winked and crossed his arms in front of his chest. "I hope you like it."

"I'm sure I will." How sweet was that? Scott had never given her a single gift. She put the bag on the kitchen counter and reached in. Clara pulled out seasons one and two of *Downton Abbey.*

"Have you ever seen it?"

"No, but I've heard about it." She scanned the back of season one. "It looks great."

"My mom and my sisters love this show. If you get into it, I can get you more seasons. They have a whole bunch at the PX." He put his keys and phone on the counter.

"Thank you so much for the DVDs."

"There's more. Dig in."

"Oh!" She dug in and pulled out three CDs this time. She lifted a sealed Roberto Carlos CD just like the one Andrew had played for her yesterday. "You got a brand new one?"

"What can I say? Can't live without Roberto anymore." He chuckled. "I've grown attached."

"Happens. The man has been in business since the fifties for a reason. I understand." She looked at the others. She recognized one from his house. "Christian music?"

He nodded. "Casting Crowns and Lauren Daigle—good stuff. I think you'll like it."

"I bet I will. Thanks." Lauren Daigle looked familiar. "Wasn't she on American Idol?"

"I think so."

Clara folded the bag and grabbed her new DVDs and CDs. "Should I put one of the new CDs in?"

"What you have on sounds good. It's up to you."

"It's NPR." National Public Radio had always been part of her life. It was her mom's absolute favorite, and her dad had enjoyed it too.

"Leave it on. It's good."

"Okay." Clara gave a half shrug and put her gifts on the bookshelf in the living room.

Andrew glanced at the books that came with the apartment and raised one eyebrow. "I like your books."

Was he serious about liking the books? She eyed titles most college students were familiar with. "Some have potential … many don't."

Andrew smiled and approached the shelf. "Between this Bible and the literature anthology, you shouldn't have to worry about the ones that don't have potential."

"True." And if things worked out at the ballet studio, she would have very little time for reading—which reminded her … "Andrew, I need a favor."

"Shoot."

"I need to be at the ballet studio tomorrow for a class that starts at ten in the morning. It's on the west side of town near the Sunland Park Mall. How can I get there? You'll be at work, right?"

"What time does it end?" He leaned against the wall by the bookshelf.

"Around noon." Clara's hands toyed with a lock of hair.

"I could come here after PT. You can drop me off at work at eight-thir-tyish and then keep the car."

"I can't."

"Why not?"

"Stick shift. It's a bad idea." She was probably the only person in the world who'd damaged the same car three times in one day, two dents and one wreck. But she wasn't going to tell him about her history with stick shift cars, not yet anyway. He would have to take her word for it.

"Well, the other option is for me to drop you off early, but it would have to be really early. Around eight-fifteen."

"That would work. I don't mind."

"That's a nice area. You should be able to find something to do. And then I can pick you up around noon."

"That'll be perfect." She was a little rusty after a couple of weeks without dancing, but she was thrilled that she would be in a studio. "Thank you."

"You're welcome." He held her hands and kissed her forehead. "Is it for the summer program?"

Clara nodded, her heart fluttering. "The program starts next week. I called to see if I could get a scholarship of some kind to help with the cost. They asked me to take a class, and then we'll discuss the options."

"That sounds good, right?"

"Yeah. It does. I'm going to be a little stiff, but I don't have anything to lose." She would be fine. "I'll just show up and dance and enjoy myself."

"Good." He crossed his ankles. "Do you have your ballet stuff?"

"Yes. I'm such a dork. I don't travel anywhere without a leotard, a skirt, ballet slippers, pointe shoes, and bun stuff. You just never know when you'll have a chance to dance. Best to be ready."

"Good." The corners of his mouth tilted up. He pulled out a slip of paper from his jeans pocket. "Since we are on the dance subject, I have a surprise for you."

"Oh?" A surprise again? She still didn't care for surprises, but the first one, *Giselle*, had been perfect.

"We are the newest students of the Shundo Ballroom Studio."

"We're what?" She covered her mouth and giggled.

He did some waltz steps toward the middle of her borrowed living room as he sang the opening of "Stars Over Texas."

Andrew was a natural dancer—or trained. Which was it? "Is that really something you want to do?"

"Yes. Why wouldn't it be?"

"I don't know. I just didn't see it coming." Definitely a guy full of surprises. "How often would we go? How does it work?"

"Thursday nights in June we learn the waltz, and then there is a social something the last Saturday of the month. Live band—big band. Kind of like in the old days."

"That sounds great." As a matter of fact, it sounded perfect. Did July have to arrive, like midnight for Cinderella? The end would be painful, wouldn't it? *Nope, Clara. Don't go there.*

"Having second thoughts?" His smile slipped.

"Nope." Enjoy the ride—that's what her mom had said. "Sounds perfect and I can't wait."

"Good." He reached for her hand and spun her around gently. Her dress flared in slow motion. "Maybe we can rent a ball gown for you for the end-of-the-month social."

"Maybe we can." Clara would ask her mom about those dresses the Brazilian dressmaker had made for her grandmother. Certainly the dresses didn't exist anymore, but maybe she could find something similar.

"Whatever you're cooking smells great."

"I hope it tastes good." Right. Cooking. Back to reality, Cinderella.

"When will I find out?" Andrew peeked over the counter, his eyes on the stove.

"When you're hungry enough not to care what it tastes like." The food *had* to be good.

"I'm that hungry already."

Clara glanced at the oven. Hot. "Well, good. Then sit and enjoy the music. Dinner will be ready in seven minutes." She got the bread out of the freezer and placed it in the oven, next to the baked pasta. The sauce was bubbling.

All was well. Then why was her heart beating like she'd just finished a difficult dance solo? She swallowed hard. It was simply dinner with someone she would probably never see again after the end of the month. Her heart skipped a beat at that thought. She had to stay in the moment. Had to enjoy the ride. Her palms were clammy now. Why was it so hard? She wasn't even supposed to like him.

Clara glanced at the living room. He'd chosen the corner armchair, the one she hadn't used yet, and he looked manlier than ever. Right ankle crossed over left knee. Relaxed and comfortable, Bible in hand. That's what was appealing about him—he had the potential to be the first noble man in her life. All others had failed. All others had lower standards. She liked high standards.

He caught her looking.

"Can I get you a can of tea or a soda?" She'd made two more trips to Dollar General after talking to her mom, to make sure she had nice things to offer him.

"Tea will be perfect. Thanks."

Clara brought the tea and placed it on the small table next to him. "What are you reading?" Was that rude to ask?

"A favorite psalm." He smiled. "I'm glad they thought of putting a Bible on the shelf."

"Me too." *I guess.*

The beep-beep-beep of the oven announced dinner was ready.

"Can I help with anything?" His strong hands reached for the tea.

"No, I've got this." Clara was already halfway to the small kitchen. *I hope.*

Well, the dish looked like the picture on the recipe—beautifully gold and cheesy. The scents of garlic, bacon, and creamy Alfredo filled the air. Did she really cook the ultimate dinner for Andrew on her very first try? Looked that way. *Awesome*, she sang the word in her head.

She placed the baked bowtie pasta on the small wooden table and a basket of garlic bread next to it. A salad would have been great. Maybe next time. The apartment had two sets of individual towels and napkins. She'd picked the cherry-colored set that matched the diner-inspired chairs. The thick green plates were not her style, but together, everything looked very good. She brought parmesan and dried parsley and basil to the table and poured fresh tea over ice in thick, tall glasses. "It's ready."

Andrew was already by her side. She looked at her beautiful table and then at him. She'd done it. She'd pulled it together. Everything was lovely.

"I thought you said you didn't cook." Andrew held Clara's chair for her, then took the other spot at the table. "This looks fantastic and smells fantastic."

"Thanks." She leaned in to smell the pasta. So good. He had no idea what a miracle that was.

His hands reached for hers, and they prayed.

He was always so comfortable and confident praying. Not her. For the first couple of years after her parents' divorce, she'd prayed every night and sometimes during the day too. She'd prayed that the woman her dad had fallen in love with would go away and that he would come home so they could be a family again. But nothing happened. Her mom knew she'd been praying and begged her to stop. It was hard to give up hope, but she did. She never prayed again. Not ever. Not for anything.

"Earth to Clara." Andrew held the bread basket in her direction.

"Sorry." She took a slice, then used the large spoon to serve the main dish. She served him before serving herself.

"Mmm. This is delicious. Thank you." He drew in a long breath.

"You're welcome." She took a forkful of pasta and satisfaction to her mouth. The food really was delicious. Beginner's luck? Talent? Who cared? She'd cooked. Yay.

Was this heaven? The smells of *her* kitchen, the sounds of NPR, his touch, the way he moved, his voice, the way he talked, the way he laughed. She wanted that—him—to be in her life forever.

Why was she so smitten? Was it because he was "noble" *and* because there hadn't been a male figure in her home in fourteen years? Hmm. Probably. And who was counting, right?

"Have you been talking to your mom?" He loaded his fork again—a bigger bite this time.

"We've talked."

"How's your grandma?"

"Grandma might have surgery because of her heart not beating right."

"Soon?"

"I guess. Mom will tell me when they know for sure."

He nodded, looking somber.

"Now get this." She took a sip of tea. "Mom wants to move back to Brazil."

"To be with her mom, of course."

"To be there forever."

"Really?"

Clara nodded. "She said she won't go if I don't want her to go, but I don't want to stop her if that's what she wants. It's her life."

"It's your life too. Does it have something to do with that date?"

Ah, so she was not the only one who suspected that. "She said it has nothing to do with that. But I think it might have. She did make an interesting point that took me by surprise. She said she's tired of having geography define her as a person."

"What does that mean?"

"She immigrated to America immediately after high school, and she said she always feels like the American who was born and raised in Brazil when she's here, and when she's in Brazil, she feels like she's the Brazilian who left and moved to the United States. She said she's tired of all that. If she moves back, eventually people will think less and less about the years she was away."

"I guess that makes sense." He took a long sip of his tea. "I heard once—I think a president said it—that one could become German and never really feel German, and one could become Italian and never really be Italian, could become Russian and not be truly Russian. But he said one could become American, and really *be* American." He shrugged. "Maybe he was wrong."

"According to my mom, that would be the case."

"So what did you tell her?"

"I didn't really say anything. I just asked a bunch of questions." Clara let a forkful of bacon Alfredo bowtie pasta fill her mouth with its comforting flavor.

"Would you go back to Cincinnati if she were to move to Brazil?"

"I guess." What a horrible thought—Cincinnati without her mom? No. She pushed her food around her plate with the long fork. "I suppose I could move out of the apartment on campus and go to the house? No, that's a terrible idea. I don't want to be there by myself. I guess we would have to sell the house. I don't want it—not like that."

"I don't blame you." He caressed her wrist with his fingertips.

Clara swallowed the lump that had formed in her throat and forced a smile.

"Thank you for dinner." Andrew picked up the napkin from his lap and folded it before using it. "You surprised me."

"You're welcome." She'd surprised herself too. "We have brownies for dessert."

"Yum." His eyes widened. "You keep this up, and I'll never go away."

A lovely idea. Something was going to happen and he would go away though. Everyone did. *Ah, the journey, Clara. Enjoy right now.*

They cleared the table and sat on the couch together, eating brownies and listening to NPR. Maybe for other people her age, that would have been bland. For Clara, it was quite perfect. They talked about the few things she knew and remembered about Brazil, and he asked questions with interest.

He was right when he'd said he was not like all the other Army people Clara knew, and she wanted to ask him about the Academy and about his work. She'd noticed his handsome graduation picture and diploma in his apartment. But she didn't want to come across as an ID-card chaser, like the girls Scott had told her about, who would do anything to marry a soldier just to enjoy housing, healthcare, PX, Commissary, and other benefits. But who cared how he perceived her? It would be over soon anyway.

They'd agreed to have an early night. Andrew stood and washed his hands in the kitchen sink. Would he kiss her? Oh, she hoped he would.

"Do you need anything?" He leaned against the wall, arms crossed in front of his strong chest.

She bit her lower lip. Her body needed to be wrapped in those arms of his, but she wasn't about to admit to that. "No. I don't need anything."

"Are you sure?"

Her head bobbed in slow motion. What would he do if she were to walk into his space? Would he wrap her in an embrace? Probably, but that would be too forward, no? Maybe she could walk past him to see if he would reach for her.

"Brownies for the road?" She made her way to the kitchen, her heart beating faster as she slowly passed him.

"Come here." He held her hand and pulled her in. "I don't need brownies. I need you, sweetheart."

Jackpot.

His lips pressed against hers, warm, moist, strong. She melted against him, like mozzarella cheese on bowtie pasta. Perfect. Oh, she wanted this to last—the kiss, the man, the tender relationship, El Paso, and maybe even the Army. Oh, the way he'd called her sweetheart, the fire in her chest. Could one month last forever? She dreamed it would, but how could it?

He brought her hand to his chest. His heart beat hard against the palm of her hand. He brought her hand to his lips and hugged her as tight as he'd ever hugged her. "I'll see you tomorrow. Can you be ready at eight?"

"Zero eight hundred hours—yes, sir. I'm punctual to a fault."

"Ooh, I love that." He retrieved his cell phone and keys.

And I love you. A great night with Andrew, good food cooked by her, ballet in the morning … That was a lovely journey. What could possibly go wrong?

Chapter 12

Clara got ready for class in the school bathroom and then went straight into the company classroom which was as large as the Cincinnati Bearcats basketball court. *Holy smokes.* The blue-gray paint on the three plain walls of the studio smelled fresh. The mirrors that covered the fourth looked spotless.

A middle-aged lady who Clara assumed was the artistic director walked her way. "Clara, right?"

"Yes, ma'am."

"I'm Anna-Marie. I'm glad you came." She tucked loose strands of her short black hair behind her ears, but they slipped out again as she talked. "I hope you enjoy the class."

"Thank you." Clara held the wooden barre and warmed her feet.

"Nice arches."

"Thanks."

"You said you studied in Cincinnati?"

"I did. I just finished my B.F.A. in Dance—with an emphasis in ballet."

"Congratulations. Any prospects yet?"

"Not really. My grandma is very ill in Brazil. My mom is there, and I'm here taking care of some family business." That wasn't the whole truth, but it wasn't a lie. She didn't have to tell her she'd been to a dozen auditions since graduation—all of which had resulted in absolutely nothing. "I'm a little out of shape."

"Out of shape happens. I'm sorry to hear about your grandmother. Are you from Brazil?"

"No, my mom is. She moved to the U.S. after high school."

"We had an exchange student from Brazil here a while back—she was very good." Anna-Marie scanned the room. About forty dancers talked and stretched, glancing their way from time to time. "I guess we had better start."

Clara recognized all the lead dancers from *Giselle* right away. All but Giselle. She wasn't there.

The simple piano stood abandoned next to a pile of stage props. Clara recognized Giselle's bench and the grave's cross. Anna-Marie approached the speaker dock and placed her iPod in it.

"We are going to start facing the barre. Parallel feet. Demi plié, roll up, demi, up, demi, up, four times, then invert up, plié, up, plié, four times. Tendu front, side, back, side, right, left, right, left. Repeat the whole thing in first, and balance."

Ooh, she'd missed that. Even simple warm-ups for the feet, ankles, and knees felt like a special treat. Someone once said a dancer could be a million miles from home but would always be at home at a barre. So true. *Home.*

Her mom longed to feel at home too—obviously. Did it have to be Brazil though?

Her arches ached every time she pointed her feet—proof that she'd been away from home too long.

And what if Clara moved to El Paso? Sure it was absurd to think of that, wasn't it? But what if? Something about her mom's desire to return to Brazil made Clara feel braver about taking a chance on Andrew. Were there flights from Brazil to El Paso? Probably not. Mom would have to fly to Dallas, then to El Paso.

Her mom had never missed a single performance, and Clara had been dancing for what? Fourteen years? Since she was eight. If her mom moved to Brazil, she would show up once or twice a year, but that would be it. Not enough for the heart—too much for the pocketbook.

The whole idea of her mom being so far away was impossible to bear. Better think of something else.

Her eyes focused on the large window between the studio and the waiting area. Would Andrew come in, or would he wait for her in the car?

She should have brought something more fun to wear. All she had was her audition attire. Pink tights and a black leotard. At least she had a black wrap skirt over the leotard. Good thing she'd thought to pack it. Faded tights cut at the ankles, a bright leotard, and a flowery wrap skirt would have been best. That's what everyone around her was wearing. Clara had three drawers full of ballet stuff at home, but nothing here. Hmm.

They were doing a different exercise now, holding the barre with one hand. She glanced at her profile in the mirror. At least her black chiffon skirt covered her derriere nicely and made her look slim. Her clothes were boring, but she looked nice. Boring but nice?

Oh, enough. She could spend the next hour and a half feeling like a stranger in her own world, or she could enjoy the ride.

The ballet studio was her home. Any ballet studio. She was home. These were her people. Anywhere in the world, these were her people. Even if her mom moved and didn't watch her as often. Even if Andrew walked in and didn't think there was anything cool about the class or her dancing. That was still her world. A world of control and beauty, fairytales and dreams, all in one magic place.

Soon they were moving faster, and the room warmed up fast too. Most of the girls put their pointe shoes on for center, and Clara followed suit.

There were only three men in class. The guys who'd played Albrecht and Hilarion in *Giselle* and the guy who'd danced the Act I peasant pas de deux.

Anna-Marie's center exercises and her music selection were for the soul— beautiful combinations set to exhilarating music that was fit for the stage and that made Clara forget about the labor involved in the movement and just dance.

"From the corner." The teacher stopped the music and showed them a new combination designed to get the dancers to move diagonally from one corner of the room to the opposite corner.

The series of piqué turns, lame ducks and chaînés was easy on the brain. Clara's perfectly-broken-in audition pointe shoes would help. She was ready. She joined the last trio of women and used the cross from the *Giselle* set to spot.

"Clara, you don't look out of shape at all. That was very good."

Good thing she hadn't had a drink the night before.

She spotted Andrew at the edge of the studio window when they were transitioning into grand allegros filled with big jumps. Talk about feeling naked. She'd never been bothered being around guys in a studio environment before. But she'd never met a guy like Andrew.

She had to focus on the class and finish well. Could she pretend he wasn't there?

Her heart beat so fast she could hear it ringing between her ears. There was her answer. Pretend he wasn't there? Not. A. Chance.

Anna-Marie marked the next exercise twice, a grand waltz filled with sissonnes and ballottés, jumps that were easy for Clara and showcased her long legs. The combination ended in tombé, pas de bourrée, glissade, grand jeté—a big split in the air.

She joined the last trio of young women again.

"Very nice, Clara. I want your legs." The teacher scanned the room. "Did you guys see how long and how beautiful her legs are?"

"Thank you." Her eyes searched the window. Still there. Andrew winked, making a wave of heat go into her cheeks.

"Let's go into a coda." Anna-Marie walked to the speaker dock.

Clara wasn't sure what they were supposed to do with it. A coda was the end of a grand pas de deux or a whole ballet. A coda often meant an opportunity for the dancers to show their best effort in bravura steps that defied gravity. For women, it often meant dizzying thirty-two fouettés, a series of turns on one leg only. Clara's weren't excellent because she rarely did the multiple turns per beat, which were so common nowadays, but they were good and clean.

"Ladies, I want to see many fouettés." Anna-Marie then looked at the three men. "You know what to do. I want to see stability."

"Clara, we do this a couple of girls at a time with one of the guys doing jetés en manège, saut de basques or whatever they feel like doing around the girls."

Clara nodded, hands on her hips. She'd seen that in a Royal Ballet class online.

Her turn came quicker than she'd expected when she noticed a girl was going to have to do the exercise alone. Clara quickly stepped in and started strong.

"Relax the head." Anna-Marie stood in the front of the room.

Was she talking to Clara? Clara focused on her head movements. The rotations were smooth. Should she try doubles? Nah, better not. Keep it clean and simple today.

"Very nice. Next."

Three more groups worked hard on their turns. Some had more success than others. Albrecht finished his last turns around the studio with a big tour en l'air and then dramatically threw himself at Clara's feet as everyone applauded.

Oh! Can't say I saw that coming, but sure—why not?

"Reverence." Anna-Marie joined them and they followed her arm movements.

Clara curtsied with all the ladies and the men bowed.

"Good. Thank you very much." The teacher curtsied as the students clapped. "Have a great day. We'll have rehearsals this weekend. I want to rehearse the corps for *Don Quixote* because for the next two weeks our time and space will be limited by the intensive."

Sweaty dancers grabbed their water bottles, warm-up clothes, and bags and exited the room quickly. Anna-Marie came straight to Clara.

"If your office skills are as good as your ballet skills, I have a deal for you."

Sweet!

Andrew stayed planted on the same spot where he'd been for the last fifteen minutes and watched Clara talk to her teacher. How could she be so beautiful? He was dating a true artist. She was amazing.

In the morning, she'd looked sad and tired. She'd probably stayed up late thinking about her mom's intention of moving to Brazil—nighttime had a way of magnifying one's troubles. But she seemed to be in great spirits now. The morning cloud that hung over her head was nowhere to be seen.

Lord, whatever they are talking about in there, let it be good for Clara.

The guy who'd played the main character in *Giselle* walked past him and sat behind the large office desk in the corner of the waiting area. He'd seemed shorter on stage, but he was as tall as Andrew, just shy of six feet. The man's curly blond hair gave him a youthful aura, but he had to be close to thirty years old if not thirty already.

Andrew knew he shouldn't just stand at the window like a statue, but what did he have to say to any of those people who were so different from him? Being there was like landing in a new country and leaving the perimeter for the first time—watching the natives, imagining their lives, stealing glances.

He sat on a bench and looked at the posters on the wall—advertisement posters from previous performances. The company danced at the Magoffin Auditorium at UTEP twice a year, just about. *Swan Lake*, *Cinderella*, *Coppelia*, *Paquita*, and a dozen other ballet names. Some he'd heard about before, some he hadn't. The girl who'd played Giselle was in every poster. Different costumes, different ballets, same girl.

The *Giselle* poster was the last on two long rows of past performances.

Could Clara end up on a poster like those one day? That big jump she'd done at the end of class would make a great poster. She was crazy talented. Why hadn't she found a place to dance yet?

The guy from *Giselle* typed something on the school's computer, and soon the printer began to spit out a tall stack of papers. What was the guy's name? Mike? Mark? There was a program on the desk. He should look up the name and maybe say something about the performance.

Clara and the teacher came out of the studio, and Andrew stood.

"This is my friend, Andrew." Clara lifted her arm in his direction. "Anna-Marie is the owner of the studio and artistic director of the company."

"Nice meeting you." Andrew stretched his hand and sensed curly hair's eyes on him.

"Nice meeting you too." Anna-Marie shook his hand. "And it was very nice meeting you, Clara. I'm looking forward to working with you."

"Me too. Thank you so much."

Anna-Marie moved to the desk, and Clara put her ballet bag on the bench. She dug a cute black dress out of the bag and put it on over her ballet clothes.

"I hope I'm not making you late for work." Clara's voice came out husky.

"No, I'll be fine." The sweet scent of her sweat made him want to kiss her, and in his mind, he could already taste her salty skin.

What was wrong with him?

The same thing that was wrong with curly hair, apparently. This was the second time Andrew caught him glancing at Clara as she got dressed. At first, Andrew had thought nothing of the man throwing himself at her feet in class, but now he wasn't so sure. Was there more to it than class fun?

Whatever happened to ballet dancers being gay? Just his luck, the one sweating next to Clara was straight.

"Mark, did you talk to the storage place?" Anna-Marie approached curly hair—Mark.

He lifted his eyes from behind the computer. "Not yet, but I did send the email about the weekend rehearsal."

"Good. Don't worry about the storage people. I'll call them."

"Let's go?" Clara put her pink bag on her shoulder and looked at him.

"Sure." He gestured for her to walk out ahead of him and placed a hand on her shoulder. His eyes met Mark's. *Sorry man. She's taken.*

Once outside the school, a small door in a long shopping strip, Clara looked and acted like a little girl, walking on clouds, eyes full of magic and light.

"That good, huh?" He opened the door of the Crossfire for her.

She nodded, eyebrows up. "I don't have to pay for the intensive," she sang.

"Oh, good!" Of course she didn't have to. She was fantastic.

"Remember the girl who played Giselle?"

"Of course." The one person he hadn't seen at the ballet school. Or what was it called? The company?

"Her name is Melody. She's auditioning in Mexico, and the school is really hurting because she also runs the office."

"Okay." He backed out of his parking space.

"So, they said I can dance as much as I want for free as long as I help with the office. I'm so excited. Wait until I tell my mom."

"That's wonderful. I'm so happy for you." And he was. But … Would she be working with Mark a lot? That guy better have a girlfriend.

"How are you going to get here? What are the hours?"

"I don't know about transportation yet. I need to arrive an hour before classes begin to check email and phone messages, then stay after class to do all the rest. I can also return calls, answer messages, and do whatever else needs to be done between classes. I'll be at the studio most of the day during the two weeks of the intensive."

"When does it start again?"

"Monday."

"We'll work something out. Let me think this through." Lest somebody else decide to give her a ride.

"Thanks." Clara leaned her head back and took in a deep breath. "I'll be hurting tomorrow."

"I bet." Andrew shifted in his seat. "That was intense in there. You looked great, by the way."

"Thanks." She shot the sweetest, happiest look his way. Ballet was definitely her thing.

"What happens if she doesn't come back?"

"Who?"

"Giselle."

"Oh, Melody." Clara shrugged. "I don't know. They will have to find someone else, I guess."

"Maybe they would ask you to stay." Would she consider it?

"The thought crossed my mind, but ..." She looked at the Franklin Mountains and then at Mexico.

"But?"

Clara smiled. "But I'm trying not to think about it right now. I'm all about trying to figure out everything all the time, but lately, I've been making an effort to just be right here, right now. Like a train trip. I don't want to be so busy thinking about the next station that I forget to look out the window and talk to the other passengers, you know?"

"Sure. That sounds wise." Just don't talk to Mark too much—that would not be wise. Andrew pulled onto Interstate 10 and moved to the left lane.

How *was* she going to get around? He could drop her off after PT and pick her up after the day was done, but his schedule was so unpredictable. "Are you sure I can't show you how to drive this car?"

"No, it's too nice. Thank you, though." She rested her hand on his leg. "I'll ask Mom if we can rent something simple now that I don't have to pay anything for the classes."

"Okay." Her touch was so gentle. She could leave her hand there all the way to the east side. He wouldn't mind it at all.

Clara put her head out by the passenger-side mirror, like a happy puppy, and closed her eyes. She must be on that train trip of hers, enjoying the ride. Maybe he should try it too.

This convertible car ride on the border of Mexico with a gorgeous ballerina, this was really happening, and it was good. It was very good.

She caught him looking at her.

"What are you going to do with yourself the rest of the day?"

"I might swim."

"Must be nice." Did she wear a one-piece bathing suit to swim? The thought sent a wave of heat into his cheeks.

"Nice indeed. Swimming is good for you, you know?" She giggled, her eyes sparkling. "You can join me after work."

"I can't. I have church tonight. Wanna come?"

"Not tonight. I'll be there on Sunday for the boys' baptism."

Andrew nodded. "I will see you tomorrow for our first waltz class then?"

"Absolutely. I can't wait."

He parked by her building and walked around the Crossfire to open Clara's door. Tatiana would have told him not to. Clara let him take care of her, and that made his heart beat faster. She was the kind of girl who enjoyed receiving what he liked to give.

"I'll see you tomorrow." She waved and turned to walk away, but he held her hand and took a step in her direction, bridging the gap between them.

"I'm all sweaty." Her voice was throaty again.

"I don't mind." He caressed her neck with his fingertips and brushed his lips against her cheek. He held her near as his kisses deepened. *Sweet, sweat, salt, life, Clara ...* Oh, how he loved holding her. When he stopped, he looked into her beautiful green eyes. Did she know he was falling in love? And how about her? She hadn't complained about the Army in a while. Were they beyond that issue?

Beyond or not, he must have done something right that day because when he got in the car, she was still standing where he'd left her, and she was wearing a Texas-sized grin on her face.

Chapter 13

A ndrew held the door of the Shundo Ballroom Dance Studio open for Clara. "After you."

The dance floor was huge—bigger than the ballet studio. One long wall was all mirrors, and the other was all glass, making the space look even larger.

The faint fragrance of a familiar perfume teased Clara's nostrils and her memory. It wasn't her mom's, but the place smelled like family and childhood. Hmm. This was going to be different.

A pretty woman in her early twenties danced alone to the fun beat of a Latin song. She stopped when she spotted them in the mirror and rushed to meet them with a smile that reminded Clara of late nights watching Miss Venezuela be crowned Miss Universe year after year. The choice of program was her mom's, not hers, but Clara didn't complain. The competition was amusing.

The woman's little black dress was too short for daytime in the city but didn't seem out of place at Shundo. She was tiny—one hundred pounds maybe. Plus chest. Make it one hundred and five.

"You must be Mr. and Mrs. James." Her voice was even younger than her face.

Mrs. James? If Andrew could have heard the juvenile giggles filling her head, she would be so embarrassed.

He winked at her with a broad smile. "I'm Andrew James, and this is Clara Malone."

"Nice meeting you. I'm Helena." She shook Clara's hand first, then Andrew's. "Let me grab your paperwork—just one second."

The dance school was on a hill, so the view of the west side of El Paso from there was phenomenal. The west side was her style—it was busy and happening, and the gorgeous UTEP campus with its vibrant population re-inforced that impression.

Helena returned with two sheets stapled together. "So, you are here to learn the waltz, and I see that you are also interested in competing. How fun!"

"We're interested in competing?" Clara choked on her question and searched Andrew's face.

"We don't have to." He shrugged. "I just thought it would be a fun thing to do one day."

"Okay, I guess." What day? In three weeks? Or was he thinking long term? He knew she was leaving on the Fourth.

Another couple had arrived and was already on the dance floor, moving effortlessly to the sound of a romantic salsa—Marc Anthony? Totally.

A man wearing designer jeans and a black shirt—their teacher?—fol-lowed them from a distance.

"Are we ready?" Helena's eyes were on the other couple too.

"How long have they been doing this?" Andrew raised both eyebrows toward the dance floor.

"Forever. They've been dancing together for more than ten years—mar-ried for twenty plus. They're regulars."

They moved as one and were into each other like high school sweethearts on prom night. "Why do they need a teacher?"

"They compete."

"Ohh …" The woman's hips moved so fluidly like Jell-O removed from the fridge fifteen minutes too soon. *Perfect.* Clara's hips were a block of ce-ment. Firm. Unmovable. The source of strength and power that allowed the rest of the body to be graceful.

"They were beginners once." Helena's eyes returned to Andrew and Clara, her smile reassuring. "We're going to learn some basic steps, and then we will play a waltz. Okay?"

"Sure." Andrew tightened his lips and stepped onto the polished dance floor. His hand reached out for Clara's. "This might be ugly. I'll apologize ahead of time."

"We work with beginners all the time." Helena stood within two feet of them. "It'll be fun."

"I will take your word for it." Andrew looked tense—like it'd just dawned on him he'd signed them up for dance classes.

Clara chuckled.

"You've never danced either, right?" Helena asked Clara.

"I have a bachelor's in fine arts in dance with an emphasis in ballet, but I've never tried ballroom dancing."

"Oh, good. You'll love it."

Why? Ballet and ballroom were nothing alike. Because dance was dance? Hmm. Helena was young and trying hard to be nice, though. It wouldn't hurt to be nice back. "I'm sure I will."

She showed them how to do a box in six counts—her fancy words for tracing a square on the ground with waltz steps—and had them practice it many, many, *many* times. Next, she taught them how to move around the dance floor. That was much harder than doing a box in place.

Poor Andrew had to think about everything—which leg to move, the music, and counting. He'd been much smoother when he'd had the freedom to improvise. Structured training was definitely harder. Clara didn't struggle much at all. Ballroom was coming to her quite naturally. Plus all she had to do was follow his lead. Easy. Should she feel guilty?

Nah, she shouldn't feel guilty, and he shouldn't feel bad. She'd been dancing forever—even if it was ballet.

"Andrew, transfer your weight more on that third count. That will help you know which leg is next. You'll only have one option, and it will be the right one."

So that's why it was happening so easily for Clara. There was never a doubt in her mind which leg was next—there was only one possibility.

"There." Helena tiptoed around them as she counted the beat. "You got it. Go around a few times to get confident, and then we'll combine the boxes with the advancing."

"For a moment, I thought I wouldn't get it." He looked at Clara, blew out his breath, and then got his legs mixed up again. His shoulders dropped. "And here we go again."

"That's okay." Helena approached. "Start over."

He did.

"Can we have music? Our music?" Clara was no ballroom genius, but surely it would help to waltz to waltz music and not to salsa music.

"Sure. I'll show you how to combine what we've learned so far and then play a slow waltz."

"Good idea." Andrew took in a deep breath.

"Take a quick break while I find the right music."

Clara let go of Andrew's hand and watched Helena walk away, her heels clicking to the rhythm of a fast Latin song Clara didn't recognize.

Andrew cupped Clara's sweaty face. "Tired?"

"A little." She panted. She hadn't noticed her heart was getting a bit of a workout. It'd been a long day already. She had to tell him about her bus adventure. Clara straightened her back and spotted Helena still looking through CDs and talking to someone. "I took the bus today."

"You did what?" Andrew searched her eyes.

"I learned to take the bus. The stop is by the apartment, then I make a quick change downtown and go all the way to the ballet studio." It wasn't fast, but she wouldn't have to depend on Andrew every day. "So that's how I'll be getting to the intensive. You won't have to worry about me at all."

"I'm worried already. That doesn't sound safe."

"It was great. Easy *and* safe."

"Why didn't you tell me you were going to ride the bus? I had no idea you were going to the studio today. I would have gone with you."

"By bus?"

"Maybe?" He raised both shoulders.

"One: You were at work. Two: You would have tried to talk me out of riding the bus."

"I probably would have." Andrew reached for her hand.

They were both warm, and his touch was like silk fresh out of the dryer. "The bus doesn't bother me at all. I use it in Cincinnati all the time. I haven't had a car since high school."

"If you'll give me your schedule, I will help whenever I can."

"I just don't want to be a burden."

"You're not a burden." He winked and squeezed her hand. "I mean it."

Helena came back to the sound of a very slow waltz with little melody to it. But the beats were nice and clear.

She showed them how to combine the steps, then asked them to do two of each.

While Andrew counted and concentrated, Clara moved to the music, letting the melody carry her to a different time, a different era. A time when life was slower, people had their license plates and names listed in a book, and young women spent time at windows dreaming of a life they didn't yet have.

Clara pictured herself at a ball in Brazil, wearing an old-Hollywood gown, and dancing like her grandmother had. She was certain her upper body positioning was a mess, but that didn't matter. Not now. She wouldn't hold back on the fun because of what she didn't yet know about the waltz. She was just going to dance.

Andrew, on the other hand, was still working hard. Would the deep lines on his forehead go away after class, or were they permanent now? "Putting that West Point education to good use, huh?"

"Funny girl, huh?" He narrowed his eyes. "You're lucky I like you. I've never worked this hard at anything before—not even Ranger School."

"Really?"

"No, not really." He chuckled. "This isn't too bad. I'll get it. You'll see."

Clara shook her head and giggled. She loved his sense of humor.

When the second waltz concluded, Helena ended the class. Together they walked to the lobby. "Practice at home. Next week we can learn turns, and by the end of the month you'll be ready for the Big Band Party."

"Sounds good." Clara eyed the trophies and competition pictures on the wall. Andrew really wanted to do that?

"We'll see you next time. Thank you." Andrew held the door open for Clara.

She tried to look at him as a performance partner but wasn't feeling it. "You really want to compete?"

"Yeah." He opened the car door for her. "Remember that movie *Shall We Dance?* with Richard Gere and Jennifer Lopez?"

"I don't think I've ever seen it."

"Now you're the one who hasn't lived."

"Because I missed a Richard Gere and J. Lo movie?"

"I'll get it this weekend. You'll see for yourself."

"Okay." J. Lo? Really? "It's a date."

"I have a unit event Saturday afternoon though. It's just a cookout at the First Sergeant's house." He cleared his throat. "Would you like to come? We could go there first, then watch the movie."

"A unit event? No way." One soldier was one thing. A unit event was something else entirely and way too much for her right now.

Andrew started the Crossfire and didn't say anything. Was he disappointed? Probably. "I'm sorry. Maybe next time?"

"Maybe next time." His phone vibrated. He looked at the screen and shook his head.

"Everything okay?" Not that it was any of her business, but it felt rude not to ask.

"Um-hum." He raked his hand through his hair and drove out of the parking lot faster than usual.

Chapter 14

Sunday church was busy again. This time Clara wore a dress and a little knitted half jacket she'd found at Dollar General. She'd done a good job. She looked like she belonged there.

She sat between Alice and Andrew, who'd just finished teaching his class. He wore a gray suit with a blue shirt and silver tie. Sharp.

Clara put away the thanks-for-being-here card her Sunday school teacher had handed to her in class and then made sure her money for the offering was handy. The teacher had tried to mail the card, but Clara hadn't put an address on her visitor's card. Of course she hadn't. On that day she didn't really have an address.

"A couple more weeks and my dad will be here." Alice squealed. "Can you believe it? I can hardly wait—I miss him so much."

"It's hard to believe he's almost here." Clara's heart tightened with the mixed feelings she now had about her time in El Paso and her future.

"I love your bracelet." Alice saw Clara's bracelet and read the words on the petals. "Is it local?"

"I think so. Andrew got it for me at the airport." Clara's cheeks warmed. "I was looking at it when we first saw each other."

"Aww." Alice looked at Andrew, who was up again, talking to one of the ushers. "He's too sweet. He said he took you to Las Cruces last night for a special pizza you missed?"

"He did—Uno Pizzeria and Grill. That was on Friday, actually. There's an Uno around the corner from my apartment on campus, and I was missing it a lot. It was a surprise, though. I had no idea why we were going to New Mexico." He'd kept her wondering all the way to the restaurant's parking lot.

Wouldn't even give her a hint. "Last night we watched a Richard Gere and J. Lo movie."

"Oh, *Shall We Dance?*—I love that movie!" Alice's eyes sparkled.

"Yep." Clara had enjoyed it more than she cared to admit.

"You guys are taking ballroom classes, right?"

"We are." Clara giggled and Alice did too.

"Sounds lovely." Alice patted Clara's hand. "Good for you."

The door by the packed choir loft opened and three men walked in. Clara recognized the young man in the middle—it was the pastor.

"I knew you guys were going to have a great time together," Alice whispered. She winked and began singing the hymn on the screen.

Clara grinned, then sang the words on the screen too.

Andrew's voice wasn't particularly beautiful, but it was strong and masculine. She remembered him sitting in the armchair and reading the Bible.

Why was that image, this voice, this man, so appealing to her? She hadn't been looking for religion. Hadn't thought about it in ages. Didn't even care for soldiers. Yet here was this guy, and she desired him. *And* she also desired his lifestyle, his faith. Where had that come from?

When it was time for the offering, everyone had that neat little envelope ready. Oops. She'd forgotten about the envelope. She put two neatly folded dollar bills on the gold plate Andrew handed to her and passed it to Alice. How much did people give? Had to be more than the cost of making the envelopes. Hmm.

The learning curve would be steep if she kept going to church. Good thing no one seemed to care about what she knew or didn't know about proper church behavior. People were always talking to her and were friendly to a fault.

Maybe she should keep showing up, at least on Sundays. She would keep an eye out for envelopes, so she could bring one ready too.

"Let's open our Bibles to Hebrews 13 this morning." The pastor drank a sip of water from a simple cup next to the pulpit while people found the passage and stood.

She should have brought the Bible from the apartment. Oops again. Andrew found the passage and held his Bible between them as they stood together. His Bible was all marked up with many passages underlined in black ink and several handwritten notes in the margins. He also had whole verses handwritten at the end of the chapter, which was also the end of the book, hence the extra white space.

"We're going to start on verse three and read down to six." The pastor's voice was young and fresh, but based on a picture of him with his family that she'd seen in the lobby, he had to be at least thirty. "'Marriage is honorable in all, and the bed undefiled: but whoremongers and adulterers God will judge. Let your conversation be without covetousness; and be content with such things as ye have: for he hath said, I will never leave thee, nor forsake thee. So that we may boldly say, The Lord is my helper, and I will not fear what man shall do unto me.' Let's pray together, and we'll get started."

Ooh. That was a lot different from the previous week. Clara bowed her head and found comfort in the pastor's prayer. He wasn't there to judge or put people on a guilt trip. He just wanted folks to get right with God if getting right was needed, so they could enjoy all the benefits of their relationship with God. Okay.

Clara hadn't broken any vows. This wasn't about her, was it?

She hadn't promised to love someone forever and then decided to love someone else instead. Scott had done that. *And* he had lied to her about his marital status. She'd walked into the relationship blind and ignorant.

He was an adulterer. She was not.

Then why was it that her heart shrank and hurt with every word the pastor said?

Virginia.

Could it be that what she'd done that one cold night in Virginia two years ago was actually a much bigger deal in God's eyes than she'd imagined?

The sermon moved in different directions, but her thoughts stayed in that one word, one place, one act. Virginia.

"Please stand up for the invitation. With every head bowed, eyes closed— no one looking around—if God has spoken to your heart this morning, you need to respond. As *Brother Jim* sings, if you need to come, come. There are people praying at the altar already. Come do business with God."

Might as well go down there wearing a scarlet letter. *I don't think so.*

She peeked at the floor as *Brother Jim* sang a beautiful hymn. Andrew was still there, and Alice was still there. There was no way she could get to the altar. Next time she would try to sit at the end of the row. Then maybe she would go.

"If you're here today and you've never been saved—you've never been born again—come talk to someone here at the altar. We have people here who can take you to a private room and show you from the Bible how you can be saved. We'll have one more verse of invitation. There's still time."

Even the hymn the man sang pierced Clara's heart. Something about God having His way and being a potter.

I want to do business with you, God. But not like this. Not right now.

"If you'll be seated, we have a few who are getting ready for baptism today."

That's right. Baptisms. Wasn't that the whole point of being there today? The Howards were no longer next to her. She spotted Alice up front with her camera. Then the boys showed up one by one in a blue gown at what she assumed was a tub at an elevated corner behind the choir area. The guy baptizing wasn't the pastor. Alice took pictures of each boy, and with each baptism, the crowd clapped and cheered.

Clara glanced at Andrew. Were his eyes moist? Sure thing. Aww.

The pastor walked up to the pulpit and pointed at Alice, who was in the front row now and standing next to another lady. "This here is the mom of the boys you just saw. Her husband is in the back helping them." Colonel Howard quickly joined his wife. "*Was* in the back—here he is. This is Alice and Max Howard. They just arrived from Baumholder, Germany, and wish to unite by letter from the Grace Baptist Church there in Baumholder. All in favor, pending their letter from Grace Baptist Church, say so by a hearty amen."

"Amen."

It was hearty. And just like that, Clara was the only outsider in their group.

Should she get baptized too? She wanted to. But she should probably get clarification on the morning's preaching first. Was she an adulteress, or was she not?

She didn't feel like one. Big, hurtful mistake? Yes. But adultery?
For him, yes. But for her? No, right?

"Ready?" Andrew had his hands in his pockets and a clean smile on his face.

"Ready." Clara's reply caught in her throat. She walked ahead of him and peeked into her bag. She opened the card her teacher had given her, just enough to look at the signature. Rachel. And her phone number was under her name. *I thought so. Good.*

Knowing she had a connection to the church warmed her still-stunned heart. She could call Rachel if she needed to.

Clara had a feeling she would need to.

Chapter 15

A ndrew stood when Clara approached their table at Ardovino's. "Looks like you survived day one."

"I did." Clara kissed his cheek and sat. He must have spent a good chunk of time outside—his face was warm and pink, almost hiding his freckles. He looked tired. "I'm beat up, but I survived."

"Glad you did. I got your text and ordered. I still wish you'd let me pick you up, though."

"How about you pick me up tomorrow?" The bus did take forever. She would much rather ride with him.

"Deal."

Clara looked at dozens of different baskets hanging from the ceiling of the pizzeria. "I think I like the Ardovino's on the west side better. It's cozier."

"You like everything better on the west side." His hands reached for hers.

"Not everything." He looked fantastic in the candlelit room. "New haircut?"

"The $7.99 special." He kissed her hand. "You like it?"

"I do."

He drank his iced tea and then pointed to her untouched one. "I assumed you wanted tea too."

"Yes, tea is perfect. Thanks." He looked handsome—he always did, but his voice and his gaze lacked the usual enthusiasm, right? Or maybe it was just her imagination. Was the whole bus thing bothering him that much? "You can pick me up every night from here on if you want. I like when you help me."

"Good. I will. I can't this Wednesday—I have a range, and we'll be out there until past dark. But all the other days should be good."

"Great." Clara tried to remember what having a range meant, but nothing came to mind. It'd been too long, and she'd been too little. "Now see. Isn't it nice that I have an alternative for Wednesday?"

"Sure." He smiled with his lips but not with his eyes.

Was this a good time to ask him about yesterday's preaching? She wanted to know more, and he always got excited when he had a chance to talk about Bible things. He would probably think she was weird, though. Maybe later.

Their pizzas arrived, and Clara finished her tea.

As Andrew prayed, Clara worked up the courage to ask.

Just ask. "Andrew?"

"Clara?" He imitated her soft tone.

"I have a question." She tucked a lock of hair behind her ear.

"I hope I have an answer." He offered her the first slice of pizza Margherita.

Clara put her plate under the slice and placed it in front of her, the smell of warm tomatoes and fresh basil filling the space between them. "Remember what the preacher was saying yesterday about adultery and getting things right with God?"

"Yeah." He took a small bite, his head cocked.

"Where does that leave my grandma? I always thought that adultery was a married person being with someone they are not married to. Is she guilty of adultery too, even though she was single and available?"

"I don't know about specific definitions. It was adultery for him and fornication for her? I'm not sure." He shifted in his seat. "But at the end of the day, adultery is an act that requires two people to be involved, and she participated. Once she learned there was a wife, she quit being an innocent victim and became a co-conspirator. Sad, but true."

Ouch. "Co-conspirator?"

"I don't mean to be judgmental—I'm sorry if it came across that way. I was just trying to answer your question."

"I know." Co-conspirator? It *was* true. Hurtful, but true.

"I feel bad for her." Andrew put another slice of pizza on his plate and finished his tea. "She was so young and had gone through so much. I bet she wishes she'd never yelled out his name from that window."

"Probably." Clara wished she'd never approached Scott, so there was a good chance that her grandma felt the same way about Mario. Adulteresses, co-conspirators. What else had he said?

"My main problem with it all is that the people getting together and having a good time, falling in love, or doing whatever they think they are doing don't seem to consider the family that's sitting at home—completely clueless about what's going on."

"I know." And she did. She often wondered if her dad would have left them if he hadn't had someone lined up, waiting to marry him.

Even though Scott went ahead and divorced, would things have been different in his marriage if he'd never met her?

Andrew cleared his throat. "Is your grandma a Christian?"

Clara nodded. "That's when she wrote the letter, a couple of months ago during another hospital stay. There was a preacher who came by the hospital just before my mom got there. He must have said something that really resonated with her. Mom said she seems to have made peace with it all. Wrote to Mario …"

"Now I'm even more curious to know what's in the letter."

"Me too." Clara took another slice of Margherita pizza. "Two more weeks."

"That's right." Andrew's phone vibrated. He glanced at it, then put it away.

Any hint of sadness was now gone. In its place, an expressionless face, then a fake smile.

"Is everything okay?" Clara stopped eating and studied him.

He nodded. "Fine. Just Army stuff. It can wait."

Clara remembered that, her dad's phone going off when most other dads, the civilian type, had left work behind at five. "Watch Mario not let us read the letter." She ate a small bite with a big basil leaf on top and enjoyed the sweet taste.

"Do you talk to your grandma often?" Andrew asked. "On the phone?"

She nodded and finished chewing. "I do, but lately she's been sleeping a lot."

"You should ask her."

"Ask her what?"

"What she wrote."

"Oh. Well, it's hard to have a long conversation. She can handle I love you, how's the weather, I miss you, but that's about it."

"I didn't know that." He rested against the wooden chair. "I'm sorry."

Clara nodded. "I think she's really fading away. There's always something off with her heart or lungs, and she's not eating well. My mom says she's 'se recolhendo'—kind of means she's turning inward? I'm not sure. Doesn't make much sense in English, I don't think."

"It does make sense." He caressed her hand, his touch as gentle as ever. "How are you holding up?"

Clara shrugged. "I'm here. Waiting for the general. Doing my part." Clara finished her meal and picked up the napkin from her lap. "I grew up in the U.S. My grandma has always been in Brazil. It's hard to grow close when you don't spend a lot of time together. That's something Mom said she wishes she'd done more. She wishes she'd taken me to Brazil more to spend time with grandparents and other family."

"I bet that's hard indeed. I don't have that problem, but I have a lot of missionary friends who say the same thing about their kids' relationship with grandparents, uncles, cousins, etcetera."

"There you go, so you know." Clara drew in a deep breath, and they finished eating.

In their silence, the word co-conspirator came back to her thoughts. It was ugly and low, and it bothered her. "What time is it?"

"Hot date?" Andrew looked at his quad watch.

Clara giggled and shook her head.

"It's eight."

Would it be too late to call her Sunday school teacher? She should call her—if not tonight, tomorrow then. She would speak more freely with a woman—someone she wasn't trying to impress.

Ooh, had she just admitted to trying to impress Andrew?

Tomorrow. Tomorrow after ballet she would call her teacher for sure. She didn't want to carry that weight around anymore.

"You look like you're deep in thought." Andrew moved his chair closer to hers.

"I am." She picked up his hand, massaging the palm. Maybe she could talk things out with Rachel and even get baptized on Sunday. Why not? She'd waited long enough.

"Thinking about me, of course." Andrew closed her hand in both of his, the cute grin on his face bringing her back to the here and now.

"Of course." That was somewhat true. She would surely not be sitting at a pizzeria thinking about God and sin and baptism if it weren't for him in her life. Maybe he was achieving his goal—he *had* said he wanted people to look at him and be inspired to know God and walk with God. Well, here she was.

The waitress came by with the check and left with Andrew's card.

"Want to catch a movie tomorrow?" Andrew folded his napkin and ran his fingers over a crease.

"I know you wake up early. We don't have to do something every night. I don't want to wear you out."

"I like being with you. Plus, I won't see you on Wednesday, will I?"

"Probably not." She didn't know anything anymore. "If I keep going out as often as we have, I will go back to Cincinnati without ever watching Downton Abbey."

"Then you can watch it there and remember me. Be here with me as much as you can and while you can."

His words hit her hard. *While you can.*

That's right. It was all temporary. Temporary apartment, temporary boyfriend, temporary job, temporary ballet company. She drew in a deep breath as hot tears pooled in her eyes. Oh, what was wrong with her? Her pinky fingers reached the outside corners of both eyes, keeping the pools from overflowing. "Sorry."

"No. I'm sorry. I didn't mean to make you cry." He cradled her cheeks with the palms of his hands and kissed her gently. "If you want to stay home tomorrow and watch Downton Abbey, you certainly can. It's okay to have alone time. We don't have to live like the world is coming to an end—well, the world *is* coming to an end, but probably not today."

She shook her head and chuckled.

Andrew held Clara's hand as they walked back to the apartment community. The warm breeze showered them with purple desert willow blooms. He caught a flower mid-flight and placed it gently on Clara's delicate hand. "Here."

"Thank you." Her green eyes sparkled.

"I love to see you smile." He shouldn't have made her cry, it hadn't been his intent at all. But at least he now knew she cared about being with him as much as he cared about being with her. When should he tell her how he felt?

She tucked the flower behind her ear. "There."

Maybe he would tell her how much he liked her the next time they met. After all that talk about adultery and her grandma, this night didn't seem right for beginnings. He felt bad for her grandma. He didn't judge the woman. But he'd been on the receiving end of betrayal and knew the hurt selfish people imposed on a marriage and a whole family. Married people who cheated and the singles who agreed to get involved with a married person were the hardest to forgive. Andrew forgave enemy combatants faster and with more ease. He took a cleansing breath and tried to enjoy the night air.

He should also try once more to get Tatiana to stay out of the way. He didn't have to check the phone anymore to know she was the cause of all the buzzing and vibrating. He could feel it again even now as they walked.

Maybe he could tell her he was going someplace for the Fourth. She wouldn't come if he weren't in town, right?

No, that meant lying. He didn't want to do that.

He studied Clara's profile—the purple flower contrasted beautifully with her tanned skin. Tatiana's appearance would be a disaster, but how could he keep it from happening? He'd run out of things to say to the woman. She was determined to visit.

"Rachel?" Clara held the phone with one hand and opened the freezer of her temporary apartment with the other.

"Yes?" There was no sound of voice recognition on the other end.

"This is Clara—from Sunday class? Do you remember me?" She placed the flower Andrew had caught midair on the top shelf of the freezer to preserve it.

"Oh, of course. Hi."

"Sorry for calling so late, but I wanted to ask you something important." A streetlight outside her bedroom window bathed the hallway with a soft yellow light. Clara walked toward it.

"Sure. That's not a problem. Ask."

She sat on the bed and looked at the painting, also bathed by the yellow streetlight. Its turquoise estuary looked darker at night. "Can I talk to you about something really bad I did a couple of years ago?"

"Of course. Will you be at church on Wednesday?"

"No. Andrew has a night range or something."

"Where are you staying?"

"Up by Sean Haggerty."

"I'm on McCombs. I can pick you up, and we'll go together. How does that sound?"

"That sounds good. Do you know where Ardovino's is?"

"Sure."

"I can wait for you in front of Ardovino's—the apartment community is a maze."

"That sounds great. How about 6:30?"

"That will work." She wasn't sure Ardovino's was the best place to wait for someone, but it was the first thing that had come to her mind. It would do.

Sooner would have been better—tonight even, but at least she would get it taken care of before seeing Andrew again for waltz class on Thursday.

Was she being silly about all this?

No. It wasn't silly. It was real, and it needed to be taken care of.

Then she could tell Andrew the truth about Scott. She wanted things to be right between her and God.

From the small speakers of her borrowed apartment's CD player, Lauren Daigle's voice pierced the night air with "How Can It Be?"

She was going to get things right and feel right. Totally doable.

Guilty, hiding, and afraid? Yes ... But one step away from God's freedom. She could almost feel it.

That's why she *had* to come to El Paso. Everything made sense now. She was going to make peace with God and come to terms with the past once and for all.

That must have been God's plan all along. Her mom, her grandma, and the Howards were just His helpers. *Brilliant.* That was it, right? The reason why she was still jobless and on this family mission. She'd been on a collision course with this moment, no?

She drew in a deep breath and turned on the bedside lamp, then the hallway light. Tea. A beautiful cup of tea would be perfect. Romantic Jasmine.

Chapter 16

Rachel pulled up to Ardovino's in a gold Honda Civic that had seen better days.

"Thanks for picking me up." Clara breathed in the welcoming soft scent of French vanilla as she got into the car.

"Not a problem."

Rachel, who had to be in her mid-thirties, wore a simple beige and brown dress that matched her oversized purse, large shades, and simple sandals. She looked nice.

The two exchanged a quiet smile.

"I'm glad you called me, Clara. How are you doing?"

Clara reached for the seatbelt and exhaled hard. "The real answer or the polite answer?"

"The real one." Rachel tapped the turn signal and exited the parking lot.

"I've been anxious since Sunday. Though I'm more hopeful now. I think I did something very bad, and I want to fix it."

Rachel put her shades on top of her curly red hair. "How can I help?"

"Three years ago, I met a guy, and I just assumed he was single."

"Okay."

"When I saw him the following day, I told him that I was incredibly happy to have met him. We'd really connected—the kind of thing you're sometimes afraid doesn't happen outside movies and romance novels, you know?"

Rachel snorted and nodded.

"We were at a park, and everything was going great, and then—" Clara's voice caught in her throat, a familiar lump formed around the words like a constrictor around its prey.

"And then?" Rachel merged onto the highway.

Clara's heart broke anew like it always did when she remembered the exchange—the words that ruined her dreams of perfect love and happily ever after. "I said, 'Please don't tell me you have a wife and two kids.'" Hot tears pooled in her eyes.

"What did he say?"

Clara cleared her throat. "He said, 'Three.'"

"Three?"

"A wife and three kids."

"No!" Rachel punched the steering wheel. "What was he thinking? Why do men do that?"

She got it. Good. "I don't know." Clara would never understand what possessed Scott to talk to her when he was not available.

"What did you do?"

"He said they were separated, so I let him tell me about how miserable he was and about everything that went wrong. The woman had turned up pregnant—that's why he'd married her." Clara had imagined him lonely and used, trapped in a relationship he'd never wanted in the first place.

"Were they separated?"

"At the time they were."

Rachel's hands gripped the steering wheel as a gust of wind shook the small car.

"Since he was divorcing her anyway, and he was only in town for a few days to take care of a family emergency, I thought we could spend some time together and then stay in touch—for when he became available." The words rolled out of her lips like a red carpet now, fast and smooth. "I was crazy about him, Rachel. I still don't know what possessed me. It was a wonderful feeling. Love was real. True love. Soul mates. People born to be together." Those few days in Cincinnati were the best of her life to that point. Long walks in the woods, marathon kissing sessions, and promises of forever. Her heart beat louder and faster even now, to the tune of remembrance. How could something so wrong have felt so right?

"Did the plan work?"

"Plan?"

"You spent time together, then stayed in touch?"

"Well, that part, yes." Clara studied the desert's horizon. "After he left, we talked on the phone almost daily and wrote long letters and equally long emails. He's a wonderful writer."

Rachel glanced at her. Her lips smiled, but her eyes didn't.

"Soon, we started making wedding plans. I was going to quit school at the end of the quarter and join him in Europe." Who would have thought that within weeks all they'd shared and all those plans would be nothing?

"Did you do that?"

Clara shook her head and lowered her gaze. "One day he didn't answer the phone. Didn't return calls. Didn't answer emails. The man went poof. I thought I was going to die, Rachel. Dramatic, I know, but it was all so real. It was a big deal."

"I believe you. I understand." She switched lanes and passed a loud grocery truck. "Did you ever hear from him again?"

"Oh, yes." Though she now almost wished she hadn't. "He finally answered the phone after four or five days of silence." Clara could still remember the tone of his voice. Solemn. Cold. As if he'd never been in love with her. As if all the passionate letters and sweet promises had only existed in her imagination. "He said he'd changed his mind. He said he wanted to try and reconcile with his wife, said he missed the kids."

"Ooh, I'm so sorry, Clara—I mean, I'm glad they chose to reconcile, but that must have been so hard for you." Rachel exhaled hard and tightened her lips. "It was probably for the best, though. Don't you think—now that a few years have passed?"

"That's not the end of the story, though." She wished it were. That's when *she* had transitioned from innocent victim to co-conspirator, as Andrew had put it.

"You don't *have* to tell me what happened next, Clara—though you may if you wish, but you can't have unconfessed sin in your life. That's probably why you've felt 'anxious'—that's conviction. If you regret whatever you did, you need to pray for forgiveness. God will forgive you. That's a promise. 'If we confess our sins, he is faithful and just to forgive us our sins, and to cleanse us from all unrighteousness.' That's a quote from First John, chapter one, verse nine."

"I want to tell you, though. I've never told anyone—not even my mom." She'd gone too far. Maybe God couldn't love her anymore. Someone had to know the truth and tell her that she would be okay. "Do you mind?"

"If it'll help you, go ahead."

Clara shifted in the seat. "So I told him I didn't accept his decision. I was nineteen and so stupid. I'm ashamed to admit that marriage didn't really mean much to me back then—I'd never seen one work out. Everyone I knew was divorced. Even my grandparents."

"I'm so sorry, Clara. That must have been hard."

"It was. My dad didn't think of me at all when he left my mom. Didn't care about Mom's feelings either. So why would I care about Scott's wife and his three kids? The kids would get over it. I did." Hadn't she? "The wife didn't deserve him—she'd trapped him into marriage with a pregnancy when she knew he was about to break up with her and disappear from her life forever. And I ... I was convinced that Scott was my soul mate, that I was born to make him happy, and that what we had was real. We would be the ones to make it, Rachel. Forever. We would be happily married—forever." Clara filled up her lungs. "Stupid girl. I'm so stupid, Rachel."

"You're not stupid. You made a very bad decision, I guess." She squeezed her hand. "You need to get right with God and then forgive yourself too."

"I know." Her voice was low, and her heart felt like the oversized cannonball sinker her dad used when fishing bottom dwellers. *Co-conspirator.* "Scott was living in Germany at the time—I think I already told you that. His wife was in England with the kids—that's where she's from. He was coming to the U.S. again in the winter for a course in Virginia, so I told him I would meet him there. He didn't object."

Rachel took the church exit. "I'll drive to the back, so we can finish talking."

"I was convinced that if we could spend more time together, he would change his mind and love me again." Should she go on? Would Rachel hate her? She had to tell someone. Had to.

"Did you see him in Virginia?"

"Yep." Clara rubbed her forehead. "I also wanted to sleep with him. I'd never been with anyone, and if I was going to lose my one true love, I wanted to have all of him first. I wanted memories to hold on to forever because surely I would never love anyone again." And she hadn't. Until Andrew.

"Oh, the heartbreak, Clara." Rachel glanced at her. "For everyone."

Clara nodded. "And it was all my idea, Rachel. I wanted him to be free from her and available to me. I didn't even feel bad doing any of it. I was convinced that she was evil for trapping him and that she needed to be out of the picture no matter what. But looking back now, I get it. What I did was awful. I was the bad guy. The woman made a mistake in her youth, but he married her, and they had three kids—they were not all unplanned."

"Everybody lost, Clara. You lost too. You were very young as well. You came from a broken family, and this is a broken world." Rachel pulled into the church parking lot. "Were you familiar with what God has to say about marriage?"

"I don't know much about the Bible. I went to VBS when I was little. That's it." Clara took the tips of her fingers to the outside corners of her eyes. Would it have helped if she knew the Bible better? Would it have caused her to walk away the moment Scott said he was married? Maybe? Probably? But what was the use of thinking about that? Too late now. She filled her lungs to capacity and exhaled slowly. "Oh, how I wish I'd stopped it all on that second day—the day I discovered that he was married."

"I can imagine." Rachel nodded and bit her lower lip. "Have you prayed about all this Clara? Have you asked for God's forgiveness?"

Big tears rolled down Clara's cheeks. "I don't think God wants anything to do with me anymore."

"That's not true. Remember the promise I told you about—if you confess, He's faithful and just to forgive." Rachel parked behind the church.

"I am so ashamed." Clara sobbed.

"That's a good place to start." Rachel squeezed Clara's hand. "We'll pray about this, and God will forgive you and start healing your heart."

Could He really do that? She took her fingertips to the corners of her eyes again. But even if God were to forgive her, could she ever forgive herself?

"You told me you're saved, right Clara?" Rachel handed her a tissue from a small plastic pack.

"Thanks." Clara straightened her back and dried her tears. "Yes, in VBS, when I was eight." Her last VBS.

"So you know for sure that if you were to die right now, you would open your eyes in heaven."

"Doesn't seem right, but I know I would." It said so in the letter she'd gotten from the church—the one still tucked in her Bible at home after all these years.

"Good." Rachel smiled.

"How did I turn out so bad, though?"

"We're all sinners, Clara." Rachel's voice was gentle, her words judgment free.

"Some are worse. I'm worse."

"To God it doesn't matter who's the worst. Remember Exodus? The Passover and the last plague?"

Clara nodded. She remembered watching an old Moses movie with her mom. It'd been a while.

"God was looking only for the blood on the door. He didn't knock to ask if the people inside were good or bad. He looked for the blood. He still does. That's the only requirement."

Clara nodded. Made sense.

"Do you want to pray on your own, or do you want to pray together?"

"I will probably bring this up in prayer on my own for years to come." She looked up at Rachel. "Today, can we pray together?"

"Of course."

Clara held the woman's hands. "Shall we?"

Rachel bowed her head.

Clara drew in a long breath, the weight of the past rolling from her chest to her hands. "Lord. Thank You for bringing me back to Your house. You know my heart. It's broken. I feel so bad about how I handled the Scott situation. Please forgive me for my stupid decisions. Forgive me for all the hurt I may have caused. Forgive me for ignoring the feelings of those kids. Of all people, I should have had compassion. But I had none. That was so wrong. Thank You for not giving up on me even though I don't deserve You. Help me do right." *Obviously all I know is how to fail and screw things up. I need lots of help. Help me with Andrew too, please. I like him.* "Amen."

"Amen."

Clara took the used-up tissue to her eyes once more.

"Good, Clara. Now don't let the enemy bring this up again and again. You can let go. Go and sin no more is what God says about situations like this. Hold on to that truth."

Rachel had a gift for saying all the right things. "Do you think I'll ever forgive myself?"

"You have to. Pray that God will help you with that too."

Clara took a deep breath. *Help me, God. Help me forgive myself.*

"Ready?"

"Ready." Clara opened the door of the Civic, a hint of energy and hope flowing through her veins. "I must be a mess," she whispered as they crossed the parking lot.

"A little. Let's sit in the balcony—plenty of tissues and fewer people."

As they walked through the back door of the auditorium, "Amazing Grace" filled the air with familiar sounds and fitting lyrics. Good.

Once at the top, Rachel grabbed a box of tissues and picked a spot close to the stairs.

Across from them, behind the altar, was the baptistry. "I should get baptized one day." Clara's eyes stayed on the waters. "My parents moved the week after VBS and divorced soon after. I never had a chance."

Rachel squeezed Clara's hand. "No, you sure didn't."

"What do I have to do?"

"Walk up at the time of invitation and say you want to do it. They will ask if you've trusted Christ as Lord and Savior, and if you have, they will take you to the back and show you where to change into a baptism gown."

"Hmm." She wanted Andrew there. "Maybe on Sunday."

"Good." The corner of Rachel's mouth quirked up.

Yep. That was what the trip was for—to get things right with God. What a wonderful feeling to be exactly where she needed to be at that precise moment.

Clara went through the whole box of tissues, as the pastor preached about a perfect God for imperfect people. Right there in Jesus's lineage was a parade of people as imperfect as her. Adulterers, liars, thieves, prostitutes. Yep, church was for her. She belonged. She examined the ceiling above her. The roof wouldn't fall on her head after all.

She would text Andrew from home and let him know she had some exciting news.

Chapter 17

Andrew and Clara spun around the dance floor of the Shundo Ballroom Dance Studio as an orange sun set over the Chihuahua Desert outside the large windows.

"You guys are looking great," Helena said. "You'll be on fire when we have our social party at the end of the month."

Andrew thought they were on fire already. "I don't know about you, but I'm loving this."

"I'm loving it too." Clara glided around the room in his arms. "You must have really practiced."

"I watched some class videos on YouTube." Many of them. "I didn't want to hold you back. It was so easy for you and so hard for me last time."

"Oh, you shouldn't have. Don't stress over this."

"I'm not stressed." He winked. "I like being good at what I do."

"You guys are too comfortable." Helena approached them. "Let's learn some poses and work on where you stand in relation to each other."

"No rest for the weary." Andrew chuckled, dropping his head.

"No rest if you want to compete." Helena giggled. "Let me pick a slower waltz."

"So what's the exciting news you need to tell me about?" he asked.

"I'll tell you after class." She tilted her head. "Have you ever heard of ... Hmm. I forgot the name of the band or whatever they are."

"Nope. I've never heard of *Hmm. I forgot the name of the band or whatever they are.*"

"Very funny."

Helena came back.

"We'll talk about it later." Clara held his hand.

"We're just full of mysteries today, aren't we?" They laughed together—how he loved her laugh. He'd missed her—even though it'd only been two days.

Should he talk to her about the Tatiana issue? He'd texted her last night again, begging her not to come. No answer. Nothing at all. Maybe she was in the field. It would be best to tell Clara that he did not want to see the woman. Then if she showed up, Clara would know that he didn't care and that he had tried to stop her from coming.

Helena showed them the new moves.

He tried the first pose she showed. "I have no words to describe how moronic I feel right now."

"You look great." Helena clapped. "Don't you think, Clara?"

Clara looked at their pose in the long wall-to-wall mirror. "She's right. You look great."

"You're mocking me."

"Am not."

"Are too."

"We will learn two more poses, and then I will let you put it all together. Okay, Mr. James?"

"Why are you singling me out?" Andrew's lips twisted.

"This is ballroom dancing. Whatever happens, it's your fault even if it's not your fault. You're leading." Helena lifted both eyebrows.

That actually made a world of sense. It was like being a company commander. Or like being the husband he hoped to be one day. He understood that. "Yes, ma'am." He *was* leading. It *was* on him.

Taking ballroom dance classes was by far the most original thing he'd ever done to win a girl. Not that he'd had many. He was pretty proud of his dance class idea and of having the guts to actually do it. He'd told his guys today that they had to hurry up because he had to make it to ballroom class. He'd expected to get all kinds of heartache for it, but most were actually curious and wanted to know more about it.

"You guys did a great job today." Helena put her hands on her hips, her bracelets jingling. "I can tell you've been practicing."

"That's right. I have." He kissed Clara's forehead. "Some of us are slacking a little, though."

"Funny." Clara tilted her head up.

""You two are cute." Helena chuckled. "You'll make beautiful babies one day, you know?"

"Well, will we?" Clara asked looking at Andrew. He was beet red.

"Yeah, your kids will have massive amounts of red hair." Helena giggled.

"If they look like their dad." Clara played with a strand of her hair. "My hair is not red. It's auburn."

"Looks pretty red to me. It's beautiful." Helena walked to the office area and grabbed a bottle of water.

The three chuckled and then Clara and Andrew said goodbye.

"Do you like gorditas?" Clara asked as they stepped out of the ballroom studio.

"I don't know." He opened her door. "What's a gordita, ginger girl?"

"Auburn." Clara's eyes narrowed. "I'm not sure I know how to explain a gordita."

Her smirk was adorable.

"Try." Andrew narrowed his eyes.

"It's like a flatbread made with cornmeal—I think it's made with cornmeal—then stuffed and fried."

"Stuffed with what?" Andrew started the engine.

"I like mine stuffed with meat, but they make different ones."

"And you know a place that makes them near here?"

"It's by the ballet studio. I was there for lunch yesterday."

"I'm game. Let's do it." Andrew pulled out of the parking spot and turned on the radio. He hadn't thought about her going out for lunch. He'd assumed she packed lunch or snacks. Did she go alone? Did that ballet guy go too? What was his name? Mark?

"You'll like it. It's very simple, but very good." Clara dug for something in her oversized purse.

"I'm sure I'll like it." They would get to hang out and talk. That was the highlight. He'd missed her. Time in the field and ranges never bothered him, but last night he wished he'd been with her. He glanced at her perfect profile. She was still looking for something. Half the contents of her purse were on her lap now—a brush, mirror, and papers. Lots of papers. What was her "exciting news," and was the concert something related to the news? Did they have the same definition of exciting news? He was ready to find out.

"Here it is." She pulled out two event tickets from the purse.

"What's that?"

"Tickets for a Christian concert—The Thirty Second Proverb? It's on the twenty-second. It's a Monday. Not next Monday, but the following Monday."

"What do they sing?" Why had he never heard of them? The fact that there's no thirty-second proverb probably had something to do with it.

"I'm not sure, but one of the girls at the intensive had a bunch of tickets that her church was handing out, so I got two for us."

"Cool." Why did he have a feeling he would end up watching people spin around, and who knows what else? *Don't judge.* "Where's it at?"

Clara read the ticket. "Abraham Chavez Theater?"

"That's by the Convention Center." He would have to look up the band. "It's a downtown theater. I've seen it."

"Well good. Here's your ticket." She held one of the two in his direction.

"Just put it under my wallet, please." He pointed at the center console. "Thank you."

"You're welcome." Clara's sweet scent reached him as she placed the ticket between them.

"So is that the exciting news? The concert?"

"No. Well, I'm excited about the concert, but that's not it." She sat taller as if looking for the place. "I'll tell you in a minute."

Andrew slowed down.

"Turn right there." Clara pointed at a corner strip mall.

"Yes, ma'am." He chuckled.

The place was small but clean. By the time they were done ordering gorditas from the simple mom and pop shop, he was all the way curious—about the food and about her. Was she leaving early? *Please no.* Staying longer? He would like that. Was she performing with the company? Was it related to her job search? Maybe she'd found a job in El Paso. How great would that be?

He wouldn't be moving for another year or two. And who knows—maybe the Army would let him stay in El Paso longer than the usual three-year tour of duty. He would stay in El Paso longer for her. He liked the church. What was it that she wanted to share?

Clara walked to the long bar-style table by the window, and Andrew pulled out a tall chair for her.

She crossed her legs and twisted to face him. "I went to church last night."

"You did?" He didn't see that coming. "How did you get there?"

"I did. Rachel picked me up. I'd called her the night before asking to talk, and she offered to meet before church."

"Okay." Andrew cocked his head and studied her expression. Her smile faded.

"Sunday's sermon hit me hard."

He nodded. That might explain why she'd seemed a little off Monday night at Ardovino's. She wasn't just tired from day one of the intensive after all.

"I've done some things I'm not really proud of." She fiddled with her small silver earrings.

"Haven't we all?" Having said that, what *had* she done?

"So, I talked to Rachel, and she helped me pray about it. She told me about God's promises on forgiveness." Her smile returned. "Then last night's sermon was perfect. It was all about a perfect God for imperfect people. He talked about the lineage of Jesus and how there were a lot of broken people in his background—liars, murderers, prostitutes, adulterers, people who were not born Jews, and all kinds of kinds."

"That's right." Which kind was she? He couldn't imagine her doing anything too horrible. Their number was called, and Andrew brought their food to the table.

"So my big news is that I got right with God, *and* I'm getting baptized this Sunday."

"Oh, wow! How exciting. I'm so happy for you." He grabbed her hands and squeezed them. "At long last." Maybe this wasn't the best time to ask what she'd done.

"At long last." She beamed.

But would there ever be a good time? They prayed, and he watched her bite into her gordita. Maybe she would tell him one day. One day soon would be good. *Please, God. I need to know. No more heartbreak.*

He took a tentative bite of his food, then a bigger one. Ooh, that was good.

"Like it?" Clara raised her chin.

"Love it." A familiar voice came through the large corner speakers.

"Roberto Carlos." They said together and giggled.

"In Spanish." Clara took a sip of her diet soda and then bit into her gordita again.

They enjoyed their meal and listened to words that he didn't understand but that she probably did. General Medeiros had once told him that most Brazilians understand Spanish well. *General Medeiros—what a character.* He missed his stories and was looking forward to seeing him soon.

Clara's smile faded like it had when she began the conversation. Was it the music? Something sad? Her gaze roamed the road beyond the windows.

"What's bothering you?"

"I want to tell you about what I did, but I'm embarrassed."

If they were to build something together, they would need to know each other's stories. But could he handle whatever it was that she was about to tell him? "If telling me about it will help you feel better, then tell me about it."

"It won't make me feel better. But I want you to know."

Andrew bobbed his head and shifted in his seat.

She closed her eyes. "Remember the guy who recognized me on post when we were outside Starbucks?" She opened them back up, lips tight in a straight line.

"Yeah. The major. Colonel Howard's XO?" Ah, one conversation—two mysteries soon to be solved. Good.

She nodded. "Scott." Her eyes avoided his and searched the streets again.

So, they had history. Baddish? Yes, but he'd already figured out that she had a past with that major—Scott. The way he'd looked at her at Freedom Crossing said it all. He'd sort of come to terms with that. He liked Clara that much. But was there more to it? There had to be for her to feel convicted and want to get right with God. A baby? An abortion? Please no. He couldn't handle that.

"Andrew, this is something I've never told anyone until last night. Not even my mom knows the whole thing."

"You don't have to tell me." But now he needed to know. He had to know what he was getting himself into. The music was faster now and almost annoying. It wasn't Roberto. His clammy hands reached for a paper napkin. "What happened?"

Clara drew in a deep breath. "I met Scott about three years ago. I wasn't supposed to go out that night. But I did. And I wasn't going to stay late. But I did. And I saw him. And a guy with a military-style haircut at a Cincinnati honky-tonk really stands out."

He couldn't even imagine Clara at a honky-tonk. Maybe she liked the dancing.

"I shouldn't have talked to him. But I did."

She didn't have to tell him anything about regret. He could see it in her face—all life drained, zero joy.

"The whole thing could have been avoided if I'd minded my own business. If I hadn't been so desperate. Girls and their daddy issues, let me tell you." She glanced up. There was life in her eyes now, but not the best kind. Anger flared. "Just like my grandma at that stupid window calling out Mario's name. She should have watched Mario pass. I should have said nothing to Scott. Everyone would have been better off."

Was she right? In her grandma's case, yes. But how about her? Was Scott married? He hadn't noticed a wedding ring.

"He had the best lines—of course I didn't know they were lines—I was nineteen and had never been with anyone other than guys from ballet who were practically family, you know?"

He didn't know, but he got the idea.

She pressed her hands against her cheeks. "I'm ruining your gordita experience, no? I'm so sorry."

"You're not ruining anything—here." He took a big bite of his food.

She finished hers without finishing the story or recovering her excitement. Her skin was unusually pale, clammy even. Maybe it was the bright lights. "Tell me what you want to tell me, so you can start feeling better."

"Well, we talked and spent time together, and it was like a fairy tale. The thing you wait for, hoping it actually exists. A strange connection. A not having to explain your emotions because he got it before I could verbalize it. I don't know how to explain it."

"Soulmates." He clenched his jaw. Did he have to hear this part of the story?

"I know you don't believe in it. But it *was* like finding my other half—how else could someone who I'd never seen or spent time with ever before know me so well and bring me to life so fully?"

He shrugged. "Soulmates really don't exist." He could bring her to life better than that clown ever could, and he knew it. Scott probably slept with her then dumped her. Typical. He had a picture of that big Italian-looking beast in his mind, and he could punch him right between his baby blue eyes.

Clara held her head in both hands. "The next day was just as beautiful. Flowers on my car, a sweet note, an afternoon date at a gorgeous state park overlooking the Ohio River. Picture perfect. Until ..." Her voice caught, and swift tears fell on the counter.

Andrew grabbed her hand and watched her lips tremble—the soft skin over her lip turning red. Her hands squeezed his. What had Scott done? He would kill him. Or hurt him badly—at least. Deep breath. Everything was great until what?

"Everything was so perfect until he confessed to having a wife and three kids." She sniffed and looked up, eyes red.

"No." Why did men do that?

"I'm so embarrassed. Embarrassed about what happened and embarrassed because I'm crying here."

Two people had been in and out. They were alone. "It's just us and the gordita guy. He's in the kitchen. He can't hear us."

She chuckled and patted her cheeks dry with a fresh napkin.

"So this joker is married with kids, broke your heart, and had the nerve to come say hi to you the other day?"

Clara tugged at her earlobe. "So much has happened, Andrew."

As Clara told him about her hurt, Scott's separation, their wedding plans, his change of heart, her disregard for the family he'd decided to save, and her trip to Virginia, Andrew knew he had to be supportive—she'd repented and confessed. But in his mind, he was an eleven-year-old boy, afraid his dad would never come back home because of the girl he'd met while on travel duty in Washington, D.C. The eleven-year-old boy he'd once been.

He'd begged God like only a young boy can beg. "He can't leave us," he'd prayed. He couldn't.

But he almost did.

God had heard his prayers though, and after three rocky months when he wasn't certain of anything, life went back to normal. No one talked about that nightmare ever again.

That'd been the worst time of his life. Worse than getting dumped by Tatiana. With Tatiana, he was the only one getting hurt. With the situation with his dad, everyone was hurt. His mom lost all joy. He was in pieces. And his sisters cried daily.

Hate was too strong a word, but what had Clara been thinking? She knew Scott was married and had three kids, and she slept with him anyway. Who would do that? *Someone who doesn't know any better.* But how could someone not know any better, Lord? Wasn't that common decency? *The heart is deceitful above all things, and desperately wicked: who can know it?* A muscle in his jaw twitched.

"I knew you would be disappointed."

"So you didn't see him after Virginia?"

"Nope." She placed her hands together on her lap. "We spoke on the phone for a few more months, but when I saw that he was serious about getting back with his family, I figured I had to cut my losses and move on."

Her losses—Scott's family's gain. Good for the kids. But wait—how about the wedding ring? Andrew was certain the man wasn't wearing one. "Is he divorced now? I didn't see a ring."

"That's what he says."

Too much damage. Another broken home. Sad. "Did he call you here?"

"He texted a couple of times, but I don't want to see him."

How were his kids? How old were they? Andrew remembered the many times he heard his sisters' tearful prayers, and a familiar heat burned the center of his chest. "Boys or girls?"

"Hmm?" Clara's eyebrows shot up.

"You said he has three kids?"

"Oh. Two boys and a girl."

How could she have ignored their feelings? Two boys and a girl without a dad at home. And Clara was at fault. Andrew ran his fingers through his hair.

"You're upset." She covered her mouth. "You don't forgive me, do you?"

"It's complicated." What should he do? That was one of those moments in life that demanded a good decision—a spiritual decision, and he knew he was about to fail.

Her jaw dropped, and her skin turned paler than before. "You don't forgive me."

He wanted to say something, but nothing came out. *It's complicated.*

"Wow." She stood and grabbed her purse.

"Where are you going?"

"How did you understand my grandmother and the general so easily? You talk about her like she's a normal person, but you're looking at me, and …" Clara shook her head. "I'm standing here, and I feel dirty all over again. You forgave my grandmother, but you can't forgive me?"

It wasn't about forgiving—it was about character. "I didn't fall in love with your grandmother. I wasn't dreaming of a future with your grandmother. There's a difference."

She tightened her lips. "Who's being judgmental now?"

He *was* being judgmental. But it was impossible not to judge. *God, help me.*

The gordita guy appeared at the counter. "I'm closing in fifteen minutes."

Andrew nodded. "Thanks."

Clara clutched her purse strap so hard her knuckles were whiter than the rest of her hand. "The first night we went out you said that sometimes Christians are the only Bible most people will ever read."

She didn't have to finish her thought for the weight of her words to hit him like a punch to the ribs.

"You're not being a very good Bible right now. You are not representing Christ well. And I don't want to be like you."

Fair. Deserved. But that was a hard one to take. She didn't say it with anger. She said it with authority, and the conviction he felt tore his heart. He wanted to be better. He wanted to behave better. But there was nothing he could resolve standing in the middle of a gordita shack that was about to close.

Clara walked to the door.

"Where are you going? Let me take you home."

"Good enough for God. But not good enough for Andrew James. I knew this was going to happen. I knew it. I'm so stupid." The last words came through tears, and then she stormed out of the place.

The gordita guy came to the door. "Go after her."

He followed her from a distance. She covered her mouth, probably crying. Why did this have to happen? She was probably walking to the ballet studio, but he doubted there would be anyone there. The studio came into view. Oh, there was light. Maybe people were still in the building.

Clara opened the door and disappeared. Would someone be able to take her home? He sure didn't want her to take the bus at night.

Andrew walked to the car but couldn't bring himself to leave without her. He parked in front of the studio, and before he had a chance to step out of the crossfire, Mark came out. Wearing sports shorts. That was all. No shirt. *Really man?*

"She's okay. I'll take her home."

Say what? "I can take her home. We just had a misunderstanding." Mark looked like something out of the movie *Top Gun*, the volleyball scene. The only thing missing was a pair of dog tags. Bleh.

"I'll take her home tonight. She can call you if she wants to."

It was official. Andrew did not like Mark. Not one bit. He leaned back. Why? The door of the studio opened and closed. Mark was gone.

Andrew's phone vibrated. *Clara.* Maybe she was texting him. Maybe she was going to let him take her home.

Tatiana.

I GOT A 4-DAY PASS. I'LL BE AT BLISS TOMORROW. IT'S A MILITARY FLIGHT. I'LL CALL WHEN WE LAND.

Chapter 18

Andrew spent the day expecting a call that didn't come. Actually, make it two. Clara hadn't returned his call, and Tatiana, who was supposed to call upon arrival, hadn't called either.

At 8:30 p.m., someone knocked on the door.

He ran his fingers through his hair, filled his lungs with air, and stood.

On the other side of the peephole, a familiar figure grinned.

"Tati?" He opened the door.

"Surprise!"

"What happened to calling?"

"I caught a ride. One of the guys who flew in with me lives here too."

"Oh, good." Was it good? He was going to take her from the airfield straight to lodging. Now what? He glanced toward Clara's apartment. Everything was dark. "Come in."

Tatiana walked in with a black duffle bag and parked it by the West Point graduation picture.

"Glad I found you alone. I was ready to fight."

"Fight?" What was she talking about?

She placed her hands on her hips and cocked her head. "You said you met someone—didn't want me to come?"

"Oh ..." Better not to talk about that. Quick—change the subject. "Wings! I see you have jump wings now." He'd noticed the parachutist badge on her uniform when he saw her through the peephole. "When did you go to airborne school?"

"Two years ago." She opened the fridge and pulled out the bottle of sweet red wine. "You were in Afghanistan when I went to Fort Benning to earn this." She tapped the badge.

"Good for you." Andrew walked to the kitchen and offered to open the wine.

She took the opener from his hands and freed the cork with ease. "We'll let it breathe while I change."

Tatiana walked to her bag, and Andrew's eyes followed her. Change into what? "Where are you staying?"

She dug a black one-piece swimming suit and a pair of shorts out of her bag. "Here." She searched the dark hallway for the bathroom and went in.

What was she doing? She couldn't stay there. And why was she putting on a swimming suit?

"Isn't it a bit late for swimming?" This had trouble written all over it. Clara or no Clara. "I'm going to call lodging, Tati. Let's do this right."

She threw the door open. "Let's do this right, let's do this right, let's do this right. Don't you ever get tired of this?"

"Tired of what?" Her uniform was in a messy pile just inside the bathroom. Her long blonde hair had the marks of the bun she'd certainly worn all day. Andrew avoided her curves and looked at her feet instead. "Nice green polish."

"Thank you." She shook her head and walked to the kitchen. "Where do you keep your wine glasses?

"There are two in the freezer."

"In the freezer?"

"Yep."

"That's new." She filled both glasses halfway and walked to him holding their drinks. "I like the way it looks."

He took one and studied her expression. No idea what to expect.

"Will you say something?"

He lifted his glass tentatively. "Cheers?"

"Cheers." She had a sip and looked relaxed savoring it. "This is very good."

"Good." Not good. Had he ever been this uncomfortable around a woman before?

Her bathing suit and shorts were so incredibly out of place. She seemed changed. She took a step in his direction, her chest almost touching his, her feminine scent and warmth inviting.

"Let's get you to lodging, Tatiana."

"Can we relax and enjoy this time?" Her voice was sweet for the first time since she'd arrived. Now she sounded like a girl, not an Army officer.

"I will enjoy it more if you put a shirt on." He could have a decent conversation if he weren't constantly avoiding staring at her pretty shape. "Please. Put something on."

"Yes, sir." She giggled and opened her bag again. Out of it came an olive green military police T-shirt—probably her unit's. "I do want to swim, though."

If they were to walk around the apartment community long enough, Clara would certainly spot them. He didn't know what to do with his feelings toward Clara and the things she told him last night, but he knew he didn't want to hurt her. "I don't want to swim. It's late, and I'm tired."

"I just flew all over the wild west to get here. You owe me a swim."

"I don't owe you anything."

"Is it because of the girl?" Her eyes narrowed. "Who *is* this girl you're seeing?"

"It doesn't matter." Did his face look as hot as it felt? "It didn't work out."

Her eyes sparkled. "Good for me, I guess."

"What do you want from me? Haven't we been through enough?" His jaw tightened. "I asked you not to come."

He watched the sparkle fade. It was replaced by a cloud that shadowed her whole face.

Maybe he should have been kinder. "Tati, what is it? What is this trip all about? I don't want to be rude, but I don't understand what you're doing."

"I'm so confused. I'm sorry." She slumped, and her eyes filled with tears.

That was unexpected. "Listen, I'm confused too. What do you want from me?"

"I don't want to lose you, but I don't think I want to quit the Army, and I definitely don't want you to be with someone else." She bit her lower lip. "It's an impossible situation."

"Jealous, huh?" He couldn't help but smile.

"One hundred percent." She sniffed hard. "You are not authorized another girl, Captain James."

He shook his head with a chuckle. He dried her tears with his fingers. She was too cute when she was vulnerable. "Come on. Don't cry on me."

She nodded, her big blue eyes reddened by emotion.

"I'll tell you what we're going to do. We'll get you checked into lodging and then go out for a late dinner, okay? You want to spend a couple of days in town, that's fine, but let's do this right."

"Yeah, let's do this right."

"Are you mocking me?" He couldn't tell.

She shook her head and watched him fold her uniform and place it in her bag.

They stepped out, and he locked his place. The night air was warm, the breeze pleasant. Andrew looked toward Clara's apartment. Everything was dark still. She was probably with her dance friends—probably with that Mark character.

He put Tatiana's bag in the back of the Crossfire and opened the door for her.

Was that Tatiana?

Clara watched them from her dark bedroom window, where she'd been gazing at the mountains and the stars.

It couldn't be. She swallowed hard and covered her mouth.

She'd seen a female soldier go up to his building when she was coming back from the laundry room, but she'd thought nothing of it. A guy had dropped her off.

The blonde girl put her hand on Andrew's neck as he pulled out of his parking spot. It *was* her. It had to be her.

But what happened to her uniform? Did they? No ... That couldn't be.

After dinner at the Denny's at Freedom Crossing, Andrew took Tatiana to her room at the Army hotel. The Howards were still staying there, waiting for their household goods to arrive from Germany.

Please let Colonel Howard and his family be asleep already.

They walked slowly through empty hallways until she stopped at one of the doors. Tatiana walked into her dark room and went straight to the window, leaving Andrew at the door.

Her hands opened the curtain revealing the beautifully lit, large swimming pool. "Wow. This is amazing. We can still swim, you know?"

Andrew approached her and looked at the pool. It was very nice, as big as an Olympic pool, plus a square that made the whole thing look like a fat capital letter "L."

He focused on a large group that was grilling and laughing by the pool. One of the guys looked like Clara's Scott, but it wasn't him.

Being at Freedom Crossing had reminded him of Clara and Scott and the big mistake they'd made.

Andrew felt Tatiana's familiar arms around his waist, and he embraced her, his eyes fixed on the palm trees waving in the soft night breeze. When had his life become so fuzzy—so complicated? What did he want? Who did he love? Would the right person ever come along, or should he just make life work with the one in front of him?

Tatiana moved her head just enough to look him in the eye. "Oh, Andrew, everything is so perfect right now. Let's do this forever. Me and you. I'm a grown woman. You're a grown man. We've known each other forever. We love each other. Let's do the grown-up thing. I'm begging you. Please." She took a step toward the king-size bed and tried to pull him with her.

"Please, Tatiana. Don't." Andrew's eyes closed. Yes, the bed was right there. Images of the two of them on it tried hard to break into his mind. His heart beat harder, his jaw tensed. It would be so easy to give in, but he couldn't. Could he?

"I've saved myself for you, you know? But I don't want to wait anymore. Waiting is not working for us."

She'd waited? He didn't know that. That meant something to him. But why? It wasn't important for her—she'd said so a million times. "Why? How about the people you've dated since deciding not to marry me?"

"Not marrying was never about other people, about guys. It was always about the Army, and how much I love serving, how much I love being an

MP." She lowered her head. "But when it comes to love, I love you. Don't you realize that?"

He hadn't. She'd been sending him mixed messages since they'd graduated from West Point.

Should they try again? She could continue to serve for a while, but once they started a family, being dual military wasn't going to work out for them. Many couples made it work, but they'd agreed that was not a lifestyle they desired. Was that the problem? Did she want to be a mom *and* serve? What if she did? Was that a deal breaker for him?

It kind of was. It very much was. More than Clara's past with Scott? Probably. His concern about Clara was likely to stay in the past. The issue with Tatiana, if he was getting it right, was a present and future issue. He didn't want the mother of his children to go to war. That was a bigger deal.

"Please make love to me tonight, Andrew. I'm begging you." She hugged him tighter.

"Stop with this." She knew him better than that. "What's with the obsession? Don't tempt me. Living out my faith is hard enough without you propositioning."

"Don't make me feel like a prostitute."

"Then don't talk like you're talking right now."

"You don't get it, do you?" She pulled away and sat on the edge of the bed.

"No, I don't."

"Even if things don't work out. I want you to be the one I saved myself for." She sniffed. "Because if I leave El Paso and our relationship is over, I know I will never find a man as good as you."

That was sweet. His eyes rested on her trembling lips. "Tati, you'll meet someone who's right for you. And when that day comes, you'll be happy you saved yourself for him."

"No one cares about that stuff anymore." She shook her head and tightened her lips.

"That's not true."

She waved her hand in dismissal. "You should go now."

Andrew filled his lungs to capacity. This would be a good time to walk away forever. She'd just said he should go. He studied her sad features.

She'd also just said that she loved him, that she'd saved herself for him, and that she knew she would never find anyone else like him. Those were things he didn't hear every day. Maybe they *could* make it work. "Can I pick you up tomorrow for some sightseeing?"

"Sightseeing?" she mumbled.

"Yes, sightseeing. There's a lot to do around here." Again with the mixed messages. What was wrong with sightseeing with the person she claimed to love?

"I came to see one thing." She didn't look at him. Her eyes were focused on the lights outside.

"How about I call you tomorrow?" She had to be exhausted. In the morning they could figure things out.

She lifted both shoulders. "Sure."

"What's wrong?"

"You just denied me. That's what's wrong."

"I'm sorry." What did she expect? He looked at her profile in the darkened room. "I'll call you tomorrow."

"Listen, Andrew, I came here with a very specific purpose in mind."

"Okay?" To lose her virginity, while he was trying to keep his?

"I want to marry you. I'm ready to resign my commission."

"You are?" She'd said she was confused.

"As ready as I'll ever be." She nodded in slow motion. "I love you."

Wow. Was that what he wanted? Marriage to Tatiana? What if they got married and then she changed her mind about being at home? What if she was miserable out of the Army?

"But before you even think about it, I have one condition."

"A condition?" So there's more to it?

"I saved myself for you because I know it's important to you." She tucked a piece of hair behind her ear. "But I don't want to wait until marriage."

"What do you mean?" She was definitely confused. That made no sense.

"Sometimes I feel like you want to get married just so you can have sex, and that bothers me."

"That's God's design—it's part of the plan."

"I want you to marry me because you're ready for a lifetime together. I don't want you to marry me because of hormones."

"What are you suggesting?"

"It's not a suggestion. If you want to go ahead and marry me, we must have sex first."

"That's absurd. I already said no a million times."

"Then maybe you're right. Maybe we do need to say goodbye forever."

"Tati, don't be ridiculous."

She stood and held his hand. "I promise I'm not trying to be difficult."

"But you are being very difficult. You are asking me to sin."

"Is it really sin? We'll get married anyway."

"Then we wait. We've waited for twenty-six years. What's another six months or however long?"

"I just want to be sure you are marrying for the right reason."

She would never get it, would she? Was she lying to him or herself? He wouldn't sleep with her then not marry her. What was the real motivation? Did she want to try sex with him to see if it was worth leaving the Army for? "I can't do this. I'm sorry."

She stood and embraced him. "Don't say you can't. Think about it." Her lips teased his neck.

"Tati!" This was not happening. "I'll call you tomorrow, okay?"

"Promise to think about it?" She took a step back.

"Sure." Was there anything to think about?

Andrew crossed the empty lobby and then the parking lot.

She wanted to play house to see if she liked it. That had to be it. Maybe she didn't realize it, but that's exactly what she was trying to do. That was the only reasonable explanation for her behavior.

What a recipe for disaster. He would end up being left behind again— only this time having lost much more.

Chapter 19

"Andrew?"

Andrew recognized Colonel Howard's voice as soon as he answered the phone.

Had they seen him at lodging last night? Maybe the call was about something completely different. "Good morning."

"Good morning—I guess."

"Is there something wrong, sir? Are the boys okay?"

"We're fine. I'm worried about you. What's going on between you and Clara?"

Andrew exhaled. "That's a bit of a long story." Had Clara called them?

"Well, I was supposed to go golfing with my XO, but he canceled because he's cooking for 'the girl from Freedom Crossing'—a.k.a. Clara."

Awesome. "Her wanting to see Scott is not exactly unexpected." It was, however, unfortunate.

"I'm glad it's not unexpected." There was a pause. "I had to warn you. I would hate to see you get hurt again."

"It's my fault." He wasn't sure what she was trying to accomplish by seeing Scott, but he had somehow pushed her into doing so. Images of her dark balcony and windows flashed through his tired head. Had she seen Tatiana yesterday? Had she been there, in the dark?

The colonel's voice jolted Andrew out of his stupor. "Do you want to go golfing? You're obviously not spending the day with Clara."

"Normally, that would be a great idea." But he was supposed to call Tatiana.

"But?"

"But Tatiana showed up in town last night—I guess we're getting togeth-er." Andrew looked out the window. Bright day, no clouds. Maybe a trip to Mesilla? Anything that would keep him far from the apartment and far from Clara and Scott. And far from the places he'd enjoyed with Clara in El Paso.

"Oh. I thought she wasn't coming until the Fourth."

"Well, I'd asked her not to come, and I guess she freaked out."

"Is she with you right now?"

"No, you might see her at breakfast." Andrew massaged his temple. "She's there at lodging."

"Wow. How much does Clara know? Andrew, please tell me you didn't break her heart. My wife will kill you—I might too."

"It's not like that. It really is a long story." He would rather be with Clara. Why couldn't they go back to the night before the gorditas? He'd been happy for the first time in a long time during those two weeks before Clara's revelation.

Forgive …

Andrew shook his head and quieted the still small voice in his head.

Colonel Howard broke the silence. "I have time. Do you want to meet me at Denny's before you go do whatever it is you're going to do?"

Back to Denny's? Andrew was tired, but breakfast with the colonel had right written all over it. Iron sharpens iron. "Sure."

"I'll see you there in an hour."

"Looking forward to it, sir."

Scott showed up right on time. He wore a button-up shirt that looked very nice, but that didn't suit the weather or their plans—grilling and catching up at his house.

Clara glanced toward Andrew's building on her way down. There was no sign of him, and the Crossfire was gone. Her heart tightened.

Scott's truck was practical, a small silver Toyota. He opened the door for her, and she climbed in.

"I'm so glad you decided to see me." Scott passed the tall fountains by the entrance of the community. "We don't have far to go. My house is just past the two elementary schools—an older neighborhood, but very nice."

Scott's looks had always impressed her. He was tall and built and Italian and masculine, but his sparkly blue eyes softened his appearance, making him the best of both worlds. Beautifully massive but tender at the same time.

"You weren't kidding about living close." Clara's eyes studied the brick façade of his beautiful home, then the neighborhood as she hopped out of the truck.

In Scott's neighborhood, they were closer to the mountain.

The houses were unique. The trees were tall and mature. The neighbors didn't look like Army lieutenants.

Scott waved at an older lady who was watering two small bushes. "Retired folks—lots of them around here."

Clara nodded. How could everything change so drastically in ten city blocks?

He opened the house door for her. "Welcome home."

"Thanks." His walls were covered with pictures of his kids. "Where are they?"

"Back in England." His smile was sad.

"Must be hard."

"It is." He walked to the kitchen, and she followed him. "But it gives me a good excuse to go to Europe every year." He pulled a bag of marinated steaks out of the fridge. "What do you want to drink?"

"Water for now."

"I'm having a beer. Would you like one?"

She didn't have class tomorrow. "Sure."

He opened two bottles of Sam Adams and set one in front of her. "Now, what in the world are you doing here, and who's the puppy dog from Freedom Crossing?"

Puppy dog? Did he mean Andrew? She wasn't sure how much she wanted to share with him, but Andrew was off-limits. She wasn't there to talk about him. "I'm delivering a letter for my grandma."

"Oh?" He cocked his head.

"Yeah. My mom is in Brazil with her." Clara pushed her beer bottle around the dark marble kitchen counter making the condensation circle wider. "I don't think she'll be around much longer."

"I'm sorry to hear that."

Clara shrugged. "A friend of hers will be arriving here soon. I have a letter for him."

"That's different." He pulled a bag of yellow potatoes from the pantry and put it in the sink.

Could they talk about something brighter? Far away kids, dying relatives—Clara was beginning to feel gloomy. She should cook. Maybe she could learn something. "Can I help?"

"No. I've got this."

There went that idea. What did they talk about when they'd first met?

Scott opened the bag and picked two large potatoes. "What's the letter about?"

She had no idea what they used to talk about. Might as well talk about her family. "I'm not sure what all is in the letter. I'm curious."

"So it's for a man? An old fling maybe?"

"I don't know." Why wasn't she comfortable talking about her grandma's life with Scott? She'd known him longer than she'd known Andrew. Clara had a sip of her beer—the rich taste was just right. "I'm just the messenger."

"Well. I'm glad—and shocked—that you're here." He opened the sliding door to the backyard. "Come on."

"Wow!" A large lagoon pool sparkled under a tall pecan tree in grounds that had to be professionally kept. "This is gorgeous." She approached one of many wall planters. "Herbs and vegetables?"

"Yeah. I like growing my own food—some of it anyway." He picked a cherry tomato and gave it to her.

"This is a great space." She rubbed the little tomato with her fingers and put it in her mouth. "Perfectly sweet."

He placed his hands on both her arms. "*You* are perfectly sweet, Clara. I can't believe we are here together again."

His touch made her tremble—his eyes still had the power to melt ice in Alaska all right. "We're here ... I'm not sure about the together part." The dry heat, the drink, and Scott's proximity made her suddenly dizzy.

"We can be as together as you want to be." He brought her into his space and enveloped her completely in his arms.

Oh, Clara remembered those arms. She exhaled and rested against his chest, thinking of their first days together and thinking also of their time in Virginia. Would they be reliving the past today?

But for whatever reason, scripture was what popped into her mind next. Verses from VBS all those years ago. *Be not conformed ... be transformed ... the will of God...*

What had Andrew done?

Maybe if she kissed Scott—her Scott—the weird voice would go away. She was in Scott's arms. He wasn't married anymore. Andrew was with Tatiana. What was one kiss? Scott was the man she'd dreamed of marrying.

She looked up, stopping shy of touching his lips. He should make the final move. After the Virginia mess, she didn't dare start anything. It was bad luck.

And make the final move he did. His warmth, his lips, his beauty, his body against hers ... It was all too much. Too much in a good way or bad? She couldn't decide. Hot tears formed in her eyes. Was this home? Had she come home? Was Scott her destiny?

He swept her off her feet and carried her back inside. He went straight to the stairs, and she knew what was next.

His eyes were fixed on hers. "Clara, I love you so much. Thank God you're here."

Thank God?

She was getting baptized in the morning. They passed more pictures of the children on their way to his bedroom.

Thank God?

Scott placed her gently on his bed. What they were about to do couldn't be God's will. Not like that.

Be ye transformed.

He moved the strap of her romper off her shoulder and kissed the spot he'd uncovered.

She couldn't. *Be transformed.* She had to stop him.

But he wanted her so badly, and she'd probably led him on. What if he hated her? She didn't want him to hate her.

His right hand traveled slowly down her hips. She wasn't sure of its intended destination, but a suffocating sensation made her gasp and reach for his hand, staying it. No more. "I can't."

"What's wrong, Clara?"

"It's not you. It's me. I'm so sorry."

"No. I'm the one who's sorry. I thought this is what we were doing. I'm so sorry. Too far too fast."

What was wrong with her? She was too broken for Andrew, and he had Tatiana, so she should make things work with Scott—at least she would be with the only man she'd ever been with.

"Let me give you a couple of minutes." He walked to the door. "I'll start the grill and see you outside when you're ready. We'll just talk."

Clara nodded, and he walked away. A dozen hot tears wet her cheeks, but she had no energy to get up. Why had his touch felt so invasive and wrong? Was she thinking marriage first? Maybe it was too far too fast. Maybe they could just talk, like he'd suggested.

Ah, but there was more to it. A snort escaped her nostrils at the realization. In her mind and her dreams, she was already Andrew's. Scott had no business touching her. Never did, and now he never would.

There. She'd said it.

An image of three smiling children wrapped around their dad's neck accused her from the nightstand. She didn't even know their names. There was no way of making that relationship right—ever. Absolutely no way.

Fresh guilt tried to settle in, but Clara remembered her teacher's words. She'd repented and God had forgiven her. She had to forgive herself and move on.

Move on ...

She couldn't possibly just walk out. Could she? She should at least eat with him. She got to her feet and looked out the window.

The fire was still high, and he had their two t-bone steaks and potatoes next to the grill. A small boom box played Brooks and Dunn, and Scott leaned against a pillar, drinking his beer to the sound of "Cowgirls Don't Cry."

Reba McEntire's voice pierced the air, sending chills up and down Clara's body.

Of course she could walk out.

But that would be so rude.

Walk out.

Rude was lying about one's marital status. Rude was planning a wedding and then dropping off the radar.

Oh, and rude was calling a man a puppy dog.

She could have walked out two years ago. Maybe back then she'd been too young and hadn't known any better. But now she knew better.

Scott looked up at the window and waved at Clara.

She waved back. Fresh tears filled her eyes, but she was certain he couldn't see them, so she smiled. *Goodbye, Scott.*

Chapter 20

Clara suspected Andrew would show up at church with Tatiana on Sunday morning.

Once Clara walked into the auditorium, her eyes went straight to Andrew's usual spot, and sure enough, there she was—between Andrew and Alice—where Clara had sat last week and the week before.

"Balcony?" Rachel led Clara to the back before she had a chance to answer, and they moved up with hurried steps.

Could Andrew and the Howards see her in the balcony? Clara sat as low as possible and offered Rachel a tentative smile. "Maybe I should get baptized some other time."

"Nonsense. This personal turmoil is the enemy's work. He does that when people are trying to get right with God. Don't give him the victory."

Rachel was right, but to stand in front of Andrew and the Howards and super gorgeous and incredibly blonde Tatiana, wearing a blue bag and feeling vulnerable was more than she could handle, wasn't it? Her eyes scanned the large congregation. "There are too many people. I can't."

"This is not about people. This is about your walk. It's about obedience. Don't you ever let any person stand in the way of your walk with God."

Rachel was right again. Clara *had* to get baptized. It'd taken her a decade, but now she was here, and she was ready. This was the day.

Andrew didn't think Clara would show up at church, but he scanned every face as the Sunday morning crowd wandered in—just to be sure. Nothing yet. Would seeing him with Tatiana break her heart? He didn't want that, but Tatiana had insisted.

Clara wouldn't want to get baptized today. Would she?

She'd waited more than ten years. Why today? She was probably still upset with him and probably still at Scott's. Andrew clenched his fists as images of Clara with that guy tormented his thoughts. No, she wouldn't be at church. She had her own way of doing things. The world's way.

Judge not.

The voice in his head was gentle but had the effect of a heavy punch, and he struggled for air. Andrew shook his head and labored to fill his lungs. Sometimes knowing too much was bad. He exhaled, feeling the warmth of his own breath. Couldn't he just be angry in peace? He had to let go.

He probably wouldn't have to worry about Clara anymore anyway. She'd probably gotten serious about church because he was serious about church, right? If it weren't for him, she wouldn't be thinking about God at all. Now that he was out of the picture, God would probably be kept out of the picture too.

Another heavy punch. More struggle for air. Was this one for thinking ill of her?

He snorted and raked his hair. The truth was that he liked himself less now that she wasn't by his side. Clara had brought out the best in him. He'd felt needed. He'd felt hope. She was sweet and funny and tender. And gorgeous. Images of her big leaps in ballet class danced in his mind.

"What are you smiling about?" Tatiana's voice was low.

He lifted his shoulder in a half shrug and studied her.

She was elegant. Her long blonde hair was in a loose bun with shorter strands framing her delicate face and lips.

The choir was complete and ready. A violinist prepared to play.

He glanced at Tatiana again from the corner of his eye. She had twenty-four hours left in El Paso, and he had a big decision to make. This was the day. He'd spent Saturday night trying to talk her out of her "marriage condition," but she was adamant about it.

Why was he even considering it? The temptation? No. That wasn't it. He was used to being tempted and dealing with it. It wasn't easy, but it was perfectly doable. Maybe what had him thinking was that she was probably right. Maybe he *was* rushing into a marriage decision to have sex. Maybe he *should* get it out of the way. His way wasn't working. Nothing was working.

His eyes rested on Tatiana's profile once more. He tilted his head. Could he even do it, though? Where would he start? Heat flooded his face, and he turned his attention to the music. All he had to do was start. Take that one step. Nature would take over from there. *One step.*

Congregational singing always filled his heart with joy. Today it didn't.

"Open your Bibles to John, chapter eight." Why did Pastor's voice mock him? No, that had to be in Andrew's head. Everything was normal.

Andrew flipped the soft pages of his old Bible to the right spot. Of course. The first stone.

He was certainly not without sin. And in a few hours, he would probably be an even bigger sinner in Tatiana's arms. But who would judge him? There's no one without sin. No, not one. There would be no one to throw stones. He would confess. God would forgive. Just like He had forgiven Clara. *Clara* ... Andrew forgave her too. He was letting go. No more anxiety and judging and trips into the past. Enough. Andrew caressed the worn pages of his Bible.

But he knew better. Yes, God would forgive, but there would be consequences—those were inevitable. Argh. What to do?

The service felt long and disjointed. Or was it him? When it finally ended, Brother Jim sang the first verse of invitation. Potter. Clay. Shape. He had to go to the altar and pray there. He needed to. His feet didn't move though, and his hands hurt as he gripped the seat in front of him.

He longed to touch Tatiana now, to undo her hair and watch it cascade over her shoulders. He swallowed hard as the image aroused him. She was right there for the taking, and he wanted to take her. No more waiting. *No more, Lord.*

"We'll sing one more verse." Pastor's serene voice was like aloe on his burning thoughts. "There's still time to come. All heads bowed. Eyes closed. No one looking around. If you need to come, come."

"No."

Tatiana shushed him.

Had he refused the invitation out loud? Wow. Apparently. Open rebellion. This was a first. *Oh, God. Rebellion is bad. I don't want to be like this. Help me. But I want to be with this woman right now. I'm tired. I should be married by now. I want to be married.*

"Well, amen."

The abrupt end of the invitation left him longing for oneness with God. More than oneness with Tatiana? Yes. Much more. He glanced at his hands, knuckles white.

"If you'll please be seated, we are getting ready to baptize."

Andrew's heart accelerated so rapidly that his extremities tingled. He let go of the seat in front of him. Was it her?

The assistant pastor got in the water and reached up to the steps. And sure enough, there she was. Her red hair cascaded over the blue baptism gown. Green eyes as shiny as ever. Oh, and that amazing smile.

"It's a joy to stir the baptismal waters this morning. Now this is Clara. When we were walking up, she asked if she could stay underwater just a little bit longer. She said she's waited a long time for this day. Ten years." He put his hand on her shoulder. "We'll let you do that."

Andrew looked in Alice's direction. She was smiling at him with tears in her eyes. She clapped her hand over her mouth and faced forward.

"Now Clara, have you trusted Christ as your personal Savior?"

"I have."

"Amen. Upon your public profession of faith, I baptize you, my sister, into this church—the body of our Lord and Savior, Jesus Christ. In the name of the Father, and of the Son, and of the Holy Spirit. Buried in the likeness of His death."

She did stay down a little longer.

"And raised in the likeness of His resurrection."

As people clapped and said amen, Andrew grinned and did nothing.

I can't do it. I can't go against my beliefs and be with Tatiana in the way she expects me to. "Sorry, Tati."

"Hum?" she asked as they stood.

"I can't." He followed her out of the pew, and they walked slowly in the direction of the main doors.

She shook her head. "I can't say I'm surprised."

"So we're good?" Was it going to be that easy?

"I get it, Andrew. I don't agree with it, but I get it." She stopped and looked around the auditorium. "This is your reality."

He jammed his hands in his front pockets and bounced on his toes.

Tatiana looked at the Howards who had also paused and were next to them, talking to the Martins. "Alice, could you guys give me a lift to lodging?"

Alice looked at her husband.

"Sure," the colonel said.

"What are you doing?" Andrew whispered. "I can give you a ride to lodging and take you to the airfield tomorrow."

"I'll try to leave today." She pressed her fingers to her lips. "Whenever I do go, today or tomorrow, I can take the shuttle."

"Just like that?" Was this goodbye for real? Ouch. But it was for the best. He'd come close to making a mistake he would have regretted forever.

"Just like that." Her eyelids drooped.

"We need to collect the boys." Alice's voice was soft and low. "You can wait here if you want."

Tatiana nodded with a half-smile that faded as fast as it had appeared.

They walked slowly and stopped near the altar. Andrew held her hands in his. Their fingers cool and clammy. Eight years had come to this.

She freed one hand and pressed it to her throat.

Andrew swallowed the painful knot that had formed in his. "At least this time around, we made it to the inside of a church—progress." His joke wasn't funny, was it?

When she spoke, her voice was tender but sure. "I hope that love and marriage—and intimacy—turn out to be all that you hope it will be."

"I pray the same will be true for you." He choked up. "I'm so sorry things didn't work out for us. I really am."

"I know." Tears rolled down her face now. "I'm sorry too." She patted her cheeks.

"I'll always remember you, Tati." Should he hug her? As a friend? He wanted the very best for her, and for the first time ever, Andrew saw her as he saw his sisters—someone important and special but not a potential wife.

"I'll remember you too." She wrapped her arms around his neck, and her body trembled. "Oh, Andrew, a part of me will love you always. I wish you the very best."

He hugged her back and kissed her blonde hair. "I wish you the very best too." He remembered a similar hug at the Academy. Tatiana would forever populate his memories of West Point—good and bad, but mostly good.

She lifted her head and gazed at the door. "There's Alice. This is it."

Andrew drew in a slow breath and followed her gaze. Alice was talking to Clara. He put his hand on Tatiana's shoulder and walked her to the door. *Help us, Lord.*

Clara probably knew who Tatiana was, but Tatiana didn't seem to suspect anything about who Clara was. But none of that mattered anymore. God would bring about the right thing.

"Congratulations," Tatiana said to Clara when they reached her and Alice.

"Thank you." Clara had twisted her long, wet hair into a simple bun.

Andrew stretched his hand toward her. "Congratulations."

Clara shook Andrew's hand but lowered her gaze.

"Shall we?" Alice placed her hand on Tatiana's back and offered her a reassuring smile. "The men are waiting in the rental."

Tatiana nodded and wrapped her arms around Andrew one more time. "We'll always have West Point. Good luck, Andrew."

"Good luck." Andrew clenched his teeth. He would go to his classroom for a while. His heart hurt. His eyes hurt. Wow. Clara was probably confused about it all. He turned around, but she was gone. He watched Tatiana walk away, then took the back hallway to his classroom, where he sat in the dark empty room and wept.

We'll always have West Point.

Chapter 21

M onday evening, Clara received two text messages from Andrew. In the first, he asked to see her. She didn't answer.

In the second, he asked if she was showing up for their waltz lesson on Thursday. She didn't answer that one either.

She was in the middle of a *Downton Abbey* marathon that had started Sunday night. By the end of season two, at almost midnight on Monday, she wanted to call Andrew. But she didn't.

When would she feel ready? Would she ever feel ready? What did he want? And above all, where was the girl? Had she left town, and now he wanted Clara back? She wasn't a toy.

She replayed the snowy, gorgeous, and perfect *Downton Abbey* proposal. Did love like that really exist? She'd thought it existed—when she was nineteen. When she was nineteen, she'd believed in a lot of things that turned out not to be true. Love, dreams, family.

Maybe Andrew was right. Maybe soul mates didn't exist. She'd loved Scott so much. Correction—she'd thought that she loved Scott so much. She'd cried a million tears for him and for their fate. But look at her now. Once she resolved that the relationship was bad and wrong and unsatisfactory, she walked away as easily as one abandons a fattening, oversized brownie and ice cream pan that needs not be eaten. Simple. Not good for her. Goodbye.

Bless him. He'd texted a million times now. She didn't want to have to explain herself. She just told him she could never be as sad as she was after Virginia ever again. That was her answer to his every question.

On the screen, Matthew Crowley proposed again and again. Oh, look at that. Look at them. It had to exist. She would go to the video store to look for season three tomorrow, after the intensive and the showcase rehearsal.

She was dancing two group dances, one modern and one classic. Each girl was also dancing a repertoire variation. She was dancing the Lilac Fairy from *Sleeping Beauty*. She was also doing a pas de deux with Mark. Anna-Marie had mentioned *Le Corsaire* at first, but Clara had never done it, so she chose the *Don Quixote* pas de deux instead. Rehearsals were going well, but they had a crazy week ahead of them to get ready for the Saturday show that would end the intensive.

The following week, the general would arrive, and her mission would be complete. Then she could move on.

Clara's phone rang during the final rehearsal on Friday.

"Hi, Clara." The happy voice was clearly Alice's.

"Mrs. Howard?" They hadn't spoken since her baptism on Sunday.

"Yes, it's Alice. How are you?!"

"Doing well. How about you?" Two more soloists would rehearse before her. Clara stepped out of the studio.

"I hear the music. You dance at UTEP tomorrow, don't you?"

"I do—at the Magoffin Auditorium there. I only have a couple of minutes. We're still rehearsing, and it's almost my turn."

"Okay. I just wanted to make sure you're tracking my dad's arrival on Tuesday."

"I am." Clara sat behind the desk in the studio's waiting area—her desk. But not for much longer. "What do you think would be a good time for me to see him?"

"How about Wednesday?"

"Okay." Clara's heart fluttered in her chest as she imagined meeting the general. "Wednesday it is."

"I'll pick you up. We're in a house now. Our household goods arrived on Monday, and I have the first floor almost completely organized."

"Oh, good for you." How exciting it must be to be in a home again after months in hotels, both in Germany and here.

"I also want to watch you dance tomorrow. Is that okay?"

"Sure. It's at seven." That would be nice. A little bit of closure.

"We'll be there. Looking forward to it."

Did *we* mean Andrew too? Her heart fluttered again.

Andrew sat with the Howards, not far from where he'd sat with Clara three weeks ago. What a difference three weeks made. He searched the program and showed the Howards her name with a giddy smile.

They hadn't talked in nine days now. He'd vowed to give her space to finish the intensive in peace, but he was a man with a plan. He was going to show up at that concert —neutral territory—and talk it out. It had to work. It would work.

He hadn't seen Scott around the apartment community at all, and Colonel Howard said the major hadn't mentioned Clara again and worked late daily. That had to mean things hadn't worked out between Scott and Clara.

She was available.

Did Andrew have reservations about her character? Yep. Could he move beyond them? Yes. He'd come so close to settling for something different from his ideal with Tatiana and sinning in a way he never thought he would. It was clear now that the fog of war was real in relationships too—cloudy thinking resulting in disastrous decisions.

The lights dimmed and the music started. He rested against the seat and filled his lungs.

If, in his late twenties and in a fairly mature walk with God, he was capable of making a huge mistake, what could he expect of a nineteen-year-old girl with little to no Bible knowledge? Of course she was easy prey for a sleek officer almost ten years her senior.

There she was. Beautiful. Andrew couldn't take his eyes off her. His breathing and heartbeat quickened. How could anyone learn so much so fast? No wonder the waltz was easy for her.

Would she let him take her to the ballroom social at the dance studio? She hadn't shown up for class on Thursday, and he'd had to practice with the instructor. But Clara would remember what to do.

People danced alone on stage now, one at a time. He'd seen that in the program. Clara was seventh. "The Lilac Fairy." He grinned in the dark audience.

Clara was one of five adults he'd seen on stage—three females and two males. Mark was one of them, of course.

Some dancers couldn't have been more than twelve or thirteen, but the majority looked like high school students.

Girl after girl showed up in big tutus—and with big dreams, he suspected.

"Clara's next," he whispered to Alice.

She took the stage in a purple and gold tutu. Lilac.

The clothing, the serene music, her confident smile—everything about Clara was so professional. He had no idea she could look that good. Her presence was commanding.

She was on stage for a minute, if that. But it was long enough to get people electrified with a move that made her look like the pendulum of a clock. He'd never seen anything like that. She spun on one leg moving the other high in the air to the side then to the back as she twisted her torso—it looked impossible. Side turn and back. Side turn and back. She must have repeated the move at least ten times, and he was dizzy just watching her. She looked like it was nothing though. Clara was as poised as she'd been when she started. Wow.

The solos that followed were pretty, but nothing like Clara's. Tough act to follow was the understatement of understatements.

The last thing on the program was her dance with Mark.

Mark. Andrew twisted his mouth. Did he hit on Clara? Was he into women? Argh.

They took the stage in black and red outfits, with fiery expressions. *Awesome.*

"She looks fantastic," Alice whispered. "And the guy is not hard on the eyes, you know."

"I'll take your word for it." Mark didn't seem gay. The more Andrew watched him, the more he was convinced the guy was straight. Andrew didn't like him.

Their dance was certainly impressive. Why couldn't Clara get a good job dancing? What else was she supposed to do? She was an artist. People were thrilled to watch her dance. He didn't understand.

"Bravo!" he shouted when the dance ended, and Alice shouted too.

Colonel Howard, who hadn't said a word all night, looked at the two of them and nodded. "She is very good."

"Isn't she?" Andrew had brought a bouquet of roses and a card, but he wasn't sure how to get it to her. "Can you guys give me a couple of minutes?"

"Sure. We'll wait right here."

He followed other people who had flowers to a small door on the side of the stage. When he got near the door, a lady stopped him.

"Are you family?"

"Not really."

"We have a lot of young dancers. It's family only. I can get these delivered for you." She buried her nose in the bouquet. "They smell pretty."

"Sure." He handed the bouquet to the woman. "For Clara."

Mark passed by and spotted Andrew at the door. "Andrew, right?"

Andrew stood straighter. "That's right."

"For Clara?" Mark lifted his chin toward the flowers.

"Yes, for Clara." Who else would they be for?

"I'll take them to her. Thanks for coming, man." Mark took the flowers from the door lady and whistled down a long corridor.

Mark ...

Chapter 22

A ndrew arrived at the Abraham Chavez Theater ten minutes before the concert. No sign of Clara. Did she have a way to get there? Was she even coming? All of a sudden, in an ocean of people, his great plan didn't seem so great. *Lord, how will I find her?*

And then there she was, browsing CDs and DVDs, wearing the red dress she'd worn the night they watched *Giselle* and also wearing the bracelet he'd given her. That had to be a good sign, right? The night of *Giselle* … That's exactly what she'd looked like then. That was also the night they'd kissed for the first time.

Could this night be as good? Could they recover what they'd lost and continue getting to know each other? Please God, let it be so. He missed her.

He approached her from the side, so she could see him coming. And see she did. At the sight of him, she opened that beautiful smile of hers, like bright sun dissolving every cloud in sight.

"Hi." His voice caught in his throat. He cleared it and tried again. Stronger this time. "Hi."

One side of her smile lifted higher now. "I had a feeling you would come."

"You did?" He craved to reach out and touch her hands and put his arms around her, but he didn't want to move too quickly. He should get a better sense of where they were—where she was in relationship to him. Did the smile mean, let's forget the past ten days or so? He wasn't sure. For now, he was happy to be standing in front of Clara, smiling Clara. "How did you know I would come?"

"I didn't know. It was just a feeling." She shrugged.

"I was at the ballet, too. On Saturday. You were beautiful." He put his hands in the pockets of his khaki pants to keep them from reaching out.

"I heard you were there." She began walking in the direction the crowd was walking. "Thank you. And thank you for the flowers."

He caught up and offered his arm. "You're welcome."

Once they sat, Clara waved to a couple of girls.

"Ballet?" he asked.

"Yep. The brunette is the one who gave me the tickets."

"Did you ever figure out what kind of music they play and who they are?" Andrew had looked them up, briefly. He'd heard a song on YouTube—a good song—and then stopped trying to figure it out.

"They're out of a church in Florida or something?" Clara crossed her legs and smoothed her dress over her knees. "I'm still not sure."

The auditorium went pitch-black dark, and what looked like star beams filled the theater from every direction and to every direction. The band started strong, bringing everyone to their feet. "Wow. We're not at my church anymore."

"No, we're not." Clara giggled, and her eyes lingered on his face as they stood together.

Andrew laughed out loud. Not his kind of event at all, but for one night, why not? Might as well make the best of it.

Clara spoke in his ear, and her sweet scent enveloped him. "My friend said you just need to come with an open mind. If people say or do something that's different from what you believe, just ignore it and do what you do."

"Open mind." Andrew held Clara's hand and sang the words on the screen with her.

Song after song, they held hands and sang. Nice. He was all about holding her hand all night. Carry on. Sing away. Open mind. He smiled in the dark.

He recognized "Break Every Chain" from the radio. All the other songs were new to him, and most were very good. How come they were not on the radio? Maybe he would get a CD on the way out if they were still out there.

The concert had to be almost over, right? They'd been there for a couple of hours. Would they have dinner downtown? He would like that.

"Don't we all have things we're holding back?" the tallest of the male singers asked. "Let's make some big decisions here tonight, El Paso. With all eyes open, everybody looking around, let's make big decisions for God."

"That's different." Andrew reached for Clara's other hand so she would face him. When she did, her eyes were heavy with tears, but she still smiled. "I judged you, and I shouldn't have. I'm so sorry."

Her tears overflowed now as she spoke. "You made me feel dirty. I feel—used to feel—bad enough about Virginia. I didn't need you to make it worse."

"I'm sorry." He shouldn't have hurt her. She had enough on her plate, and it wasn't right to judge, no buts. *Keep talking. Open* ... "Fifteen years into my parents' marriage, my dad grew selfish. He fell in love with someone else. I was eleven."

Clara squeezed both his hands.

"They almost got a divorce, Clara. I was so scared. I thought my family was going to dissolve. I thought we were done—life as we knew it, over. That's why your story hit me so hard."

Her lips trembled. "I'm so sorry that happened to you. I'm sorry you were scared. But I'm glad their marriage and your family survived the storm. I'm really glad for you."

Andrew filled his lungs with the air of many prayers. "God did come through in a major way for us. My parents made a comeback, fell in love again, and they're still happy and together. I was lucky."

She nodded, her lips pressed together as fresh tears filled her eyes once more.

"Do you forgive me for judging you and looking down on you and making you feel bad?"

"I think so. I just need some time to process everything." She exhaled.

He understood that. Of course she needed time. "Can we waltz on Thursday?"

"I don't know. I'm getting ready to meet the general on Wednesday ... I'm just doing one thing at a time."

Andrew nodded as the worship leader got back to the mic announcing a prayer corridor.

Clara's eyes lit up. "Let's do it!" She jerked his hand and began walking down the steps before he had a chance to protest.

A prayer corridor? He looked at the people already there. The idea of having dozens of strangers put their hands on him in a tight human corridor was as appealing as a small arms firefight in a crowded Afghan market. But disappointing her would be worse right now, wouldn't it? "Let's do it," he mumbled, certain that she didn't hear or care about his response.

"Remember, open mind." She squeezed his hand, and they began the speed walk down the prayer corridor.

Hands touched his back, his shoulders, and his head to the sound of many prayers. His open mind was reaching the night's limit. He was there. Might as well pray.

Lord, I'm trusting you with all my heart. Put this girl permanently in my life if she's to be good for me and if I'm to be good for her. I'm giving the relationship to you. You decide. In Jesus' name. Amen.

Chapter 23

A lice drove Clara through the Cassidy Gate Wednesday afternoon to the sound of Casting Crowns' "Broken Together." Must be the most popular Christian song right now. It was always on.

A thin cloud cover was a welcome change to the always-blue skies of El Paso and Fort Bliss. The trees that lined officers' row looked even more majestic in the softer light.

Alice drove slowly past all the bungalows.

"I thought you guys were living in one of those." Clara twisted in her seat to look at the one-story square buildings they'd left behind.

"We were supposed to, but we ended up with a two-story brick house by Noel Field." She lowered her window and extended her arm, letting the slow breeze dance through her fingers.

Clara lowered her window too and remembered the night Andrew took her to the parade field. The women looked at each other and giggled as the breeze of opened windows disheveled their hair. Neither made a move to control their hair or close the windows.

"Hard to believe we're in the desert, isn't it?" Alice drew in a slow, long breath.

Clara nodded, looking at the purple and pink flowers raining from the desert willows that neighbored most oaks. "How is it that these flowers fall constantly, but the trees never run out?" One landed on the windshield.

"I don't know. I've wondered the same thing." Alice stuck half her head out the window and looked up. "It's like they are always overflowing."

"Exactly."

"Their cup runneth over ... My cup runneth over ... This is us." She pointed at a home with a West Point flag and an American flag by the entrance.

A West Pointer too.

"The driveway is in the back." Alice drove around the house and then up the long driveway. She closed her window, and Clara followed suit.

In the spacious yard, a wicker bench, chairs, and coffee table rested comfortably under a large tree. And on the bench an old gentleman rested just as comfortably. Everything belonged together.

"And that's my dad—General Mario Medeiros."

Wow. He wore a stylish beach hat, a light-yellow polo that reminded Clara of Andrew's car, and beige pants. Was he looking at them? She couldn't tell. Time stopped as she studied the man.

"You've waited a long time. Go." Alice squeezed Clara's hand.

Clara pulled the jasmine-scented, maple-gold envelope from her bag and looked at Alice.

"Should I give you guys some time alone?" Alice asked, still in the car.

"I would like that." Was she not at all mad about the hurt Clara's family had inflicted on hers? "How can you be so kind about it all?"

"He's suffered enough. He would have done things differently—much differently—if he had a do-over. I'm sure your grandma would've too."

"I'm sure she would have." Just like Clara would have. She stepped out of the vehicle and walked to the shaded area with a quick look back at Alice, who wiped her cheeks with her fingertips.

The soft green grass of the Howards' backyard tickled Clara's sandaled feet.

General Medeiros sat straighter when he saw Clara walking in his direction and stood with ease when she got near him.

"Eu conheço esse sorriso." He held both arms out.

Something about her smile? She reached for his hands. They were cool to the touch, despite the warmth of the day. "Meu Português não é bom." Her accent was thick, and Clara was certain she'd butchered half the words she'd used.

He smiled, and his eyes lit up. "I said that I know that smile."

"People say I look a bit like Grandma."

He gestured for her to sit in one of the chairs.

She did. Clara pulled the letter out—probably for the last time. This was it.

"Is that my letter?" He sat and pointed at the envelope in Clara's hand.

She nodded and handed it to him. Her hands wavered, and her voice did too. "You've waited a long time."

He touched the handwriting on the envelope. He cleared his throat and spoke slowly. "Yes, I have."

"Should I give you a moment to read it?"

"Would you mind?" he asked. "There is a pitcher of iced tea on the kitchen counter. I forgot to bring it out."

"I'll give you some time and then bring out the tea." She watched him open the envelope.

"Would you like to read it to me?" He lifted the folded paper in her direction.

"I can't ... Portuguese."

"That's too bad."

She wasn't sure she would have wanted to read it to him, even if she had known the language. Wasn't that their business? Clara smiled once more, then walked to the house.

Colonel Howard and the boys didn't seem to be home. A shower running was the only sound in the otherwise quiet house. Must be Alice. The kitchen smelled of limes, oranges, and all things citrus.

She helped herself to a glass of iced tea and watched General Medeiros from the kitchen window. The silver hair under the rim of his hat was nicely trimmed. Shoulders down. The weight of a life gone by? Hmm.

He leaned back in the chair and folded his hands on his chest, holding the letter against his heart.

Had it been worth the wait? What did Grandma write? Clara fixed him a glass of tea and walked out to meet him again. Would he tell her?

His eyes were closed. Small rays of sunshine lit his satisfied expression.

"Worth the wait?"

He opened one eye and nodded once. "Worth the wait."

"I brought you some tea."

"Want to trade?" He sat tall and offered her the letter.

She took the letter and gave him the tea. "Can I look at it?"

"You should." He studied her face.

She should? Clara unfolded the page. Her grandmother's handwriting was shaky, and she struggled to round the tops and bottoms of every letter. Did she just write the letter, or had she had it written for a while? It looked recent.

Clara touched the greeting. *Meu Amor.* Portuguese was so beautiful. She should find someone to practice Portuguese with. She knew most of the words on the text, but she had no idea how to go about pronouncing them.

Paralysis is how I deal with hardship. When my dad died, my mouth stopped. When I left you, everything stopped. I couldn't forgive. I couldn't forget. I couldn't move on. I just stopped. Thank you for coming back and setting me free.

Wait a minute. Wasn't this supposed to be a forgiveness letter? What did she mean by thank you for coming back? Did her mom know anything about this *coming back* business?

I never regretted refusing you when you came back all those years later.

How many years later? She remembered the Roberto Carlos song and pieces of lyrics flashed through her mind as she searched the letter. Missing her, wanting to see her walk by. The obsession with the song made more sense.

But I felt sorry for you and for how we ruined your life and your family. I'm so sorry.

I promised, so here it goes. Yes. Julio made me very happy—that crazy Italian.

Clara's grandpa, Julio Tomaselli.

He was different. An artist. A free spirit. He loved me, and I loved him—in a unique way. When it didn't work out after our girl was grown, we were sad to part ways but satisfied with what we'd lived together.

So, there it is. I was happy with Julio. But you were and will always be my one true love.

Soul mates?

Our Sofia talked to your Alice when she located you in Germany. She said she wasn't sure if you'd gotten right with God.

Our Sofia? Why did Grandma call Mom "our Sofia" in a letter to Mario Medeiros? And why the emphasis on God? Where had that come from? Okay. Clara was lost. What was this letter really about? What was going on? She took a deep breath and tried to make out the words again. The words. Maybe it was her Portuguese that was playing tricks on her. The letter made no sense.

I beg you, my love, if you haven't, do it.

Haven't what? She looked at the previous sentence again. Oh, gotten right with God.

That's my final request to you. I don't think I've ever asked for much. But this I ask. Trust Jesus with your eternal destiny. Do it because hell is real, and it hurts me to think of you there. Do it because you'll find peace and rest for your heart. You really will. I don't know how it works, but it works.

But above all, do it for me. Heaven won't be complete without you. Do it for me. Selfish request? Maybe. But who knows? Maybe in eternity we get to spend time together. I miss talking to you the most. Here's to never giving up ...

Clara laughed through tears. Oh, bless her. Teardrops stained the signature—old and new. Clara's in addition to her grandmother's and possibly Mario's too.

Saudades sempre,

Tua Renatinha

He'd come back, and she refused him? "When did you see her last?"

"Summer of 1950." He finished his tea. "My wife never forgave me. We were never a couple again after that engagement party."

That was a long time ago. Did anger stay that intense for that long? Maybe not anger, but humiliation and disappointment might. Thoughts of Andrew and his plea for forgiveness wandered across her thoughts. No emotion justified holding on to mistakes. She should forgive him and fast.

"What I did was terrible. I hurt a lot of people—there's no doubt about it. But I thought one day I would be able to move forward again."

"Why did you look for Grandma again?"

"I went to spy on her. I'd expected to find her married and with kids, but she was all alone. Her mom had just died. It'd been ten years since we'd seen each other. Ten."

"And she wasn't married, and you were in a tough situation at home."

He nodded. "My career was very important to me—generations and generations of Army officers, but at that point, I was ready to finish what I'd started. Kill the marriage and be with Renata. My wife and I were miserable. The kids were miserable. We were all miserable. Renata was too."

"What happened?" Was Grandma already realizing the whole thing had been a mistake? Did she leave Mario like Clara had left Scott?

"At first she was happy to see me, but then the next day she wouldn't have me."

Hmm. What could have changed in one day? A finch landed on the coffee table.

"She was older. Older and wiser." Mario pulled a bag of bread crumbs from his pocket and tossed a few of them on the small table. The little bird went after each morsel. "She said that she wanted to be with me but that she 'couldn't do it anymore ever again'—her exact words. I never forgot them. She said that if I tried to be nice, my wife would come around one day, but that never happened—I tried."

"I'm sorry." His visit must have been good for her grandma, though, because she married soon after, and then her mom was born.

Wait a minute. Was her mom—"their Sofia"—the general's daughter too? No. Her mom was born in the fall of 1951. Mario said he saw Grandma in the summer of 1950. They couldn't possibly be related. A hint of sadness clouded her heart. Did she want to be part of the general's family? An illegitimate branch of the tree? She couldn't possibly in good conscience want that. But she'd always wanted a big family, and she liked the Howards a great deal. They seemed to like her right back, but the math was off by six months. Wishful thinking. Now could the general become a Christian, or was that wishful thinking too?

"How about Grandma's request?" Clara pointed at the letter.

"Christ?"

Clara nodded.

The general lifted both shoulders. "That boy, Andrew, tried to have that conversation with me in Germany once or twice."

"Maybe you should hear him out." Should she tell him about her grandma's surgery? That could give him a sense of urgency. "There's no telling how many days we've got left on this earth."

He snorted. "Tell me about it."

Alice appeared next to Clara and startled her.

"Did I hear the name Andrew mentioned?"

"You sure did. Grandma wants your dad to become a Christian."

Alice beamed. "Now he'll do it—he'll do anything for Renata."

"I can't just 'do it,' Alice." Mario chuckled. "Last I checked you have to believe with your heart and confess with your mouth or something?"

"Have you been reading my Bible, Dad?"

His wrinkled cheeks reddened, and he stumbled on a word or two before something coherent came out. "No, but those church tracts are all over the house."

"Well, Andrew got my husband to believe. I'm sure he can get you too if you'll listen."

"They were in a combat zone. Guys will believe in the tooth fairy if it makes them feel less miserable."

"Do we need to volunteer you for deployment then, Dad?"

The three laughed together. Clara watched father and daughter exchange a sweet look—she was probably the only family member who was sweet to him. The world needed more Alices.

Alice grabbed Clara's hand but continued looking at her dad. "Andrew's coming for dinner on Friday. Maybe he can talk to you then."

"Maybe." General Medeiros twisted his mouth. "You should come too, Clara. I hear you're at the same apartment community where Andrew's at."

Was she ready to be around Andrew again? She could try. She would be leaving town soon anyway. "Grandma's having surgery Friday. If all goes well, it should be okay."

Mario's expression sobered. "What is she having done?"

"Something with the heart—it's weak and doesn't beat right."

"Will you call us when she's out of surgery?" His hands were pressed together now as if in prayer.

"Sure."

His expression softened again. "And then you'll come dine with us?"

"Okay." She could do that—if all went well with Grandma. What if all didn't go well? No, best not to think about that.

"Vó?" Clara asked.

Clara didn't hear a reply.

"She's nodding," her mom said. "Just speak loudly."

"I saw Mario today. He looks good."

"She's really nodding now." They all giggled. "Só um pouquinho—just a second."

Clara was pretty sure she wouldn't see her grandma in this life again. A tight pain wrapped around her throat. She should have visited more.

"She's asking about the letter—about her request."

"Working on it. He's not a believer, Mom, but Andrew will talk to him Friday night."

"Oh." Her mom's voice perked up. "So you and Andrew are talking again?"

"Starting to."

"Good. Are you guys going to that ball on Saturday?"

"We might." Clara couldn't make up her mind about the Big Band Party. She mostly wanted to go. But what was the point, if they had so little time left? A goodbye dance? How sad.

"Só um pouquinho—só um pouquinho."

She heard her grandma talking to her mom. Something about a gown.

"She's asking if you have a gown picked out?"

"I don't have anything figured out, Mom."

"She said you should wear lavender. Her favorite gown was lavender with little flowers."

"I remember." Clara had always loved that picture of her grandma—soft smile, delicate dress, perfect blonde hair. "We have a picture at home."

"Ela lembra." Her mom's voice was louder now. "She's smiling."

Clara swallowed the lump that had formed in her throat. Was it just her, or did this phone call feel a bit like goodbye too? Better change subjects. "Is everything looking good for surgery?"

"Clara, please get a beautiful gown and go to this ball, okay?"

Either her mom wasn't ready to change subjects, or she didn't want to talk about the surgery with Grandma awake and near. "You don't want to say anything about the surgery in front of her?"

"Uh-hum. Use my credit card."

Clara blinked back tears now.

"She wants to talk to you." Mom sounded as excited as ever. You could always count on her to keep things upbeat, no matter what.

Her grandma's voice was weak but surprisingly clear. "Dança uma valsa bonita com teu soldadinho por mim."

Clara nodded but didn't utter a word. She didn't dare speak. Grandma couldn't know she was crying.

Her mom jumped in. "She said to dance a beautiful waltz with your little soldier—for her."

"I understood." Clara sniffled hard. "Ask her which waltz? It's a big band party, so they should have singers and most instruments she knows."

"Let me ask."

"Fascinação." She heard her grandma say with difficulty.

"Fascination?" Clara was pretty sure that's what she'd said.

"She's nodding."

"Okay. I'll do that." She had to. For Grandma. "And you call me on Friday."

"I will, *Princesa*."

Clara cleared her throat. "Let me say bye to her."

"Here. Remember to speak loudly."

"Vó, eu te amo," Clara shouted as fresh tears filled her eyes.

Her grandma's voice was labored now, but Clara heard her loud and clear. "Eu também te amo."

Oh, God, please take care of her.

Clara ended the call and looked at the clock. She had to get moving, or she would be late for ballet.

The intensive was over, but she'd fallen in love with the studio, and they'd let her continue with classes. She was still helping in the office too.

Not for long, though. Anna-Marie had said something about wanting to talk after class. Melody was probably on her way back to El Paso—back to her job. If she'd made it into the Mexican company she was auditioning for, Clara would have heard something by now, right?

Too many goodbyes. Could she handle it?

She couldn't. There was no way.

Ballet, the Howards, Andrew, El Paso, Grandma, Mom possibly moving to Brazil. Too much. God, I can't. Help me. Please.

Chapter 24

The following evening, Clara knocked on Andrew's door—full of news, hope, and dog hair. What a difference a day made.

She wrapped the leash around her hand twice, put one foot forward, and leaned back. Her right hand held the doorknob when Andrew tried to open the door. "Don't open it all the way."

"Hmm, okay." He opened the door an inch. "Hi?"

"I have a surprise for you, but I don't want you to freak out." Clara leaned further back to keep Gigolo from pushing his way in.

"You've got my curiosity." Andrew chuckled.

"If you don't like the surprise, I'll keep it." She grunted and squeezed her hand on the leash as a drop of sweat rolled down her back. "Okay. You can open now."

As the young brindle boxer threatened to drag her in, Andrew laughed the deepest laugh she'd ever heard out of him. "No, you didn't. Is he for me?"

Clara continued the tug-of-war with the leash. "Bad idea?"

"Hey, boy." Andrew knelt by the door and let the dog put his paws on his thighs and lick his hands. He scratched the animal's soft ears. "This isn't Gigolo, is it?"

Clara relaxed her hands and wiggled her fingers now that the tension on the leash had eased. "He is."

"No way. Wow." Andrew stood. "Come in."

"I thought you'd never ask." She let out a harsh breath and laughed. "Can I get him off this leash?"

"Sure. Let him explore. Maybe he'll kill the fish."

"Andrew!" Was he serious? Maybe she should adopt the fish.

"I'm kidding—sort of."

Clara shook her head and released the beast.

"So you got a dog?" He squinted. "What's going on?"

She bounced on her toes and watched Gigolo as he sniffed every inch of Andrew's living room. "Do you want him?"

"I do, but remember what I said about ranges and field time and deployments?"

"Are you deploying again?"

"Not soon but eventually, and there're field problems and ranges." His voice trailed off.

"Well, I got him because ..." Would he like her news? Her palms were sweaty, throat tight. He would be happy, right?

"Because?" Andrew lifted both eyebrows.

"Because I can help. The girl who played Giselle, Melody, got into a company in Mexico, and I'm taking over her place in the company, and teaching, and doing admin work at the studio."

He beamed. "You're moving to El Paso?"

Yay, good reaction. "Looks that way. I'm moving to an apartment near UTEP. I was just there this morning. They don't mind pets. I've checked. So Gigolo can stay with me when you're out. I'm buying Melody's car too." Her mouth was dry now. "I think that about covers it. That's all my news."

"Congratulations, Clara." He put his arms around her. "That's wonderful news—all of it."

"Isn't it? I have a job, a dancing job, at last."

"You should rent here, though." He squeezed her.

"Too expensive and too far." And she didn't want him to feel obligated to date her just because she was in town. "Plus, I'm used to campus life. It seems natural to move from one college neighborhood to another."

"That makes sense, I guess." Andrew took a step back and held both of Clara's hands. "Wow. Wonderful, wonderful news."

She squeezed his warm hands. Her cheeks hurt from so much smiling. What a wonderful problem to have. She could get used to that.

Gigolo barked at the fish. "That's my boy. Need some fish for your new apartment? My dog hates fish."

Clara chuckled. She would take the fish if he really wanted her to.

"Thank you for the dog." Andrew lifted his chin toward the couch.

She followed his gaze and smiled at the sight of Gigolo, turning around three times and flopping down on the sunniest spot. "You're welcome."

Andrew looked at the kitchen clock, then at her again. "Should we go to waltz class?"

Clara wasn't thinking about class or anything other than the comfort of that moment. "We would never make it on time." She was ready to be with him again—pick up where they'd left off. Was he ready?

"But we're going to the Big Band Party Saturday night, right?"

"Sure." She didn't sound sure, did she? But she'd promised her grandma. Oops—the dress—she would have to go dress shopping immediately.

"It'll be fun."

"I know." It would. It was just a lot going on all at once.

"Oh, come here, sweetheart." He brought her close. "I'm so happy."

Clara felt his arms around her once more. Not a celebratory or a thank-you hug now, but an *I want to be close* hold. Good. Their eyes locked. That was the closest she'd been to his lips in two weeks, and she'd missed it—the closeness, the kissing, the companionship ... him. "Am I still forgiven?"

"Of course." Andrew's smile faded. "I'm really sorry—"

"Shhh." Clara covered his mouth. "I know."

The corners of his eyes crinkled.

"I've had time to think now—to process what happened to us." She caressed the space where his clavicles almost met and rested her eyes there. "I can do this if you still want to—mainly now that I'm staying."

"Of course I still want to," he whispered. "I missed you."

"I missed you too." The distance between them was down to less than an inch now. "Please kiss me, Andrew."

He breathed her in and teased her with little kisses on her cheek, then on the corner of her mouth. "If you insist."

"Oh, I do, I—" His lips stopped her words and melted her heart. She was here to stay. She had a place and a job and Andrew and the Howards—a family of sorts. *Thank you, Lord.* Clara surrendered to his arms and kissed him right back.

"I love you, Clara."

"I love you too." If her heart were to beat any crazier, she would be the one needing heart surgery in the morning, not her grandma.

Chapter 25

"She's out of surgery. Things went as expected." Clara's mom exhaled on the other end of the line. "She's sleeping—as a matter of fact, she's been sleeping since you guys talked yesterday."

"Wow. I'm glad she's out of surgery, but that's a lot of sleeping, isn't it?" Clara glanced at herself in one of the many mirrors of the bridal boutique one of her ballet friends had recommended for a ball gown. Her fingertips reached for the tense spot between her brows. "Did she sleep through surgery prep and all?"

"She sure did. The doctors said that happens sometimes. Don't worry."

Her mom's voice was serene. Good. She wouldn't worry. Clara drew in a slow breath. "Guess what I'm doing?"

"I have no idea. What are you doing?"

"Buying a dress for the ball tomorrow." She studied the delicate details in the many flowing layers of chiffon over a full skirt that would float as she danced. "Looks a bit like grandma's. It's lavender."

"Oh, be sure to take pictures. She *has* to see that."

"I will."

"Are you having dinner at Alice's tonight?"

"Yes, we all are." A family of sorts. Clara snorted. They would probably see each other more often now that Clara was staying in the area. She had to start thinking about moving. She didn't have much, but she had to go to Ohio and finally close her college apartment—box up some stuff, donate the rest. Maybe when her mom came back from Brazil. Even if her mom decided to move there, she too would have to box things, give things, close things. "Mom, are you staying there for good?"

"I don't know. I feel better about the idea now that you have some wonderful things happening for you there." Her mom sniffed, and her voice trembled. "You're officially all grown up."

"Oh, don't cry, Mom." Clara put her hand to her throat, and her eyes swam with tears. She *was* all grown up, wasn't she?

"Maybe we can talk about it when you're not dress shopping?" She sniffed again. "Tell me more about this dress. Did you pick out a nice formal cape and shoes to go with it?"

"Cape? It's one hundred degrees, Mom." Clara laughed at the notion. "Shoes, yes."

"That's right. It's summer there. This surgery and hospital life is turning my brain into mush. We're freezing here. It might even snow in Gramado over the weekend."

She'd forgotten that in Brazil the seasons were backward. "Do you have enough warm stuff?"

"I do. I'm fine, *Princesa*. I've got to go—Grandma's doctor is here. Text me a picture of your dress, will you?"

"Of course, Mom." Clara smoothed down the skirt. "Andrew's talking to General Medeiros about Grandma's request tonight, so be praying, or whatever you do."

"Oh, good! Keep us posted. I'll pray."

She'd never seen her mom pray, but if she said she would, she would. "Thanks, Mom."

Dinner at the Howards felt like a party. The dining room table and the food looked like a feast out of her mom's beloved Martha Stewart magazines. Navy and burgundy linen and décor made delicate white plates whiter and slim silver utensils shinier. They had enough food to feed a platoon. Or so she thought. Within five minutes, their three growing boys had most of it moved from platters to plates.

"Clara, you'll do well around us." Colonel Howard pointed to her full plate. "Never hesitate to serve yourself quickly when my boys are at the table."

She giggled and glanced at the boys' full plates. The three sat side-by-side opposite her and ate in silence. Was this an every-day dinner for a big family? Whenever everyone was home, it was special?

Her eyes rested on Andrew's profile and Mario's still-handsome face. Her love and her grandma's love. Andrew wanted a big family—he'd made that clear at the Magic Bistro when they first went out.

Could she picture herself in a family like this? To her left, Alice shared a funny story with her husband, who roared with laughter. Something to do with a text message gone wrong in the hands of autocorrect, but Clara hadn't caught the whole story.

As each boy finished, they asked to be excused. Alice's reply was always the same. "In a minute."

Of course Clara could picture herself in that kind of family. She would love it.

"All right, boys." Alice's voice was firm. "Dessert will be out in about twenty minutes. You may be excused."

The boys went straight to the backyard. Andrew squeezed Clara's hand, then walked down a dark hallway with General Medeiros, and the two disappeared into a room to the right. *Please help them, God.*

Colonel Howard excused himself, and Alice and Clara cleared the table.

"You can sit down. The rest is easy." Alice pointed to the barstools in the kitchen and began loading the dishwasher. "How's your mom, Clara?"

"Cold. I forgot it's winter in Brazil."

"Oh, yeah. If Dad had it his way, he would spend the Brazilian summer there and the American summer here. Then he could be warm year round."

The Brazilian summer ... Mario saw Grandma in the summer of 1950 in Brazil. Not mid-year, but sometime between December and February. Mom was born in September of 1951. If they'd got together in December of 1950, then he was her grandpa. But if they'd seen each other in January or February of 1950? Then no.

"I finished putting the dessert out—Clara, are you okay?" Alice approached her. "You're pale."

"Alice, is your dad my grandfather?"

She nodded in slow motion. "Do you think you can be okay with that?" Her voice was hardly above a whisper.

"When I first landed here, I couldn't have handled it." But so much had changed. She had come to love the Howards, had learned her grandma's story, had come face to face with the reality of what she'd done with Scott, and had gotten right with God. "But now I can. I had some suspicions, but I was off on the math because of the inverted seasons. Are *you* okay with that? Does Mom know?"

"I'm so glad you're okay with it." Alice put her arms around Clara and squeezed. "Your mom and I have known it for a while. It took some getting used to, but not much. We both love our parents so much, and we've seen them suffer a great deal. We couldn't give them any more grief."

"Why didn't you tell me right away?"

"Your mom thought it was best for you to meet us all first."

"She was probably right." Clara snorted. "Does Andrew know?"

"Oh, no." Alice smirked. "You'll get to tell him he's dating a general's granddaughter."

"The way he loves the Army, he's going to love that." Clara giggled.

Colonel Howard stuck his head into the kitchen. "Should we dig in without them?"

"We can." Alice walked back to the dining room, and Clara followed.

As soon as they sat, the general emerged from the hallway with Andrew right behind him. Andrew smiled and nodded. Then everyone smiled.

The oldest boy jumped up. "Really, Grandpa?" He didn't wait for an answer and wrapped his skinny arms around the general.

General Medeiros patted the boy's shoulder. "We don't need to make a big fuss, right? But yes." His mouth curved into a smile too.

Colonel Howard stood and used his spoon to tap his cup and halt all chatter. "So, all eight of us here at this table are citizens of heaven—children of God. And young man"—he pointed at Andrew—"that wouldn't be the case if it weren't for you."

"Praise God." Andrew's eyes were red, but that was the only evidence of his emotions.

"Thank you, Andrew."

"You're welcome, sir."

After dessert, Mario came to Clara, who was in the backyard texting a dress picture to her mom. "I know the truth." Clara typed. "I'm not mad. I'm actually happy."

"Are you going to call them?"

"I will. We need to tell Grandma you'll go to heaven one day. I'm just trying to get this picture to Mom first." Clara sent the message and then handed the phone to Mario, so he could see the picture.

He extended his arm and blinked twice at the phone screen. "I remember a dress just like it."

"That's why I got it." Her eyes rested on Mario—his blue eyes turned bluer in the night light.

He returned the phone to Clara and sat at the same spot where he'd sat the day she met him. "What truth do you know?"

"Our Sofia." Clara should have known right then. She sat next to him, folded her hands in her lap, and kept her gaze on her trembling fingers. "You saw Grandma in the summer of 1950—summer in Brazil—winter here. Nine months later, Mom was born."

He cupped and lifted her face gently. "See now why we couldn't let you leave El Paso?"

She did. But the words didn't come out. She nodded twice as hot tears pooled in her eyes. "Did Grandpa know?"

"Julio knew." Mario leaned back and put his arm around Clara. "As you probably know, your Grandpa Julio comes from a very traditional Italian family. They didn't much agree with his artist lifestyle, and a marriage and a baby were his ticket to peace and a healthy inheritance."

Clara had heard some of the stories. The family was well known indeed, but the money wasn't real. There was some, but they were not exactly wealthy by the time Grandpa received his inheritance.

"That arrangement had me worried, but Renata swore she knew him well and that it was just a different kind of love. She was content with the union and didn't want to be 'mad in love'—her words. She just wanted her baby and peace."

That was sad but made sense. She had the baby from the man she loved and had security and a marriage from Grandpa—who knew the truth. "But didn't Grandma write she had refused you?"

"She did, but I kept showing up just to see her from a distance." He squeezed Clara's shoulder. "It sounds weird now, but it was innocent back then."

None of that sounded innocent, but she'd let go of bitterness. No more.

"Then she told me about Julio. That's when she asked me to disappear and stay that way. I did. Until Sofia located me. But before leaving I'd told her I wanted her to be insanely happy and that she should find a way of telling me one day that she was indeed happy with Julio. I wanted that for her."

"So that's why she wrote that again and again." She was never sure why they'd divorced. Her mom had said they didn't love each other anymore, but had they ever? What changed? Maybe she'd just wanted Sofia to have a dad. Once Mom was grown and in the States, they lost the will to fight for the union? Who knew?

"I ruined your grandma's life, Clara. I'm so sorry." He sniffed hard.

"I know." She understood regret and immaturity and selfishness. She really did. Clara's phone vibrated. Her mom's pink zinnia brightened the screen, the Argentine tango filled the air with Spanish sounds.

"'Libertango'—Astor Piazzolla." Mario drew in a long breath and closed his eyes.

"Mom?" Had she read her message? "I just sent a picture and a message. Did you get them?"

"I did." Her voice was low and slow—as if she'd been asleep.

Was Grandma sleeping? Were they okay? "Grandma got her wish. Her Mario accepted Christ."

"He did? At what time?"

What time? Not exactly the expected reaction. "I don't know. Thirty minutes ago?"

Her mom sniffed. "A vózinha se foi. She passed away about thirty minutes ago."

Clara put her hand to her mouth. "She was just waiting." She couldn't control the achy sobs that followed.

"She died in her sleep, *Princesa*. She didn't suffer."

Clara felt a hand on her shoulder and turned. Andrew. Everyone was around her now.

Everyone but General Mario Medeiros. He walked slowly under the desert willows and into the night, toward the parade field.

Chapter 26

The Paso del Norte Big Band was already playing when Clara and Andrew arrived at the Shundo Ballroom Dance Studio. It looked different when it was dark out. The city lights and the silver moon over the desert filled the room with wonder.

A dozen musicians played a Gershwin piece, and guests filled two rows of small round tables bordering the dimly lit dance floor.

"Hi, Clara."

Clara turned around to see Helena coming their way.

"Hi, Mr. James. I thought we'd lost you guys forever."

"Just a lot going on." Andrew shook her hand. "We'll be back to class next week, right?"

"Sure." Clara forced a smile. If she hadn't promised her grandma that she would go to the ball, she would have stayed home.

"Well you guys look great. Enjoy."

"Thank you." Andrew touched Helena's arm. "Helena, I need a favor."

"Yes."

"Clara's grandma just passed away."

Clara's eyes filled with tears. Would she cry all night? She didn't get all dressed up for that.

"I'm so sorry."

"She wants to dance her grandma's favorite waltz in her honor."

"Of course," Helena said. "If the band knows it."

"Fascination." Clara's voice was strong. Good.

"Oh, I'm sure they know it. Just write it down here." Helena took a piece of paper and a pen from a nearby table and handed both to Andrew.

He wrote a lot more than the name of a song and placed the note in Helena's hand. "Can you read my handwriting?"

Helena nodded with tears in her eyes.

"Thank you, Helena."

Andrew found an available table near the mirror and pulled out a chair for Clara. "Can I get you something to drink? I didn't think of bringing wine, but they have sodas and water."

"Water would be great." She studied the many couples already on the dance floor. Every age group was represented—the youngest couple was in their twenties. The oldest in their eighties—easily. Seemed like every ethnicity too. Dance had the power to bridge differences like few other things on earth.

Maybe they could bring Mario one day—her grandpa.

She couldn't believe she had a new family and a job dancing. Who would have thought? El Paso, Texas. She shook her head.

"Are you okay?" Andrew opened her bottle of water and handed it to her.

"Yes." She straightened. "Andrew, should I feel guilty for being kind of happy?"

"Kind of happy?"

"I like that Mario is my grandpa, but I feel like it's wrong to feel that way."

Andrew scooted his chair closer to hers and held her hand. "You shouldn't feel guilty for being happy. What you're feeling lines up with scripture—it's the joy of the Lord, the joy of living in His will."

Clara rested her head on his shoulder, and he put his arm around her.

"This is nicer than I'd expected." Andrew placed his soda on the small table. "I thought I would be overdressed."

"You look nice." He looked younger all dressed up. *Ginger.* Young and beautiful in his fancy tux.

"I may look nice—but you? Wow. I feel like I'm out with a movie star."

"Thank you." She giggled and turned her face to hide the heat his comment had brought to her cheeks. Her eyes studied the dance floor, and she imagined what it would have been like for her grandma to arrive at a ball, to dance with her dad, to be a town's royalty. She'd seen a lot in her life. Clara remembered the "Boi Barroso" song. Renata was with her dad now.

One day, Mario would be there too. Her grandpa …

"We received a very special request tonight." The lead singer looked at the crowd. "One of our new waltz students lost her grandmother last night." People at the tables and on the dance floor looked around amid empathetic sounds. "Her grandma, Renata, loved dancing—she loved balls—and made her granddaughter promise that she would be here tonight. She also loved a certain Brazilian officer, a General Mario Medeiros who lives here in El Paso now. She will be waiting for the general in heaven. In the meantime, her granddaughter Clara and her boyfriend will dance to 'Fascination,' Renata's favorite waltz."

Andrew led Clara to the dance floor.

"Thank you," she mouthed. *This is for you, Grandma.*

The slow waltz brought back memories of childhood trips to Brazil, of her grandma's tidy apartment, and of her wonderful cooking—her stove never stopped. She had no idea her grandma had gone through so much. Good thing Andrew had asked her to listen. She should have started listening much earlier. How many other stories were there? Stories she would never hear now.

All she could do was hold on to what little she knew.

She knew her Grandma Renata had loved and been loved.

She knew Renata wasn't bitter.

And she knew her grandma wanted Clara to dance with her soldier. *Dance a beautiful waltz with your little soldier for me.*

Clara let Andrew spin her around the dance floor, and the band members nodded when they passed the stage. She saw their reflection in the mirror and the way Andrew held her and led her. She saw her grandma's gown move to the rhythm of her novice steps. She saw the reflection of the moon over El Paso in that dance floor where movement and beauty met, and where tonight the big band era was alive and well.

And there—right there—only a day after her grandmother's death, she saw what she'd only imagined, what she'd experienced only partially. Dream and reality. Dream and reality occupied the same space.

Dança uma valsa bonita com teu soldadinho por mim.

THE END